SHARELLE
JOHN NEUFELD

A SIGNET VISTA BOOK

NEW AMERICAN LIBRARY
PUBLISHED BY
THE NEW AMERICAN LIBRARY
OF CANADA LIMITED

NAL BOOKS ARE AVAILABLE AT QUANTITY DISCOUNTS
WHEN USED TO PROMOTE PRODUCTS OR SERVICES. FOR
INFORMATION PLEASE WRITE TO PREMIUM MARKETING DIVISION,
THE NEW AMERICAN LIBRARY, INC., 1633 BROADWAY,
NEW YORK, NEW YORK 10019.

RL 5/IL 6+

SIGNET VISTA TRADEMARK REG. U.S. PAT. OFF. AND FOREIGN
COUNTRIES REGISTERED TRADEMARK—MARCA REGISTRADA
HECHO EN WINNIPEG, CANADA

First Signet Vista Printing, February, 1984

2   3   4   5   6   7   8   9

SIGNET, SIGNET CLASSIC, MENTOR, PLUME, MERIDIAN
and NAL BOOKS are published in Canada by The New American
Library of Canada, Limited, Scarborough, Ontario
PRINTED IN CANADA
COVER PRINTED IN U.S.A.

for K. M. O'B.

PART
ONE

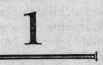

1

THE sea before her was slate gray, and calm.

Despite what she knew she had to do, Sharelle Marston felt strangely calm, too. She wondered if she shouldn't be tearful, or shaking. Perhaps even angry. But the flatness of the water reflected the resignation in her soul.

Everything had begun there, at the beach. Forget about being a California girl, she thought. Your life looks to be a long way from sun-bleached and Dr. Pepper-ed. There are no surfboards in your past. No cheerful campfires.

She shook her head. There had been one campfire. And look what had happened because she'd been the last girl around the coals.

No, that wasn't fair, either. What happened had not been all someone else's fault. If she came to think about it, she had been foolish. She should have guessed what Dallas had on his mind. But after all, he was her own sister's fiancé. Who ever would have thought . . . ?

She blinked quickly. There was no point in going back, in figuring things out now. What was done was done and, at a certain point, you had to accept responsibility.

Well, O.K., that was all right. She could do that, she told herself. Even though she had been barely fourteen, it was she who had decided to go through with it all, rain or shine. Alone or not. It was she who'd discovered, afterwards, the holes in her mother's life, the weaknesses. Not that she hadn't already suspected them, but before, well, before they hadn't made such a difference.

But when you had a child, things like that did matter.

She smiled sadly, looking out over the beach, almost as gray as the water in mid-winter. Not that she hadn't tried. She hinted quietly. She'd argued a little. Finally, she had shouted at her mother. But it was all for nothing. Some people couldn't change, and that was that, like it or not. She guessed what she'd learned would be what some people called "a lesson." Well, Sharelle didn't feel grateful, particularly, for that sort of learning, and she certainly didn't feel all that much smarter, either.

Overhead the sun made a weak attempt at breaking through the San Diego haze. There was a moment, then one more, when Sharelle could feel its heat and promised blessing. It was enough to make her sit back against the bench, loosen her grip on the small, tightly wrapped package in her lap, and close her eyes, her face tilted upwards towards warmth.

And then, without meaning to let them loose, Sharelle Marston's memories surfaced and began to replay, on the insides of her sun-spotted eyelids, the changes in her life that led her to this beach on a February afternoon, determined to give away what she loved more than anything.

2

A lifetime ago.

Almost Thanksgiving, Christmas on the horizon—"only thirty-seven more shopping days"—yards of white tulle and veiling covering beds and bureau top and chairs in Annette's room; white shoes, a belt, lingerie. A suitcase, a new winter coat. And noise, constant: telephone calls, doorbell ringing, cars and trucks pulling up outside, shouts from Melba below, arguments between Annette and her mother. "But we don't want this kind of wedding!" "You're lucky to get any kind at all, as far as I can see!" "But they're *your* friends!" "Never look a gift horse in the mouth!"

Forgotten amid all this, trying hard to step quickly and quietly around the excitement and confusion, Sharelle tiptoed through that autumn, studying, staying out of the way. There were no boys in her life yet. Annette had always been surrounded by them but Annette was also four years older than Sharelle, and "developed." Sharelle had decided not to worry over her unattached state. There was time. She could afford to wait for the day Melba promised, *swore* would come when Sharelle's chest filled out, when her hair shone a little of its own accord, when her complexion would worry her less than it did now, which was, approximately, every time she passed a mirror and sometimes even when she determinedly ignored one hanging on a nearby wall.

At night, in bed in her own small room off the back stairway, Sharelle would listen to—she couldn't help but hear—Melba downstairs going on at Annette about everything from her posture to learning to cook. And secretly Sharelle felt glad to be out of all that. She had her own life to lead, her own plans.

So she wasn't any movie star. Still, she was tall and agile, and a good athlete. Her grades were a whole lot better than Annette's had ever been. There was no way Annette was ever going to go to college, even if she hadn't met Dallas Edwards and decided to get married. Sharelle intended to. Maybe on a scholarship, if she was lucky. The last thing she wanted was to be indebted to Melba for anything more than she was: food, clothing, shelter, an occasional joke. Melba's life was *too* full. There was a lot of her to spread around, and Melba spread it. Sharelle never begrudged her mother her aching for fun, for parties, for just that one tiny extra drink that would take her "way over." After all, Melba worked hard. She'd been accountant and general manager for San Diego Paint and Home Repair Center for as long as Sharelle could remember. And if sometimes Melba invited one of the company's salesmen or contractors around of an evening for a nightcap, as she called it, and if that gentleman's socks (let alone the rest of him) were still in evidence the next morning, well, her mother deserved a little fun. After all, as Melba never tired of telling anyone who would listen, she was still a ripe, young woman; she was only thirty-five. She had her whole life ahead of her. As far as she was concerned, that meant having some fun and sharing it, too.

Sharelle had once overheard her mother, maybe a little high, a little tipsy, ushering a gaggle of girl friends out the door one Thursday night, laughing and bragging, braying on the front stoop: "What the hell, honey! It ain't anything I'm gonna run out of fast!"

6

Not that Melba didn't do her fair share of good works. Or volunteer Annette and Sharelle to do them for her. There was church, of course, and whatever special crusades the Reverend Lee dreamed up: helping the homeless off the streets, a course for recovering alcoholics, a workshop to help parents and children recognize the dangers of drug addiction, visits to old-folks homes, hot lunches for shut-ins, fund-raising for a bazaar or for air-conditioning the sanctuary. Melba was among the first to volunteer. Annette and Sharelle shuddered every time they heard her high, clear voice asking to be recognized. It was *they* who would canvass, deliver, wrap and warm and feed. Their mother's life was expanded by their own living of it.

There had been times when Melba volunteered to raise money for the Republicans; when she had stepped forward to be counted in a drive for cleaner streets, better street-lighting, more police; to gather signatures for various ballot propositions. There was a brass plaque atop the wooden mantel in her small front parlor that attested to her status as a concerned and caring citizen, courtesy of the local chapter of the American Red Cross. A blood drive. Melba had given no blood, no time, no shoe-leather. Sharelle and Annette had been sent out into the neighborhood, across town even, to Mission Bay. Sharelle had caught a head cold. Annette met Dallas Edwards for the first time.

He was thin and rangy, and bouncy. He couldn't seem to stand still for more than a few seconds at a time. His eyes roved constantly, out to the street, back again to Annette, once or twice slyly and sideways at Sharelle. He wore a suede shirt, jeans, and running shoes, all of which made his frame seem narrower and taller than it was. He seemed to have a lot of confidence. He could be crude, too, Sharelle thought.

She and Annette had been outside Dallas' mother's

door, asking for blood donors, Annette making the pitch, Sharelle by her presence offering little but support and company.

"I'd give you a whole lot more than that, little lady," said Dallas Edwards with a crooked smile. "And I wouldn't expect to be paid for it, neither."

"We don't accept blood for money any longer," Annette said coolly. "It leads to disease."

"Ho!" Dallas laughed, throwing his head back and blinking up at the sun. "*That*, too, huh?"

"Well, thanks very much for your time," said Annette, turning away quickly and motioning for Sharelle to follow.

"Hey, now, little fox," called Dallas after her. "I didn't mean nothin' disrespectful."

Annette turned and regarded him a moment. "How old are you?" she asked simply.

"Twenty-one, -two next week."

Annette nodded. "And how come you're home and not working?"

"Four-day week," Dallas said, his crooked smile straightening out into something a little less playful. "I choose my own hours, make my own schedule."

"Doing what?" asked Annette.

"Driving," said Dallas. "I deliver beer."

Annette nodded, seeming to be satisfied. Sharelle wondered whether all this was playacting or whether her sister really did discover something important.

Then, without looking again at Sharelle, Annette marched back up the front walkway and handed Dallas Edwards a card. "In case you change your mind," she suggested. "We need a lot of help."

Sharelle had longed for months to ask Annette how she had made up her mind so quickly, why, what she had seen that made her do that. What made her let Dallas call, take her out, drive her around, spend whole days at the beach together or with his friends. But that particular summer seemed to pass by so quickly that when autumn came, when it was time for Sharelle to go back to school, she had lived with her curiosity for so long that she had forgotten about satisfying it. Besides, Annette and Dallas had become engaged.

Melba was thrilled. "A teamster! Honey, they make a fortune!"

Meanly, Sharelle wondered if her mother's joy wasn't relief in disguise, one less to worry over, more room in her own life for friends and causes, for spreading it around. But this suspicion gave way as she saw her mother overtaken by sentimentality, some of it liquidly induced, as together she and Annette planned a Thanksgiving wedding.

During all this Sharelle herself was largely assumed to be somewhere around the house, going about her own life, attending school, following through alone on one or another of Melba's volunteer missions.

The only person who seemed to see her clearly when she was standing quietly at the kitchen threshold listening to Melba go on about her day's scouting of furniture stores, of silversmiths and dress shops, was Dallas Edwards, who sat nursing a long beer and listening, sometimes holding hands with Annette as her mother regaled them with the bargains sought, fought for and won, and every so often, just every once in a while, looking up under his eyebrows at Sharelle across the way, fixing her with a look Sharelle couldn't read, really, but which made her blush and smile a little with pleasure.

3

AND the parties! Nothing lavish. No country clubs or brunches. Planned get-togethers with Dallas and Annette's friends, sometimes including their parents and families, sometimes not. Cookouts behind someone's home; beach parties on weekends; once a dress-up cocktail party to which Sharelle was allowed to go on the proviso she stick to iced tea or soda. She chose soda. It was white, and with a cut of lime in it, appeared as lethal as any gin-and-tonic or vodka. Not that she had any opportunity to play grown-up sophisticated lady. The people who spoke to her at all turned out to be members of her own family, aunts and uncles and cousins. Still and all, she felt she could hardly be considered fourteen, leaning against a bookcase and holding her drink to her lips, looking over the rim of her glass at all the people around, smiling a little but hiding it behind the curve of crystal.

The summer weather miraculously held. The cloudy days, the mists that so often in October came in from the ocean and seeped through walls and jackets and skins held off, stayed out in mid-sea, letting the sun continue to beat down without cooling. And the rains people expected each October refused to fall, too. There was an odd sense of falseness in the atmosphere; at any moment, reality might descend and turn the landscape into flood tides of debris and waste and muddy water.

Sharelle went to school each day. She worked hard,

despite the occasional moments of wondering whether—when the time came—her own wedding preparations would seem as carefree, as adventurous as Annette's. Whether her mother would be as pleased with Sharelle's choice as she seemed to be about Dallas. Whether she would even be in San Diego when that time came. Secretly, she hoped not.

Not that San Diego was small town or unpleasant. It wasn't. But something in Sharelle ached to see snow in winter, and colored leaves in fall. She knew she didn't want to marry as quickly as Annette was doing. She wanted some time to herself, freedom, a job. And sometimes her daydreams revolved around that, The Job—in a lab, dressed in starched white, rustling as she went from table to table, measuring, noting, compiling. Or in front of a class, teaching . . . math? Science, computer programming? Sharelle knew her strong points. She was better at hard facts, at firm, unalterable laws of nature or science than she was with anything human, anything that could be changed by something as magical and confusing and undependable as emotion.

Sometimes she looked out of her school windows and wondered about God. Was there one? More important, was there One who knew about *her*? Who watched and understood, who heard her secret thoughts, knew her private prayers and hopes, was ready to reward or punish her own peculiar errors? Not sins. Sharelle tried hard not to sin, though the boundaries around sin weren't all that clear.

She did wish—and had prayed—that she weren't so shy. That she had—besides Monica Ruskin, whose information about life was half-gossip, half-guesswork, and not often trustworthy—someone to whom she could talk, confide in, learn from. Her mother was too scattered, her own life too full to allow more than actual posturing in a role that Sharelle understood and sympathized with, both. Since her husband's disappearance and with Melba really and truly not being *that* old, it was natural that she should want her life to go at full speed, to be filled with excitement and fun as well as the hard work and long hours San Diego Paint and Home Repair Center demanded. Melba had, after all, given her husband good years. She couldn't get them back, but she could try to fill up what remained with the luxuries and appliances and gifts and clothing she had felt deprived of, and for which she herself worked so diligently.

But Sharelle didn't fit into Melba's round of fun. And, it seemed, Melba had no need to confide in her younger daughter, either. There were few moments, apart from breakfast, when the two even inhabited the same room without being surrounded by other people. There were no mother-and-daughter teas or lunches, or even moments when Melba felt compelled to ask how her daughter was. As long as Sharelle caused no trouble, was quiet and, when required, obedient, as long as she needed nothing more than Melba in the regular course of time was inclined to give, the two got on as well as either would have expected.

As for Annette, there was just enough difference between eighteen and fourteen to keep her purposely separate from her sister. Not for her a tag-along. And Sharelle could not work herself up into feeling that Annette was selfish that way. They *couldn't* do the same things; they didn't have friends in common; they weren't even in the same school. They could go to church together. They could (and were forced to) abet their mother's charitable urges. They could stand around and make drinks for their mother's friends. But outside this, Annette's life was mysterious to Sharelle. Who picked her up for school? Who brought her home? Who took her to basketball games? Who went with her to buy clothes? How far did she go with boys on dates? What made her pick one boy over another? What made her choose Dallas so quickly, so certainly?

Not that he wasn't good-looking in his own way. He was confident and tall, a little loose, gangly, almost like Sharelle herself. His smile was quick and teasingly secretive, his laugh easy and relaxed. His eyes seemed to Sharelle to be his most curious feature: not their color, which was plain deep brown, but what she imagined she saw in them: shadows, figures moving. They were sly sometimes, questioning. Testing.

The most Sharelle could hope for was to overhear, answer her own questions by listening to other people. But in the hustle and rush and confusion of the coming wedding, it seemed to her what she most would like to hear was what was whispered about between Annette and Melba, between Annette and her friends, between Melba and *her* friends. Whenever Sharelle came within hearing range, or into sight at all, people seemed to make an effort to return to normal. If they had been laughing, they coughed and became serious. If they had been thoughtful, they smiled and asked her silly questions about school or boys. If Sharelle had been a different person, she might have imagined this abrupt change in behavior was because *she* had been the one talked about, the one laughed over. But she didn't. She was just there, as she had been for so much of her life, an extra, except that now everything people did seemed to be reminding her how young she was, how little she knew.

Still, she *was* included in the festivities. As part of the family, as Annette's sister, as Melba's daughter she got to go to dinners and showers, and she knew there would be a real, honest-to-God place card at her chair when Dallas and his mother hosted the pre-nuptial dinner the night before the wedding. She would even have a new dress for the occasion, selected by Annette and Melba.

But that all took place *after* the final rowdy young people's beach picnic. It was Dallas who told Annette to bring along Sharelle, that she might meet someone. Annette grimaced, but along with four other people,

13

Sharelle had been jammed into someone's station wagon and driven out to the beach where, at sunset, a fire was built and the pop of beer and soda cans was heard, and laughter erupted in tiny, surprised spasms from groups Sharelle could barely make out in the deepening dusk. Other friends of Dallas or Annette made the rendezvous; there must have been thirty-five people scattered throughout the shadows around the fire. Two people had brought big powerful radio sets and the competing music battled relentlessly: Diana Ross, Lionel Richie, Rod Stewart, even a little new-wave rock.

A lot of laughing and teasing went on, but Sharelle was neither target nor instigator. She had been given a can of beer by Dallas and had settled just out of the flickering lights of the fire by herself, hugging her knees and occasionally sipping, watching, listening, sorting out. She saw couples drift off towards the darkness and heard the ensuing scuffles. She heard the barely stifled laughter and protests that came from girls around her, and though she couldn't make out the exact wording of their pleas, the boys' desires were all too urgent and obvious.

Once in a while, from her vantage, she saw the fleeting shadow of an evening jogger running along the water's edge not far away. Occasionally someone—Annette or Dallas or one of their better-meaning friends—stopped by and patted her head, asked her how she was doing, knelt a moment to ask innocuous questions. Dallas made sure she had a fresh beer whenever she wanted, or whenever he thought she should have one, and the celebration continued around her.

Sharelle's head began to nod and she could hardly keep her eyes open. Her mind drifted away from the firelight and the whispers. Then suddenly, with a start, her eyes snapped open and what she didn't hear alarmed her. She couldn't hear Annette anywhere. She couldn't hear Dallas teasing, or the giggles of the girls that before had seemed musical and almost soothing. She could hear the crackle

14

of the fire still, and a few muffled sounds outside its circle of light, but other than these, she felt suddenly alone, abandoned, frightened. She stood up shakily, finding her balance on the sand, and called out, "Annette?"

Her sister did not reply. Instead, Dallas materialized out of the shadows and came towards her, smiling, walking slowly, rhythmically, his fingers clicking a little to some tune he seemed to hear in his head.

"Where's Annette?" Sharelle demanded, shaking both because she was now cold and from nervousness.

"She and Jeannine and some of the others left," Dallas told her, reaching down to pick up a blanket that had been left in the sand.

"She did?" was all Sharelle could think to say.

Dallas nodded. "*You* know," he confided with a wink that startled Sharelle, "they have a lot to do. For tomorrow, for Saturday."

"But—" Sharelle started to object.

"Hey, don't worry, little sister," Dallas comforted, wrapping the blanket around Sharelle's shoulders. The weight of his hands on her made her take a step backwards, put her off-balance, and in order not to fall she had to grasp on to Dallas's waist. He seemed not to notice.

"Here now," he said soothingly, "I told your sister I'd see you got home. There's nothing to worry about. Here" —and he turned away, kneeling down to a cooler that still held beer and wine—"why not have some of this to warm yourself up?" He poured without waiting for Sharelle to agree, and handed a paper cup full of white wine up to her. She took it. "Just sit right down here," Dallas suggested, patting the sand not too far away from the fire, "and let yourself enjoy the air and the stars." He looked up at her, waiting for her to obey, the firelight animating his eyes. Sharelle sat, staring at him, examining him, hoping to see what went on in his mind when he looked at her. But she could not.

15

"That's *good*," judged Dallas. "You can still hear the surf from here."

"Yes," Sharelle said, wondering why she felt she had to speak at all.

"Now then," Dallas announced, getting to his feet, "you stay right here, dig yourself right in and relax. I'll be back in a minute." He grinned. "You know, we should know each other better, Sharelle. We're family. Almost anyway. And there's a long time ahead of us."

Sharelle nodded, feeling uneasy. She told herself quickly, as Dallas disappeared beyond the edge of firelight, that there wasn't going to be any long time between them. As soon as she could, Sharelle was going to graduate and go off to college and probably never come back to San Diego at all.

She sipped at the wine, deciding she liked it a little better than beer. She wondered if she was tipsy. She had never had much liquor of any kind before, just a sip now and then when Melba was being publicly tolerant and advanced in front of her friends. Then in her imagination Sharelle heard her mother's laugh: "Never mix, never worry!" Melba would call out, and Sharelle wondered if that included beer with wine. Still, there at the beach, that night, everyone seemed to think drinking was natural and fun. Maybe it was. She took another sip and then, still swaddled in her blanket, leaned over to the cooler and poured herself some more.

She tried to listen for the whoosh of the surf. With the sun down and the wind quiet, the water too, somewhere out there in the blackness, seemed to have lost force. She strained but could distinguish only the slightest wash on pebbles and sand. She sipped her wine.

Dallas came towards her, his smile broad and reflected in the firelight, and his eyes wide. He knelt down first at Sharelle's side and then allowed himself to sink more deeply into the sand, nestling against her side. For

16

warmth. He was carrying his own can of beer from which he took a swallow. Sharelle did not watch.

She felt Dallas' arm over her shoulders. "You're going to be so much prettier than Annette," Dallas offered softly. "I don't know, I guess maybe it's style. You know? You're so cool, so distant."

Sharelle still did not turn to look at him. She was uncertain whether to speak. She decided finally that she would. "Thank you," she said.

"I bet you don't believe me, do you?" Dallas guessed shrewdly. "I bet no one's ever told you your good points before."

Sharelle sat motionless. She felt tears begin to fill her eyes. She swallowed to hold them back. Dallas had hit her very hard.

It was not by chance. Dallas watched her carefully, patting her shoulder. "I bet you don't even know how pretty you are," he whispered. "You got the kind of face that's always going to make men stop and stare, you know that, Sharelle?"

Sharelle did not know that. She smiled and raised her cup of wine.

She coughed but was able to stop quickly. With a shy look at Dallas, her eyes clear again, she said, "You don't have to make up to me, Dallas. I'm not Annette, you know."

He laughed gently. "I don't make up to Annette, little girl," he told her. "And I'm not doing that with you, either. I'm just telling you some truths no one else will."

Sharelle finished her wine. Dallas reached out for the half-gallon jug and refilled her container. He put it back in the cooler and, as he settled once again near her, he opened his own blanket and put a corner of it around Sharelle's shoulders, bringing her closer to him, his hand running smoothly up and down her sweatered arm. It felt nice, but Sharelle didn't want to say so. "I'm nothing special," she said instead.

Dallas waited a moment and then hugged her. "You are to me, pretty girl. You are to me."

"Why?"

Dallas put his can of beer down in the sand and squiggled around so that he was facing her, both of his hands on her shoulders, his face only inches away from her own. "Because you are. Not because of Annette. Because of you. You're going to grow up special and go places and do things, important things. I knew that the first time I saw you. Most people could see that, too, if they only took the trouble to really look."

Sharelle stared into Dallas' eyes, half-believing what he said, *needing* to believe it all.

Dallas was staring back at her. Sharelle felt she should definitely say something now, but could not get her throat to work. She glanced quickly to one side and then the other, seeing no one else about. She looked back at Dallas.

"Pretty, pretty, pretty," he whispered, coming still closer until his lips brushed hers.

Sharelle shut her eyes and believed.

Dallas whispered in her ear even as he gently edged her back into the sand, atop her own blanket, and as his hands began to unbutton the blouse beneath her sweater.

"Pretty, pretty, pretty," he said over and over, softly, gently, adoringly.

Sharelle felt as though she were starring in one of her own dreams.

"Pretty, pretty, pretty," Dallas repeated.

His words meant so much to Sharelle. They covered the soft sound of surf. She smiled to herself, closing her eyes, and concentrated on their echo in her starving soul.

4

THE next two days were the most agonizing of Sharelle's life.

She watched for signs, for signals, for anything from Dallas that indicated he knew how much he meant to her, how much she cared.

There was nothing.

To be fair, she told herself the following night in bed, after Dallas' family had played host at the rehearsal dinner in a small Italian restaurant, he really hadn't ever had a free moment to do anything except maybe smile at her. But his smiles told her nothing. They were normal everyday Dallas smiles—full of slyness and secrets. All around him were friends and family, teasing, joking, needling— grabbing his arm and then bending close to his ear to whisper advice or a dirty joke or a reminiscence of what had happened years before on their own peculiar voyages to wedded bliss. And he *had* to look out for Annette. Not to mention for Melba, who was always unhappy if a moment came when the spotlight shone away from her onto someone she imagined less deserving.

Hadn't it meant anything to him? Sharelle asked herself. It must have!

How could he keep grinning, keep playing a part, when all along he must know what he meant to her, how he himself had felt the night before, what they had done together?

That night before Annette's wedding—for Sharelle had, in a few hours, changed the label of this event to make it her sister's alone; Dallas had no part in it— Sharelle's mind whirled. Images of the apartment she knew Dallas and Annette had leased floated through her mind, only in her imagination it was *she* who stood at its threshold to welcome Dallas home after a long, tiring trip. It was she who cooked in its tiny kitchen; she who dusted and vacuumed and changed sheets and arranged flowers. It was she in a silver photograph frame on an end table, wreathed in white, smiling out at the world, beaming out at the man she loved.

As she finally drifted into sleep, still hearing in her mind the sound of toasts at dinner and laughter and the clinking of glasses, the wonderful stunning moment when the Reverend Lee would ask the assembly if any man knew wherefore these two should not be united in holy matrimony came to her, and she saw, she *felt* Dallas turn away from Annette to look down the aisle at *her*, at *Sharelle*, and to motion to her, pulling her up from her place towards his own at the altar.

That Saturday the weather was all that Sharelle could have wished: overcast, threatening rain. Only she knew what an omen this was. She could hardly bear to look at Annette without weeping for her coming disappointment. She smiled and helped her mother and her sister whenever they said they needed it, but beneath her usual cooperativeness was still the certainty that the day was hers, not Annette's at all, that it would turn out to be a day Annette wanted erased from every calendar in the world.

It wasn't until her mother had declared herself satisfied with the way Annette's dress draped, the way her veil covered just the top of her face, the wrap of the dress's waist—she wanted no gossip at *her* daughter's wedding— that Sharelle was able to hide away and dress herself, making herself up into whatever it was that Dallas had so admired two nights before. When at last, to the accompaniment of her mother's raucous shouting from the driveway, Sharelle descended the back stairs and walked through the house towards the car, she felt as though she were saying good-bye forever to her childhood.

The wedding party was small; the church enormous. Annette and Melba along with the rest of the female side of the bridal party retired to a small antechamber off an aisle and proceeded to primp, preen, and pinch each other in excitement. Sharelle stood in one corner of this tiny room, watching, tingling in her own way, wondering how Dallas would be dressed, floating on anticipation. She smoothed down the satin front and back of her dress, trying to iron out wrinkles caused by squeezing into the back of Melba's Camaro. She stood tall and outwardly calm, her hands on the material at her sides, a smile on her lips. She watched and heard Annette and Melba and Annette's friends, but no single word of their speech registered or remained with her.

Sharelle heard the church organist limbering up and her body tensed as she heard the first strains of real music a few seconds later. The room hushed and then everyone broke into what seemed to be one huge smile that covered a secret, but shared, knowledge. Melba reached out to hug Annette to her bosom and then turned to leave the room, to be ushered down the white satin-covered aisle to her seat in a pew near the altar. Annette and her party assembled in order, as they had practiced for hours the day before, and Sharelle took her position in the procession that would lead the bride to her fate.

Annette had vetoed being escorted down the aisle by Melba's current "best friend" and instead had chosen her mother's brother, Jack, to give her away. She followed her bridal party from the family room off the main aisle and delicately laid her hand on Jack's arm. Together they walked slowly and in tempo to the music of the organ towards the altar.

As she marched beside one of Annette's friends, Sharelle was aware of the whispers, smiles, and nods on both sides of the aisle. She felt as though she were floating, as though she were a swan serenely gliding on a still pond, her reflection giving as much pleasure to sightseers on land as her own body.

She halted at the appointed spot and stepped to one side, as her counterpart did on the other, and then they turned to watch Annette and Jack approach. Sharelle couldn't help herself. She glanced quickly across the space between the bride's side and the groom's to see Dallas standing there, tall, looking bulkier than she remembered because of the suit he was wearing. His face was shining and his eyes were riveted firmly on Annette as she drew closer. Sharelle knew the excitement Dallas was feeling, *knew* that the moment she had dreamed about was at hand. She admired him tremendously for being so cool-looking, so calm, when in just a few minutes all hell would break loose and the real lovers would be united before God and man.

In a daze, but exactly as she had been rehearsed, Sharelle turned as Annette passed her, and took her position beside the railing to watch. Dallas stepped forward to take Annette's hand and then to turn her towards Reverend Lee, who smiled out broadly at them both. The ceremony began.

It ended.

Abruptly Sharelle felt perspiration in the center of her back and on her upper lip. Nothing bad happened. Dallas had betrayed her. He had said nothing. When the moment came, he had remained silent, leaving Sharelle desolate and more alone than she had ever felt in her life.

The music all around her swelled and tumbled. Annette and Dallas had parted and turned back up the aisle and were leading the procession out into new, hazy sunshine.

Like a robot Sharelle followed. With her partner, she walked slowly—achingly—after the bridal couple and through the tall-ceilinged hallway, out double doors to stand on the steps of the church to be photographed. Sharelle closed her eyes against the sun, against the pain. The camera snapped and people around her laughed and applauded. Cars began pulling up to carry wedding guests back to Melba's house for the reception.

Sharelle was jostled and pushed and finally folded into someone's car for the short ride home. No one seemed to notice she was silent, close to tears. The car was jammed. People sat on top of other people, and laughter accompanied them all down the street and around the corner.

Sharelle was aware of the body beneath her own. She felt someone's hands on her legs but her brain signaled this was only an effort to stay stable as the car took another, sharper turn. Then she was being pushed out on her own tiny front lawn and swept into the house along with the others.

But where some people stopped in the front room and looked around for something to eat or drink, Sharelle kept right on moving through the house, through the kitchen (ignoring the caterer and her assistant) and up the back stairs to her own room. She slammed the door behind herself and stood a moment, breathing heavily, silent tears bursting from her eyes.

She began to unbutton her dress. She kicked off her shoes and wriggled out of her slip. She grabbed a pair of jeans and a sweat shirt and put them on, and then, finally, her finery in a pile at the door, she fell forward onto her bed and sobbed into her pillow.

She could hear the merriment downstairs. She knew she was not missed. And knowing this as certainly as she did made her cry even harder. She pulled her pillow over her head and wept into her mattress.

Suddenly she stopped. She sat up, listening hard, swinging her legs off the side of the bed. There were shouts and laughter from below as before, but now she heard people leaving the house. The noises continued but came now from the front lawn. In her bare feet Sharelle rushed to her door and ran down the back stairs and through the kitchen.

On the lawn, just a few feet from Dallas' car, Annette and Dallas stood smiling and waving. Sharelle saw people taking pictures and throwing handfuls of rice at the pair. She edged through the crowd and stood to one side in the front ranks of happy celebrants, staring at Dallas. He waved at people, his other arm around Annette's waist, and from time to time he would pull her towards him in a squeeze. Sharelle felt every one of those gestures, felt every pound of pressure from Dallas' hands. And waited.

And waited. Dallas suddenly turned Annette to face him and gave her a long, lingering, and almost embarrassing kiss. It *had* to be for the camera bugs in the crowd. It had to be. A cheer went up from the watching families and friends. Sharelle closed her eyes, feeling weak. She opened them again when another cheer rose. Annette and Dallas were taking the steps towards his car that they needed to begin their honeymoon.

Dallas waited patiently as Annette arranged herself in the front seat. Annette had not changed clothing, despite the "going away" wardrobe Melba had insisted on purchasing during the previous weeks. Instead, she had packed everything she wanted or needed before the wedding and stowed her suitcases in the trunk of Dallas' car the night before so that their "getaway" would be swift and make-believe sudden.

Dallas closed Annette's door and she rolled down her window to wave at the crowd on the lawn. Her mother rushed forward, pushing Dallas to one side, to kiss her. Dallas turned back to smile at his friends. And he saw Sharelle.

They looked at each other.

Sharelle wanted to scream, to reach out, to tear at Dallas' clothing, to hold him.

He stared at her, the shadows in his eyes as dark and confusing as ever. There was affection in them, but mostly they seemed cautious, counseling silence. He nodded at her. He winked.

Sharelle felt as though someone had slapped her. A wink? Was that all she got? A wink?

PART
TWO

5

IN the weeks following Annette's honeymoon, Sharelle lay in bed angry. Not angry enough to imagine revenge, to picture taking Annette aside some bright sunny Sunday afternoon and telling her that her husband had done more than simply marry and glide off into the sunset. After all, Sharelle was fond of Annette; Annette was just plain ignorant if she expected Dallas to be other than what he was.

Still, Sharelle was angry.

Although, as she turned the event over in her mind, no real harm had been done.

How did she feel about *that?* she asked herself. Well, she wasn't sure. She didn't feel so much different. Whatever physical discomfort there had been had passed, leaving her only with memories and dashed plans. She certainly didn't feel superior to her schoolmates.

She had felt inferior a few months earlier when everyone in her gym class had experienced a period and Sharelle was still fibbing, still waiting. When at last it had happened to her, too, the relief was short-lived in the face of understanding that this sort of thing went on for years and years and was, mostly, just one extra, large pain.

She did not feel on fire for more of the same, for another nighttime tussle on the blanket and sand. Maybe that was because what she had allowed herself to feel for Dallas was, now, so clearly her own feeling only—there was nothing coming back from him to support her daydreams. Once bitten, twice shy, as Melba liked to say. (Melba, of course, would add laughingly that what *she* meant was that she was afraid she'd never get a second bite!)

Sharelle reasoned that the sensations, the romance she read about were out there somewhere, waiting. There was no point in searching, in substituting, in looking for another such moment purposely. When she was ready, when a boy was ready—someone who actually did make her feel good and special and warm and loved rather than just a smoothie like Dallas taking advantage of someone younger—well, maybe, maybe then. Not before.

There were some difficult family times on the horizon, what with Christmas and New Year's just ahead. Annette and Dallas were all aglow with arranging their apartment for the holidays, planning a large family dinner to which Melba and Sharelle would have to go. There were presents to be exchanged, news and gossip and pictures to look at from Dallas and Annette's trip to San Francisco. There were long silent moments when Melba would stare at Annette proudly and shake her head in pleasure that she had done so well by her. Whenever Melba looked at Sharelle and shook her head, it seemed more in despair than in hope or pride.

But Sharelle was used to this after so many years and made plans to be away from home as often as possible during her two-week break. She had nowhere special to go, nor anyone special to hang out with. She just wanted to remove herself from Melba's field of vision. Who knew what sudden well-meaning and/or charitable plan her mother might hatch during the Holy Season: decorating the Reverend Lee's altar for Christmas-night services, helping in the soup kitchens downtown, collecting toys for needy children?

Sharelle was not in the Christmas spirit. She was somewhere deep inside herself, testing, running her fingers over her imagined bruises, pushing down gently to see whether they still hurt. She had no one around whom she trusted to tell what had happened to her. So she spent a good deal of time that holiday sitting quietly and as inconspicuously as possible at the back of a church that wasn't hers. She watched as women of that parish decorated the aisles and stairway to the altar, as they polished the pews and dusted the tiny stools people knelt on during services, as they wrapped polished rags around their hands and walked slowly, reverently along the communion rail. She knew she was noticed, but the sense of peace and silence Sharelle found there was more pleasing than anything else she could imagine—certainly more than worrying about assignments due January 4th, or ducking Melba's long arm of parental insistence.

It might have seemed as though Sharelle were praying in the church, but really she was just there, sitting, watching.

Which was how she felt about life in general just then: it was slow and sort of pointless and not very exciting. Her school work had always taken care of itself and would when the time came. She was safe and out of the way. No one expected anything of her, or missed her. In spite of feeling relieved to be so independent, every once in a while Sharelle admitted to herself, sometimes with tears in her eyes, that she felt alone. Terribly, miserably alone.

"Just a phase," Melba would say to any well-intentioned friend about Sharelle's silences. "Goodness, when I was her age, I was just on fire for life, for everything I could get my hands on. But kids today, well, you know, they've got so many new pressures. I wouldn't want to grow up again for anything in this world!"

Time passed and school began again and everything about Sharelle's life seemed once more to assume familiar shape.

That she had missed two periods was a fact of which she was hardly aware, and certainly nothing that made her worry. She had so recently joined the club of "mature" teenaged girls that the cessation of one of life's bodily signs was a relief and more easily accepted than puzzling. She had not yet begun to plan around those times when she must take extra precautions. In fact, whenever her time had come, she was surprised. She had forgotten about it. She was almost always unprepared and had to ask among her classmates for help, for extra tampons. She always promised to pay them back, to buy some for herself, but she would forget a few days after and be taken by surprise all over again a month later. To be normal to Sharelle meant not being bothered by anything so unpleasant.

It wasn't until Monica—her one single sort-of best friend at school, a rounded little bundle of energy—complimented Sharelle on finally getting her act together that Sharelle even considered what, if anything, this holiday from discomfort might mean.

"What do you mean you don't do it anymore?" Monica asked with astonishment. "You *have* to. I mean, that doesn't stop unless you're nearly fifty or something and all played out."

"All I know is that I don't have to worry anymore," Sharelle said, standing by her school locker.

Monica squinted her big eyes and touched Sharelle's shoulder. "Sharelle, honey"—and she smiled broadly—"you're still a good girl, I hope."

When Sharelle looked blankly at her, Monica rejected her own suggestion. "Well, then, who knows? The only three things I know stop the curse are age, cancer, and being pregnant."

Sharelle's eyes widened. Cancer!

Monica saw her concern. "Listen, why not drop in on your doctor?" she offered. "Just to make sure, I mean.

Everything's so easy and private these days. Better that than worrying."

"But I wasn't worrying," Sharelle protested.

"And maybe you don't have to," Monica relented. "But just in case."

The hall bells rang.

In English class, Monica's three possibilities before her, it was cancer Sharelle focused on. It was natural. There were so many things in the air, so many things people ate. So much smog and pollution in the city. So many additives and chemicals in food. After all, her great-aunt Cissy had dried up and died almost within a month from it, and no one ever seemed to know where it came from or where it was. It was mysterious and frightening. Aged fourteen, seated on a hard chair in class, your whole life could be changing inside. And you'd never know until it was too late!

Being pregnant was unimaginable. After all, it had happened only once. That sort of stuff might go on in movies and books but not in real life. Besides, she was smarter than that. It couldn't happen to her. And Dallas —well, he certainly knew his way around. Surely he had taken some precaution. He couldn't have expected her to. She hadn't planned anything. It was her first time. No matter how much you thought about those things, unless you were ready to actually go ahead and do it, there wasn't any reason to prepare.

It had to be cancer.

The odd thing was, as Sharelle considered this, cold sweat running between her shoulders, that in her mind's eye she saw people with cancer wasting away, growing thinner minute by minute, the disease eating up every ounce of energy and reserve fat in one's body. Like Aunt Cissy. But Sharelle was still eating. Eating more than before, maybe. Nothing weird, just larger amounts than usual. Well, what was there to do? She was studying, hiding out, keeping clear of Melba. So what if she took extra Twinkies and Cokes upstairs to help her concentrate? What was abnormal about that?

No, it had to be cancer.

But how to be sure?

6

"MONICA!"

"What?" Monica gathered her books and her purse and stood at her desk, looking at Sharelle.

"Can I go to your doctor?"

"What for?"

"For what you said."

Monica's eyes narrowed. "Which?"

"Cancer," Sharelle whispered.

Monica softened. "Your own has all the records and things."

"Who keeps records of cancer?" Sharelle scoffed. "Will you?"

"What?"

"Make an appointment. Please."

Monica considered. "O.K.," she said finally. "When?"

Sharelle shrugged. "As soon as possible, don't you think?"

"O.K., I'll call when I get home." Monica started towards the door. "You going to the Valentine's dance?"

Sharelle shook her head. "No one's asked me."

"No one has to, silly." Monica smiled. "That's what Women's Lib is all about. No more hanging on, waiting to *be* asked. You just go. You pack your bag, pick up your rifle, aim, and fire. It's us who do the shooting now, not just the boys."

"I never thought of it that way. Who else is going?"

Monica shrugged. "A whole bunch of us. Dutch treat."

She grinned wickedly. "We're going to hang out in a corner and point and stare and whisper, just like the boys."

"Well, I don't know. I'd rather take care of this other first."

Monica sobered. "Oh, Sharelle," she said, her voice lowering dramatically as she went through the door and out into the hallway, "I sure hope I was wrong."

"So do I," admitted Sharelle.

"It would be so tragic," Monica intoned.

And that was the mood in which Sharelle operated for the next few days. She was a tragic heroine, never given enough time, never to be given enough time to live her life fully, fruitfully. She would be cut off in her prime, before she had a chance to make a difference to the world.

It was this idea more than the abstraction of death that consumed her: that no one would ever have known how wonderful she could be, what a great physician, healer, teacher, scientist she could have been. A life of promise never allowed to flower.

She ate while waiting for the afternoon of the appointment Monica had made for her. She had begun to gain weight—a happy sign, she decided, in view of her certain demise. The stronger she could make herself now, the better chance she had with chemotherapy. She began reading magazine articles and supplements on health care, on rehabilitative programs, on support groups. She wondered how Melba would take the news. Thinking about this almost gave her pleasure. She wouldn't be happy to see her mother saddened. It was just that, for a change, even if only for a short time, the focus in Melba's life would have to be on her, Sharelle. Sharelle thought it was just about time for this, anyway, although she was sorry for the reason.

The afternoon of her doctor's appointment, Sharelle allowed Monica to accompany her.

"Well, I wouldn't want to go through this alone,"

Monica said as they walked along the street. "I mean, you need a friend now, you really do."

Sharelle nodded, uncertain exactly what having a friend could do against such a final, fatal sentence. Still, she felt stronger going into a strange doctor's office building with Monica at her side.

When the examination was over, when she came back into the waiting room to pick up her coat and purse and books, she was still dazed. She tried to smile, was determined to smile, and did—weakly.

"Good news!" Monica guessed. "I knew it, I just knew it. What did he say?"

Sharelle shrugged into her coat, avoiding looking directly into Monica's face. "He doesn't think it's cancer."

"Whew!" Monica fanned herself. "So, what is it?"

"He isn't sure," Sharelle allowed herself to say. "He's making some tests."

"Well, at least we know it's not the end," Monica said triumphantly.

Sharelle nodded and started for the door. She wasn't at all sure.

"Now," Monica chirped brightly as they walked away from the doctor's park, "you're free to concentrate on Valentine's Day. All you have to do is pick some hunky guy and zero in. And don't forget that if there's any rejecting to be done, it's you who does it."

"What?" Sharelle asked, not having heard.

"I *said*," Monica repeated, "that *we* get into the gym and size *them* up, not the other way around. It's going to be gang-busters. You know what Marcella Douglas is doing? She's organizing a boys' beauty pageant. The guys have to wear swimming suits, and then a coat and tie, and they have to answer questions and do all kinds of things to win."

"To win what?"

"The crown, the cape," Monica explained. "Saint Valentine!"

37

Monica saw that her friend's mind was wandering. "When do you get the test results?"

Sharelle turned to look at Monica, suddenly sorry she had chosen to share her anxiety even a little with her; Monica, she realized, would hover like a hawk. "Monday," she answered tonelessly.

"Well then, there's time to live! Live and be merry!" Sharelle tried.

She went to the dance.

She tried to smile, to giggle and gossip, to pick at and poke the boys there who had allowed themselves good-naturedly to be put on display, pushed by their girlfriends or teased into it by teammates. She stood around in Monica's group and listened and tried to laugh, to ogle and criticize. But her attention flew, her thoughts splintered.

"*My* vote would go to Pat Fitzroy," Monica whispered to Sharelle. "If only he'd go along with all this."

"Who's he?"

Monica's eyebrows went ceilingward. "The most considerate, the sweetest boy in school. Also, the most gorgeous, the sexiest, the humpiest, the—"

"Which one is he, Monica?" Sharelle interrupted.

Monica pointed.

In a far corner, alone, leaning against monkey bars and looking at the dancing with a slight smile on his face, stood a tall, fair-haired boy with translucent skin and very high color. His arms were folded across his chest and his lower body swayed to keep time to the beat of the recorded music that filled the gymnasium. He wore a letter-sweater, jeans, and running shoes, and seemed somehow distant from all the pink-and-white revelry.

"So, what's a Patrick Fitzroy?" Sharelle asked.

"Just the best-looking senior around," Monica answered, turning to stare at the boy across the way while talking from the side of her mouth to Sharelle. "One

38

thing, though. He drives people absolutely bananas. He's smart, straight A's, a terrific athlete, captain of the basketball team, for God's sakes. He's polite to *everyone* and he takes out the prettiest girls. But no one can get near him."

"What do you mean?"

"What I mean is he could have any girl in this gym, in the whole school, including me. And he doesn't seem to care. He sure doesn't date anyone in particular."

"Maybe he's gay," Sharelle suggested.

Monica shook her head violently. "Not a chance. He's just, well, unique. He *cares* about other people, I think. He's even spoken to me a couple of times. I guess he just has other things on his mind, you know? He's everyone's friend and no one's lover, if you know what I mean."

"It sounds to me like *you're* hooked," Sharelle said. "Besides, unless you go along on those dates he does have, how do you know he doesn't do it?"

"Because I am positively certain that if he made out with someone, just out of pride and joy the girl would shout everything about it to the entire world."

"Would you?"

"Like a shot!" Monica admitted eagerly. "He's a *star*, Sharelle. But no one hates him for it. It's amazing. He's so good with people, from us freshmen up, no one can find anything bad to say about him."

"There must be something."

Monica shook her head again. "Nope. He just wants us to feel good about ourselves, I guess. You sort of feel if Patrick likes you, you can't be all bad."

"I could sure use some of that," Sharelle admitted almost under her breath, looking with deeper interest across the floor at the boy. "He does have beautiful hands," Sharelle whispered. "I mean, even from here."

"Wait till you get up close," Monica advised. "He's got more than a pair of hands on him." She laughed. "Anyway, he won't dance. At least not with me. So"—she

39

shrugged—"it's out into the jungle then for me, sweetie. I'm coming back with a skin of *some* kind!"

Sharelle stepped back to watch her friend begin to mingle and sink into the swirling bodies on the basketball floor.

There was a punch table to one side of where she stood, draped in pink-and-white tablecloths. Sharelle was suddenly thirsty and very hot and there was no crowd around it. She turned and reached out, not for punch but for a can of soda.

The music in her ears seemed suddenly to grow very loud, very clear. The voices from the crowd not far away became clearer, too, as though everything anyone said was shouted directly at her. She began to perspire and to feel just a little weak-kneed. Her stomach made a rumbling sound.

She put down her tin of soda and looked frantically for an exit. There, the door to the girls' lockerroom. She started to walk towards it, purposely moving slowly, struggling against the urge she felt to run, to get away from the oppressiveness of the party. She passed Patrick Fitzroy without looking up at him.

He watched her go, a slight frown creasing his forehead between his eyes. He shifted his stance.

Inside the washroom, Sharelle leaned against a sink, looking above it into a mirror. Her hair was scraggly from perspiration, her make-up shiny. "*What* a pretty girl," she said unpleasantly to her image and then, almost as though she were being thrown across the space, she ran for a john and vomited into it, her knees surrounding the bowl, its disinfectant shocking her nose.

She knelt that way for a moment or two more, waiting, hoping the urge would pass. It did finally, and slowly she pulled up and away and went back to the washbasin to pat cool water on her face. She reached for a paper towel and dabbed the moisture from her skin, again looking into the mirror. What she saw this time she could not avoid. She knew, finally. It was *too* much like movies and television. People didn't throw up unless there was a good reason. Sharelle knew she had exactly that, although she had fought the doctor's diagnosis, had refused to accept it until now.

She wanted to cry. She wanted to be alone and to talk to herself, to hug herself and damn Dallas Edwards to the skies. She wanted to pray, somehow to make a bargain with God about the whole affair. If she could find and make the right promise, maybe everything would just stop where it was before it got out of hand.

The first thing to do was to get out of there before someone else came in. Before Monica tried to find her and ask a lot of questions. The first thing was to go home.

Sharelle brushed her hair quickly, made speedy repairs to her face and eyes, and then approached the door carefully, pulling it open slowly to survey the route to the double door that would lead to freedom and darkness.

She emerged from the women's dressing room and elbowed her way carefully and slowly towards the doorway. A hand suddenly landed on one of her shoulders, and she jumped. She looked directly up at Patrick Fitzroy.

"Are you all right?" he asked sincerely. "Are you ill? Is there anything I can do?"

Sharelle stood, rooted to the floor, wide-eyed. Despite the secret she carried, she was clearheaded and cleareyed enough to look at this young man and to decide he was the most perfectly beautiful boy she had ever seen. His longish blond hair was parted on the left, a shock of it falling over a part of his forehead. His skin was unblemished, colored by the gymnasium lights, but white and gold; his eyes were blue, light blue, and oddly deep for their color. And his eyelashes were the longest and most arresting Sharelle had ever seen. Patrick's mouth was what she focused on as she tried to speak: he had perfectly formed lips, like those of a small child. When he smiled, as he did now expectantly and with concern, she saw that his perfect teeth were not quite that at all, that one of them was discolored a bit, as though it had been damaged in playing football or basketball. In the fraction of a second before she spoke, she had time—she had a sensation there was enough time to categorize everything about Patrick, that he would wait patiently, unselfconsciously, while she did so—even to spot the small brown mole on his left cheek. "I'm all right," she said finally.

"You look a little shaky," Patrick said. "Is there anything I can get you? Would you like a drink?"

Sharelle shook her head. "I thought I'd go home. It's a little close in here, is all. Maybe I'm coming down with something."

Patrick nodded and smiled just slightly. "I'd be happy to drive you, if you like. My name is Pat Fitzroy. My car's just outside."

Sharelle flashed on an idea, a way out, and then rejected it instantly. She couldn't bag him if no one else had been able to. She stood a moment more facing Patrick. Still, she told herself, if she did, he would never know.

No, she couldn't. Never. That would be as bad as what Dallas had done to *her*.

She tried to smile, thinking then that Monica would have died for this opportunity. "No thanks, really," she said. "I'll be fine. I don't live very far from here."

"Still, it's dark out there. You'd be safer in my car."

Sharelle decided this was true. Let Monica eat her heart out. "All right. I appreciate it. Yes."

The two turned and started towards the gym doors.

"My name's Sharelle, Sharelle Marston," Sharelle said as Patrick opened the door for her.

Which was all she said for the few moments it took Patrick to drive to her house. He helped her into the car, got in his own side, looked sideways at her once with a nice smile and started the car's ignition. She came to life once with a start to point and say, "Take a right, there," and then finally, "O.K., this is it." But they did not chat, or try to *make* talk.

Sharelle noticed how clean the car was, not tricked out with all the gimmicks and hanging doodads that Dallas and Annette's friends had. Once she looked over to see Patrick's hands on the steering wheel, again admiring the strength and length of his fingers but afraid to raise her eyes to his face.

"Thank you," she said as he pulled the car to the curb in front of Melba's house.

"Are you feeling any better?" Patrick asked. "Would you like me to go in with you?"

Sharelle would have liked that very much, but the thought of Melba at home and the excited little scene she might treat her daughter's friend to made her shake her head. "No, I'm going to be fine, really. You should go back to the party."

Patrick smiled and shook his head. "I've had it," he said quietly. "It was fun to see, but it's not really my scene."

Sharelle turned then to look directly at him and felt a sudden, thrilling hollow in her stomach as Patrick looked back at her. He made no motion, gave no sign he was interested in her other than as someone who might have needed help. But Sharelle felt powerful and powerless at the same time, glowed inside, and felt committed— and also hopeless.

"Thank you," she said softly as she got out of the car.

"See you," Patrick called out.

Sharelle nodded.

And as she walked up the short walkway to the front of her house, her eyes clouded and her lower lip trembled, and both reactions had nothing to do with the idea she now carried with certainty, that she was pregnant.

43

7

ON Palm Sunday, one week before Easter, Sharelle sat in her mother's dining room, forced to listen.

Annette was pregnant.

Melba thought that was a mistake. "Not a mistake, honey, so much as bad timing," she corrected, smoking at her end of the table before Sharelle or her sister had finished their dinner.

"Look," Melba explained, leaning both her elbows on the table, pointing her chin towards her older daughter, "you're young, you're pretty. You've got a go-ahead man. What makes you think he wants a baby now? That he won't take a look, one good long look at you when you're about eight months along, and decide, hell, *I* don't need this?"

"Mama," Annette said weakly, "I know what you're saying. I just don't know what to do."

"You do, too," Melba said firmly, exhaling a cloud of smoke and leaning back in her chair. "Even Sharelle here would know what to do."

But Sharelle there didn't.

She had been waiting. She couldn't have said for what. Time was passing. She could feel changes. She was grateful that morning sickness did not seem to be her lot. Or, on those occasions when it was, that Melba was already up, out of the house, on her way to work. She didn't ap-

44

pear to have gained much weight, and what did show only made Melba smile and say, "See, I told you it was all a matter of time before you filled out."

"Mama," Annette said then, "I can't do that."

"Why not?" asked Melba. "Lot's of women do. It's just a matter of putting things off for a bit, waiting till a better time."

"But it's killing someone," Annette protested. "I can't do that. I couldn't ever."

"Better that," Melba replied, stubbing out her cigarette, "than killing your married life. Which is what having babies too soon does, believe you me. You think I'd be alone all this time if I'd known? You think having you, Annette, was such a terrific favor for me?"

"Mama," Annette said softly, smiling tolerantly, "I *know* you don't mean that."

Melba relented. "You're right. I did want you, you little mouse. That's what you were, that's exactly what you looked like."

"Well, if you couldn't, then how could I?" asked Annette.

"*I* couldn't," Melba answered quickly, "because I didn't know enough. All the . . . the technology wasn't available. It was a sin then, a real honest-to-God sin even to think about it. But today, baby, no one even gives it a second thought."

Sharelle had. "What does Dallas say?" she asked quietly.

Annette turned to face her sister. "He says whatever I want is O.K. by him. Maybe secretly he's hoping something will go wrong. I don't know."

"You *see*," Melba interrupted. "At least he's got sense, that boy. I knew it the minute you told me what he did for a living. That's an ambitious boy, Annette, and having a child now is just going to take the steam out of him. You think he'll work so hard, take extra trips the way he does now? Not on your life! The only long haul he might

45

make is out of here, to Mexico or Canada or somewhere, and that'd be the last you'd see of him."

"I don't believe that, Mama," Annette defended. "Dallas is working overtime now for things we want, things that'll make our life a little nicer. Why wouldn't he feel the same about working hard for a baby, to give *him* the same kinds of things?"

"He might, but don't bet on it," Melba retorted. "Now, I'm not sayin' what I say is Gospel, but you got to admit, around men I've had a little extra time, a little more experience."

"I do, Mama," Annette said diplomatically. "That's what I'm doing here, after all. Trying to find out what you think I should do."

"Well, you know what I think," Melba toughened, lighting another cigarette. "It's not like you got married because of this, Annette. No one is counting back. You can do it any time you choose. That's the miracle of life today, honey. That you *can* choose."

Sharelle had a thought there, but held it.

"You don't think Sharelle would hesitate a minute, do you, if, God forbid, something like this should happen to her?" Melba asked then.

"Mama, Sharelle's a child. She's not married. Of course, she'd think about it. *I* think about it, Mama. I just can't convince myself it's the right thing."

"The right thing to do changes all the time," Melba announced certainly. "What's wrong yesterday is O.K. today. I mean, look around. See what's happenin'. You think I'd have let you go out and get a job at McDonald's like Sharelle when you were her age? Not on your life. But Sharelle's determined, Annette. She's not like you, floatin' through life, looking good. She's got a head on her shoulders. She wants to be something. Working for her is a way of storing up so that when college comes, she can help instead of just take. And I appreciate that, honey, I really do," Melba added, reaching out to pat the top of Sharelle's hand.

Sharelle nodded and tried to smile.

The reason she had gotten a work permit and started her part-time job was to put money aside, in case. Not for college. Just for *in case*.

"Mama," Annette said somewhat testily, "I didn't want to go to college. I'm not that smart."

"No, that's not true, honey," her mother said, swinging quickly back to her normal order of preference. "You're plenty smart. Look at you, Annette. You got a husband! You latched hold of someone who makes good money, a lot of it. You don't think that's smart?"

"I think it was lucky," Annette decided.

"I won't argue with that!" Melba laughed. Sharelle watched the leftover lungful of smoke emerge from her mother's mouth in short spurts. Then, after a second, she stood up to begin clearing the table.

She wasn't as lucky as Annette. Or as pretty or popular. Nobody had ever taken one good long look and loved her on the spot, as Dallas must have with Annette.

Which caused her to look up from the sink where she was rinsing plates, and to look sightlessly out the back window into a neighbor's yard.

Dallas.

Sharelle had first heard the news of Annette's impending event while she was standing at the same window. Dallas and Annette were in the dining room with Melba, and Sharelle's ears burned and tears came to her eyes when she overheard them. She had pulled herself together. She knew she would have to go back to the table to be told what she already knew, and that she would have to pretend it was a surprise and a delight.

But she was angry. Not at Annette. After all she was her own sister, and if having that creep's baby was what she wanted, more power to her. But Dallas!

Who did he think he was, flitting over the countryside, getting people pregnant without thought or feeling or even knowing what he was doing?

She had dried her eyes then and stayed in the kitchen as long as she could. She would be long dead in her grave, she decided, before she let Dallas know about this other baby-to-be. If this child ever saw the light of day, it was going to be hers, and hers alone, period. She might have to struggle, she would have to change plans, she wouldn't be free any longer. But the one thing she *would* be was *loved*. That little kid, boy or girl, *had* to love her, for herself, with all her faults. It would depend on her and wait for her and play with her and laugh at her and learn for her and obey. And she would know, deep down, that the love she saw in those tiny bright eyes would never change, could never change. No matter what she did, whether she was rich or poor, that child was hers and would love and respect her and admire her for herself always.

If Dallas thought he was going to get even a part of that baby, he was crazy! He wanted his own, fine. Sharelle never doubted that Dallas felt something for Annette, a lot more than he ever felt for her. So if that was what they wanted, O.K. But not her child. Hers was hers if it was going to be at all.

That had been easy to say weeks before because Sharelle had been angry. Now, time had passed, and if she were honest, she would have admitted to feeling more trapped and forlorn. She had the power now to make other people angry and unhappy, to cause someone else's marriage to split, to disappoint and shame her mother. That power for destruction was about the only idea these days that gave her any pleasure, secretly to be sure, but made her smile to herself just the same. Boy, could she drop a couple of bombs!

She knew the solution was simple. Life *could* be easy again. And because she knew this she worked after school and on weekends at McDonald's. Suppose she did make the decision Melba was pushing at Annette? Who on earth could she expect to pay for it? She couldn't ask Melba without being shouted at or worse. Annette would make demands, want to know too much. And she could hardly go around soliciting for one of Melba's charities and then run off with the proceeds to have the operation. Where could she go? What would she live on?

She had thought, once, of enlisting her grandmother's help. But then she went to visit her one evening and saw her with unblinking eyes. True, the old woman lived alone and seemed to have extra room and many comforts. But also true, her grandmother wasn't well. She had emphysema (you'd have thought Melba would understand and change her habits, but then that wouldn't be Melba) and she needed oxygen everyday and some nights just to get through, and she didn't eat well or even seem to remember how to cook. Her hospital and doctors' bills were enormous. Melba complained at home about how she and Jack were being burdened and drained when it would have been so simple years ago for her mother to have taken out insurance of some kind. To get some now was almost impossible and hugely expensive, and neither of her children could afford to do that without causing their own families hardship.

Sharelle sat that night and talked with the old woman, seeing her as a possible refuge, just in case. She tried to imagine what her grandmother would say if she were told she was about to be a great-grandmother. Sharelle thought she might be more pleased than angry, but probably because she wouldn't really understand what that meant—that her fourteen-year-old granddaughter had been taken by surprise and didn't know what to do about it, about anything.

Sharelle knew a decision had to be made. Monica's doctor, after the last time Sharelle had been examined by him and had been told that she was definitely carrying a child, had suggested that she tell her own family

49

doctor and ask to be put on a supplementary diet, and that she make a complete schedule of regular visits with him. If she needed more help, Monica's doctor had advised kindly, there were family-planning clinics around the city to which she could apply, and she should certainly investigate MediCal because it was not cheap to have a baby these days. He had smiled sweetly then at her, recalling that having children had never been cheap in the first place—an idea Sharelle grasped quickly as she paid her bill.

But MediCal sounded to Sharelle like something for old people. Worse, it and the clinics, too, sounded like Welfare. And in the Marston family, Welfare was, had always been, a dirty word. Besides, the few kids Sharelle knew whose families were receiving some sort of government aid always complained about how getting it— lining up, filling out forms, being visited by people who had no business in your own house and yet were always snooping around—was demeaning and embarrassing and something no one in his right mind should ever do. And Sharelle felt she couldn't do it, either. She couldn't imagine that kind of surrender. Whether or not she had the child, she was positive that the one thing she had to do was work her way *back*, make amends, so that she could look at herself in a mirror proudly, knowing she was clean and alive and strong.

So she waited, and hoped.

She didn't expect to fall down a flight of stairs. She didn't imagine a mysterious virus invading her body. But she just couldn't quite let the idea go that everything was a bad dream and that, some day soon, she would awake and smile with relief and gratitude, back to normal.

Besides, there was still time.

8

TIME ran out behind the counter at McDonald's.

One Saturday, in the mall to which McDonald's was attached, a large white van rolled in and parked; a blue cross and the call letters of a San Diego television station were stenciled on its side. An awning was put over the doors to the van, and placards on easels announced *Health Fair*. Free X-rays, Blood Tests, Immunizations.

Sharelle had been aware vaguely of the week-long campaign, a combination of good citizenship and advertising that the station had promoted on all its news programs. The idea that she herself could take advantage of the services offered had not occurred to her. But it did increasingly as the day—flavored by the smell of oil and french-fried potatoes, of melting cheese and charred beef —progressed. In fact, Sharelle had not been feeling as strong as she was used to lately, and working at McDonald's—which she intended to do as long as she could— was harder and harder, on her legs, on her back.

Happily, school would soon be over for the year. She could stop worrying about whether anyone there, especially Monica Ruskin, suspected her condition. She could stop getting up a few minutes early each morning to assemble a wardrobe that covered what had to be covered, not just from her classmates but from Melba as well.

Melba was too self-absorbed to do more than take a quick glance each morning at her daughter as she rushed

51

out the side door to her car on her way to work. She waved, or shouted something about needing items from the store, or told her daughter to have a good day, work hard, be a good girl. Sharelle nodded and waved back and then breathed more freely as she heard Melba's Camaro start, cough, sputter, and then calm to a roar that was probably against sound-abatement rules and regulations for residential neighborhoods.

As far as Sharelle was concerned, she had only one reason to congratulate herself. She carried extra weight without showing it: her height made the new pounds seem well-distributed. That they were centered at her abdomen instead of elswhere, as she had hoped in seventh and eighth grades, was just one of those things.

Sharelle worked all Saturday morning and through noon, watching the parking lot whenever she had a free moment, seeing lines of people—elderly, middle-aged, young with children—line up outside the van for whatever it was they felt they needed to have checked. Frequently reporters with television cameras approached the line and did quick interviews that would show up later on the four-thirty, five-thirty, and eleven-o'clock newscasts.

At four, when Sharelle finished working, she wrapped a light sweater about her shoulders and said good-bye to her new but not really personal friends at McDonald's, and left the shop. She circled the block once and then came to the van from a direction not easily visible from where she worked. She waited in line, a short one, for by that time people were beginning to hurry away home to prepare for whatever big Saturday night doings they planned. She mounted the two shallow steps of the van and entered it, surprised at once that so much heavy medical equipment could be installed in such a small space.

Just inside the door, to her right, sat a young woman who seemed not much older than Annette. She looked up at Sharelle and smiled. "Well, there's time for one more, I guess," she said, clearly tired but pleasant to the end. "What's your problem?"

Sharelle went cold. She had never said this out loud. "I'm pregnant," she said nervously.

The young woman's forehead furrowed and her smile faltered for a second but then returned, forced. "Well, you're certainly lucky," she said. "You look like you're making it through in a breeze."

"That's what I need to know," Sharelle said. "Am I?"

"How do you mean?" asked the woman. "Do you mean, uh, developmentally, or nutritionally, or what?"

Sharelle shrugged. 'I was thinking about an . . . an abortion."

The woman inhaled, looking away for a second. "How far gone are you?" she asked.

"Pardon me?"

"How long ago did this happen? How many months ago did you *get* pregnant?"

Sharelle counted back. "About six, I think."

"Six months?"

Sharelle nodded. "I guess.".

The woman sighed.

A man's voice came from behind a wall of dials and lights. "Maggie? How many more?"

"Not too many, Jimbo," the young woman called back, "Take a break. I can hold the fort for a while."

"Right," said the voice. There was a scurry and then a young man in white appeared at an edge of the van's interior. "Want some coffee?" he asked, looking quickly at Sharelle.

"No, thanks. You go," said Maggie. "I'll wait till later."

"Right you are," said Jim, and slipped down the steps to the mall's parking lot, heading towards McDonald's.

"Would you like to sit down?" Maggie asked Sharelle.

"No, I'm all right. What I need to know is . . . is . . . does it hurt?"

53

"You don't need to know that, dear," Maggie replied. "But tell me, does your family know you're pregnant?"

"No. Not yet."

"You'd better tell them then, and soon," said Maggie seriously.

"No, I don't want to," Sharelle argued. "That's why I came here. To find out about . . . about . . ."

"You're too late for that, I'm afraid."

"Why, what do you mean?" Sharelle wondered. "Do I have to come back tomorrow?"

Maggie smiled sympathetically. "No, honey, that's not what I mean. What I'm trying to say is that you're way past the time for doing anything like that. Don't you know? Didn't anyone ever tell you?"

"Tell me what?" Sharelle demanded.

"That you can't abort after a certain period of time's gone by. That it becomes dangerous then. That there's a certain point of no return, unless you want to go through some pretty expensive, painful surgery. And then what would you do? Suppose the baby lived? Could you take care of it?"

Sharelle felt dizzy. "I don't get it," she said quietly. "You mean I *have* to have it now?"

"Well, I think so," said Maggie. "At least, from everything we know, having it is less dangerous now than not."

"Oh, God!" Sharelle moaned.

Maggie leaned back in her chair and looked up at her visitor. "Have you even been to a doctor?"

Sharelle nodded.

"Well, what did he say?"

Sharelle shrugged. "He gave me some vitamins."

"Is that all?"

Sharelle shook her head. "I haven't— My own doctor, my mother's, I mean, well, I just never got . . ."

". . . around to it" said Maggie, completing Sharelle's thought. "I think maybe the time has come for you to tell your mother."

"I can't!" Sharelle gasped. "She'd kill me!"

"She might not," Maggie counseled. "She might be angry at first, or hurt. But you're still her child. And that's still her grandson or -daughter. Don't underestimate the help your family can give."

Sharelle smiled thinly. "I don't think I am."

Maggie examined Sharelle. "Perhaps you're right," she said then. "But I hope not. Now, though, I guess there's not much we can do for you here. Oh, we can take some blood, make sure you're not anemic. We can give you some things to read, if you'd like, that might explain things a little." She ducked her head and swiveled around to open a shallow file drawer. "Will you take these?" she asked, holding out several pamphlets towards Sharelle. "And, also, I'd feel awfully pleased if you'd take *my* card, just in case there are other things you wonder about. I'm available almost every day. I'd like very much to help, if I can. If you'll let me."

Sharelle accepted the packet of materials and put Maggie's card without reading it into her purse. "I'm not afraid to ask for help," she said after a moment. "I'm just not sure there's anything you can do."

"Well, just in case, then." Maggie smiled. "Would you like me to draw some blood and send it out?"

Sharelle shook her head. "I'm all right. A little tired, maybe, but that's all."

"Well, that's what the test would show, too. I mean, if you were tired, run-down a little. You've got to balance a diet when you're pregnant, you know."

Sharelle nodded, having heard this before.

"You're sure there isn't anything I could do—I mean, the other thing . . . ?" Sharelle asked again.

Maggie shook her head. "I'm afraid not. Certainly not here, not outside a hospital. You really should talk to your own doctor. Even if you won't tell your parents. Perhaps *he* could explain to them for you."

Sharelle smiled sweetly. "I don't imagine there's much

my mother doesn't understand about these things," she said slyly. "Thanks, anyway."

She stepped back out of the van the way she came, rather than following the brightly painted red arrows that led to another exit. The sun was still shining. People were milling about, making last-minute runs into the Safeway or a drugstore or the liquor store, stocking up for the weekend.

Sharelle stood a moment beneath the awning looking across the parking lot. She watched as an old-fashioned convertible, shiny and polished and obviously well-cared-for, wheeled into the area and pulled to a stop before McDonald's. She counted six, then seven, little kids, none of them older than eight, spilling out onto the pavement, running into McDonald's with what seemed like money clenched in their small hands. The kids looked dusty and grimy and tired, but happy, and seemed to come from every conceivable neighborhood: black, Chicano, Chinese, white. Old Mother Hubbard, Sharelle said to herself and smiled.

Then she recognized the mob's driver. It was Patrick Fitzroy.

She watched as he pulled himself up to sit on the back of the front seat, directing his troops, waving, shouting, laughing at them. They in turn gave as good as they got: they teased, shouted back, disappeared, reappeared to leap back up into the car, tiny hands full of smearing catsup and mustard and spilling soft drinks. None of this seemed to trouble Patrick. He laughed and brushed back his blond hair from his forehead and sank back down behind the steering wheel of his car. A song floated upwards from the convertible as it waited a second at the curb of the mall's lot, before turning into traffic and drifting away towards the ocean.

Inside, Sharelle shouted: Wait! Take me with you! Take me along!

She stood a while longer in the shade of the awning,

wondering about Patrick. She remembered vividly how concerned he had seemed the night of the Valentine's Day dance, how gentle he had been, how thoughtful. Also, she recalled now, how calm, how distant.

She had caught sight of him in the halls at school every so often since then but had never come face to face with him, or had to embarrass herself by discovering whether he remembered her. He was ever the senior star, still perplexing Monica and her friends, a four-letter man in basketball, captain of the team, good student, quiet man. Sharelle had not gone to the Senior Prom. No one invited her; she knew hardly anyone in that class, anyway. But now she wondered whom Patrick had taken.

She could imagine the pride of being his date, of standing beside him. She would have bet a nickel he would be a good dancer. He was agile on the court (she had gone to the final two games of the season, not to see Patrick play but just to escape Melba), and graceful despite his height and the slightly pigeon-toed lope he employed to hustle the ball down the wooden floor.

In the fading sunlight of the mall, Sharelle remembered the texture and color of Patrick's skin in his basketball jersey, and the sense of strength in his sinews and tendons. If *she* could have been his date for the Prom, she would have expected nothing, would have been joyous just to stand beside him, to fill his arms in a friendly, affectionate way, expecting nothing more than sweetness and care. She would have been proud.

She remembered then with a smile Monica's suspicion that any girl who managed to sleep with Patrick, or even get close to him, would be unable not to boast. Sharelle decided Monica was probably right, but that if ever she had the chance, she would fight like anything not to do that.

And the chances? she asked herself as she thoughtfully started walking home. None. Absolutely none.

There was enough light left as she walked to pull out

57

of her purse the pamphlets that had been given to her at the Health Fair. Idly she looked at their titles: "Proper Nutrition for Your Baby," "Child Development: Knowing What to Expect and When," "Public Aid Program for Needy Families."

She didn't have a needy family. Yet. She didn't think she needed to know what and when to expect a child to do anything. If she had to go ahead and have the baby, she—she stopped short on the sidewalk. She hadn't even thought what sort of child she wanted. The few times she'd allowed herself to come close enough to the prospect that lay in shadows somewhere ahead, all she had envisioned were beautiful clothes, petite, tiny things carefully made and tended, laid out neatly and colorfully in a tiny bureau.

What did she want?

Not to have a baby?

No. Sharelle shook her head. Finally, no. She wanted to have the baby. Secretly she was relieved not to have to explore abortion. What had happened happened because of Dallas' greed and her own silliness. There was no need to punish an innocent child for either.

She put the leaflets back into her purse and walked straight ahead, her neck stiff, her eyes clear. She wondered if she really could tell her mother. She might. She just might. But not about one thing. Her mother must never know *who*. Annette must never know, either. It would break her heart.

As for Dallas, he knew he had been the first. But Sharelle doubted he was quick enough, or responsible enough, to figure everything out. He'd probably decide she'd been seeing boys her own age. Since clearly he thought sex was normal and everyday, there wouldn't be any reason for him to think that *her* doing the same was shameful or selfish.

Besides, Sharelle wanted nothing more to do with him, ever. Not just because of what had happened on the beach. But also because, in her heart, she still felt betrayed. There had been that one moment when Dallas could have stood tall and straight as a man and taken her hand and together they could have faced down the world. He didn't. Sharelle now thought the idea had probably never even crossed his mind. He had been horny and on the make, and she had been stupid enough not to see this and take precautions. Or even to say, No.

That night—"Hey! Saturday Night in the Big Town!" —Melba went out with a group of friends, leaving Sharelle to entertain herself with television or a book. Melba did stand at the threshold of the living room just before leaving and, seeing Sharelle sprawled on a couch in front of the television screen, teased her younger daughter. "After all the time you ached to have 'em" she said laughingly, "here you are, hidin' 'em!" And she laughed again and shook her head. "I ever tell you how you got your name, honey?" Melba asked, swinging her hips a little in time to music from years past. "There were only two groups I liked when I was a kid. One was called the Beach Boys, and the other the Shirelles. Well, I couldn't hardly call you Beach Boy Marston, could I?" She giggled, happy and excited, anticipating the evening ahead. "Beach Boy Marston! Boy, that would have been something! Beach Boy Marston!"

Sharelle smiled obligingly and nodded. Her mother had told her that before. As well as how the "a" in her name came to be substituted for the "i" her mother intended: a non-musical county registrar. She kept her eyes on the television set and waited to hear the front door close. It did, and Sharelle snuggled into the corner of the couch.

Melba really wasn't being fair. It wasn't that Sharelle wouldn't like to go out, wouldn't like to have a boyfriend. But it wasn't entirely up to her. True, her breasts had grown lately, and the breadth of her shoulders seemed no longer so disproportionate since she was filling out.

59

Still, what was needed was someone to look at her, to see her the way Dallas said *he* had. Until then, Sharelle thought, she would wait. She didn't really feel "awakened," a word she had read in some article. She wasn't eager for more experience just yet. She hadn't been all that excited about the experience to begin with. And now that she'd had it, there was no longer any doubt in her mind of its consequences.

There wasn't anything on the tube she wanted to watch. The Saturday-night movies were ones she'd already seen. She sighed and sat up. Actually, she was tired, bone-weary. Maybe she'd just make a sandwich, take a bath, and go to bed. Maybe look at those leaflets again.

The long day came to an end as Sharelle nodded off, her bedside lamp still glowing, the top covers of her bed scattered with pamphlets about breast-feeding, resumption of sexual activity, liquid formulae and diets, pediatricians. Her dreams did not include visions of herself as a mother. Instead, she smiled in her sleep to see again the gaggle of little boys piling out of Patrick's car, looking for all the world like multicolored clowns at the circus exploding from the world's tiniest car.

Some while later Melba's Camaro growled into the driveway and grew silent. Two sets of footsteps echoed on the short, paved walk to the house, and two figures entered stealthily—afraid, it seemed, to make a sound for the sleeping girl upstairs.

Melba ushered her new-found friend Frank into her parlor and asked what he wanted to drink. "I'll stick to the same poison," Frank replied, looking approvingly around the small room, swaying just a little, spotting the couch and collapsing quickly onto it. "Bourbon and branch-water, honey," he added unnecessarily. They had both been knocking back the same combination with regularity for hours.

Melba put her finger to her mouth to counsel silence

as she turned to walk into the kitchen to make the drinks. She walked securely, steadily, confident since this was her house and it was unlikely there were new corners or treacherous turnings.

She returned a few minutes later carrying two glasses, one of which she handed to her friend. Frank was drowsy, or looked so, but he managed to raise his hand to take the drink and to smile up at Melba in a silent toast. She raised her glass in return and sipped, thinking to herself that Frank wasn't to die for, but he was certainly good enough to live for for an hour or two longer. He was older than she by a few years, still relatively trim though with just the slightest roundness below his belt as befits a man of forty in a sedentary occupation. His hair was thinning but not yet seriously, and Melba liked both his height and his hands, long and narrow, tapered and flexible.

Melba took another swallow and then put her glass atop an end table. "I'd better check on the kid," she said quietly. "Her lights were still on."

Frank nodded and said, "Um-hmm, right," and drank again. Melba smiled and left the room.

At the top of the backstairs landing Melba stood a moment to collect herself, clear her eyes, straighten her slip beneath her skirt. Light shone from beneath Sharelle's door. Melba tiptoed forward and put her ear to the wood panel to listen. Nothing. Ever so gently she touched the door handle and turned slowly. The door opened.

The brightness of the bedside lamp made Melba blink her eyes. When she saw clearly, what she saw she approved. Her stay-at-home had been studying. Good; at least one of her children was determined to *be* something. The idea of having a child in college sometimes appealed to her. Actually she was a bit in awe of this second daughter, whom she knew she had largely ignored as she struggled to put down roots of her own, financially and socially, and who was always willing to do whatever she was told. She had been a placid baby, almost trouble-free, dependable. Best of all, Sharelle had never made Melba feel guilty about the way she lived, or the choices she felt forced to make. Whatever guilt Melba *did* feel was entirely her own, and she was not unhappy to recognize it since Sharelle herself seemed so able to get by in life independently.

It was with something close to tenderness that Melba approached her daughter's bedside and reached out to remove from its coverlet the pages Sharelle had apparently fallen asleep over. She shuffled them neatly into a pile and put them on the table beside the map. As she leaned over to switch off the lamp, unable to look directly into its glare, her eyes fell on the top leaflet. "Pregnancy Is Not a Sickness," was its headline.

Melba's eyes opened a bit wider and her gentle, reflective smile wavered. She reached out again for the pile of paper and straightened up to thumb through it. "Picking a Family Doctor." "The Importance of Nutrition in Child-Rearing." "When to Call Your Doctor, and When Not To." "The First Two Years."

She tapped the packet against her hand and stood a moment without moving. Then, still undecided, she put everything back on the table and turned quickly to leave the room, not touching the controls of the lamp.

She found herself in the kitchen and realized she had no recollection of coming down the stairs.

In the living room, Frank had loosened his tie and undone the top two buttons of his shirt. He was smoking now, his long legs stretched out in front of him, crossed at the ankles. He looked up lazily as Melba stood in the doorway. "Everything cool?" he asked, winking.

Everything was *not* cool. Melba looked at the man and had to make a conscious effort to identify him, then to make the connection between who he was and what he was doing in her home.

She took a few steps into the room in order to get

closer to her drink. She bent down and lifted the glass to her lips. She let out a chestful of air loudly, put the glass down again, and went to get her cigarettes from her purse. She lit one and finally turned back to look at Frank.

"The little bitch!" she whispered.

"What?"

"That dishonest, ungrateful goddamn slut! Who the hell is it? That's what I want to know!"

"What's the matter, honey?" Frank asked, a little more alert suddenly. In fact, a little edgy. He sat up on the couch, looking at Melba.

"Jesus, I should have known!" Melba half-shouted, waving an arm. "My God, I was absolutely blind! Why else would she go get a job? Having a baby's expensive, for God's sakes! Why else would she sneak around, being helpful and pretending to care about things? She's got to have someone to lean on, somewhere to live; Who in hell is the boy, that's what I want to know! Where is *he*, I'd like to know! What was she thinking of? I mean, she's bright, she knows her way around. She knows how things happen. How could she do this? How could she do this to me? And what about the boy, I want to know! What's *he* going to do? God, the disgrace! I mean, after everything I taught her, after everything I've done for her, to turn around and dump *this* on me! And where in hell is the father, that's what I want to know! Ohmygod! Maybe she doesn't even know who the father is!"

"Easy there, baby," cautioned Frank, almost completely clear-eyed now. "Who you talking about? Who's got you so all fired up?"

But Melba seemed not to hear. She was still on a roll, gathering a head of steam and finding as its gauge inched upwards to an invisible red line that relief was still nowhere ahead.

"I mean, how long did she think she could hide this? After all, sooner or later you can see this sort of thing, can't you?" Melba stopped suddenly, inhaled on her cigarette and reached again for her drink. "Maybe it's not too late," she said almost in a whisper. "Maybe that's why I never noticed. I mean, if she's only a little way along, we can stop the whole thing."

Frank's eyes went from one exit of the room to another, from the threshold that led to the kitchen to the front door at his right. "That's right," he said comfortingly. "Maybe you're just over-reacting."

"Over-reacting!" Melba shouted. "I'll give you over-react!"

And she whirled on her heel and marched back into the kitchen.

Frank didn't wait to hear the sound of her heels on the back stairs. He grabbed his jacket and swiveled right, reaching out for the front door handle a dozen feet before his hand could connect with its brass.

Sharelle did not even hear the blow. Her mother's open hand swung down and caught her sharply on the side of her face, against her ear. Her eyes opened in fear and her ear began to ring before she was even aware she had been hit. She brought her hand to her cheek and swung up quickly out of bed at the same time. Her mother was inches from her face, her mouth open. It took a second for Sharelle to hear her clearly.

". . . whoring around, that's what I want to know!" Melba was shouting. "Right under my own roof, I suppose! What gives you the right, that's what I want to know? Who do you think you are that you can play fast and loose and expect to get away with it?"

Sharelle stared not at her mother's face but at her upraised hand. Her room was so small. There was no place to run, to hide.

"Who is he?" Melba shouted, her hand cleaving the air. Sharelle ducked instinctively and Melba's blow skimmed off the top of her head. "Or do you even know who it is, missy?" demanded Melba. "Maybe that's it.

64

You don't know! How could you tell anyone if you didn't know? How long is it? How long?"

"What . . . what do you mean?" Sharelle asked, afraid but aware also that there was something besides fear building up inside her.

"What I mean is that maybe it's not too late. We can have it taken care of. Get an operation. Now, how long ago was it?"

"I don't know, exactly," Sharelle lied.

"Ohmygod!" Melba moaned. "I was right! She doesn't even know what boy it was!"

"Yes, I do!" Sharelle said quickly, regretting it instantly.

Melba's eyes widened and her hands went to her hips. "All right, then, Little Miss Sophisticated, who was it?"

"I can't tell you," Sharelle replied.

"You mean you won't."

"I mean I can't and I won't," Sharelle said. "It doesn't matter anyway."

"Well, it sure as hell matters to me!" Melba shouted. "You telling me he's going to get off scot-free?"

Sharelle shrugged and tried to move away, but Melba reached out and grabbed her shoulder. "Sharelle!"

Sharelle was spun around. "Yes, he is getting off!" she replied angrily. "And it's none of your business, either."

"Oh ho!" Melba crowed. "That's what you think, missy! You think you can come slinking home carrying somebody's little bastard and expect me to look the other way?"

"No, I don't expect that!" Sharelle shouted, the anger that had been lit finally flashing into flame. "If I had, I'd had told you about this, wouldn't I?"

"God alone knows!" Melba shouted back.

"I didn't want this, you know," Sharelle went on. "It's not my idea of heaven, you want to know."

"Well, at least there's some sense left in your tiny brain, then," Melba said, lowering her voice finally.

65

"The whole thing . . . everything, I mean . . ." Sharelle turned away, beginning to cry despite her resolve. "I wanted *more!*"

Melba watched a minute. "I wanted more for you," she admitted softly. She paused. "Sharelle, honey, don't have it."

Sharelle shook her head. "It's too late," she told her mother.

"Ohmygod!" Melba whispered. Then: "What on earth were you thinking of, I'd like to know? I mean, maybe we never did get around to talking about all this, drawing diagrams and looking at picture books, but surely you knew? Surely?"

"Mama!" Sharelle wept openly. "I didn't think it would happen. I wasn't planning it. It just happened!"

Melba nodded firmly. "How many times? How many boys?"

Sharelle's tears stopped and she stared at her mother. "Mama," she half-screamed, "look at me! Do you think I'm even halfway pretty enough for that kind of thing? Look at me!"

Melba looked but didn't see. "I never thought," she said slowly, "it never occurred to me how jealous of Annette you were."

"Annette?" Sharelle shouted. "You have to be kidding! I wouldn't be Annette for anything in the world!"

"Of course," Melba continued, almost talking to herself, "it's understandable. The older daughter gets married, gets a lot of attention. No one pays you any mind. I suppose it's almost natural to want to seem important to someone, no matter who, when all that's going on."

"Mama! You're not paying attention!" Sharelle was exasperated. "I'm asking you for help and you're playing psychiatrist."

"Help?" Melba repeated a little foggily. "Help? Is that what's going on here, when my own daughter can't come to me when she's in trouble?"

"All right, Mama, I admit that," Sharelle said. "I didn't. I was scared. I kept hoping I was wrong, that something would happen. I didn't want you to be hurt, or angry."

"Well, for someone who didn't want that, I'd say you did a pretty good job of making sure that was exactly what I was!"

Sharelle sighed loudly and turned away. "Come on, Mama, what about me? What about me?"

Melba reached out and grabbed Sharelle's shoulders, swinging her around. "You?" she screamed. "You? You're turning my hair gray! You're crucifying me!"

"And what do I get?" Sharelle shouted in return. "No college, no boyfriends, no career, no fun—a dirty little kid to carry around and pick up after and feed and change and stay home with for the rest of my life!"

"You don't think you deserve that?" Melba yelled. "After what you've done?" She pushed Sharelle roughly and her daughter fell back atop her bed. "No one in our fam'y has ever had to get married, young lady! And if you don't know who's responsible, if no one *wants* you for anything but a quick lay on a warm night, then as far as I can see you got exactly what you deserve Don't expect anything from me!"

Melba turned instantly and stamped out of the room and down the back stairs. Sharelle was tempted to cry but did not. She lay, listening. She heard the refrigerator being pulled open, she heard the clink of ice cubes falling into a glass. She nodded to herself, oddly satisfied. Talk about getting what you deserve, she said to herself with a wicked but rather small smile.

Then she turned over and wept into her pillow, asking over and over again in her mind what she was going to do now.

9

SHARELLE woke late the next morning. She opened her eyes and saw the bedside lamp was still burning. Fine with her. She rolled over in bed and lay listening. She heard nothing out of the ordinary: birds, cars, a few kids on the street below.

No sound from Melba.

Which wasn't unusual. After a night's "entertainment," Melba frequently slept in. Annette and Sharelle had both been taught to tread softly on Sunday mornings.

There was sun outside. Sharelle could see it through her shades, almost feel its warmth. She raised the shade closest to her bed and squinted out. She was aware suddenly that she had a headache and that her stomach hurt a little.

She swung out of bed and went to the bathroom, washed, brushed her teeth, and put on a robe. Barefoot, she slipped down the back stairs and went to the refrigerator and pulled out a Fresca. She thought maybe the bubbles in it would help her stomach.

She walked out into the living room and looked around. Melba's purse was on a table, and there were two liquor glasses, one half-full, making rings on another. She lifted them both and carried them back into the kitchen and put them in the dishwasher. She remembered the Sunday paper, so she tiptoed back through the living room to the front door and opened it, expecting to lean out and bring it in. It wasn't there.

Sharelle stood in the doorway, thinking. Maybe Melba had it, upstairs. No, she'd never do that. She hardly ever looked at the thing, anyway.

She was hungry. She turned and went back into the kitchen, swallowing some more Fresca as she stood looking into the refrigerator. She ought to eat something healthy, she thought. Eggs. Muffins. Maybe some juice. She reached in and pulled out what she wanted and was laying it all neatly on a sinkboard in order when she heard the front door close. She froze.

The footsteps she heard were identifiable, as ever. She did not turn around. She waited.

"Good morning," said Melba. "Sleep well?"

Sharelle turned. Her mother was still wearing her party clothes from the night before. Sharelle stared at her.

Melba smiled a little apologetically and shrugged. "I slept at Jack's house," she explained. "Really. I managed to make it over there last night after we . . . after we talked."

Sharelle nodded. She felt she had nothing to say.

"I talked a lot to Jack." Melba announced then, pushing Sharelle away from the sideboard. "Here," she said, "let me do all that. You sit down."

Sharelle did as she was told, and sat at the kitchen table watching her mother efficiently organize an entire meal and coffee. She could not remember ever seeing her mother moving so easily and directly in the kitchen before. Usually, she and Annette cooked and laid the table, cleaned and shopped.

Melba talked as she worked, seeming almost afraid to turn and face Sharelle directly. "Jack had a lot of good things to say, Sharelle," she said first. "I must admit, I was a fright and probably scared a year's growth out of him when I got there. But this morning we sat and talked."

"Yes?" Sharelle said. Her mother's voice had faltered and Sharelle had the sense she needed to be urged forward a little.

69

"I'm going to stand by you," Melba said then flatly.

Sharelle said nothing.

"You could say thank you," Melba suggested.

"Thank you," Sharelle parroted.

"It's not funny, you know," Melba said sharply, scrambling eggs in a bowl vigorously.

"I never said it was."

"No, you didn't. And it isn't. It's going to be very hard, for both of us. I don't necessarily want to start raising a child all over again at my age. I thought that was all finished."

"It's not your child," Sharelle reminded.

Melba smiled bitterly. "If you only knew," she cautioned. "Anyway," she sighed, continuing, "I can help, a lot. I mean, just to start, you need a roof over your head. You need enough food for two, of the right kind. I still remember a lot, you know. You'll need clothes and diapers and shoes and shots and God knows what all. And I'll help with all that. After all, even though I don't know who the father is, I *do* know the mother. And I love her."

Melba was still facing away from Sharelle.

"Mother . . ." Sharelle started to say.

"No," Melba shook her head, "let me finish. Now, when are you due?"

"August, I think," Sharelle said. "The second week."

"Thank God for that," Melba said quickly. "I mean, you've been able to get through the whole year at school undetected. Just ride it out and then you're safe."

"From what?"

"You don't think your teachers and principal want a pregnant student on their hands, do you?"

"I imagine they've seen such monsters before," Sharelle said sharply.

"Don't be smart," her mother warned. "I'm only thinking of what's best. So, anyway, you'll have finished the year. Now, Jack tells me there are places where you can get day-care for a baby and still continue your education."

"There are?"

"That's what he says. You wouldn't have to drop out that way. But it's up to you. What do you want?"

Sharelle was silent. She didn't know at all what she wanted. "I don't know," she admitted. "I've never had to think about any of this before."

"Well, it's bloody well time you started, then, missy," said Melba sternly.

"You're not talking about some sort of . . . of halfway house, are you?" Sharelle asked. "Like, I mean, for drug addicts and such?"

"No, I'm not. This is all part of the public schools. Or so Jack tells me. Your school counselor would know."

"I have to tell him?"

"I don't imagine you could find out what you needed to know otherwise, do you?"

Sharelle shook her head.

"Now, the first thing is, I think you're covered under my health insurance at work. I'm not sure, but I think so. I'll check tomorrow. If you are, then we can breathe a little easier. Otherwise, or maybe this is something you'd want to do in any case, you just keep working until it gets uncomfortable for you. You can help with the medical expenses if you want. Or not. The money is useful one way or another, God knows."

Sharelle listened. She felt light-headed, oddly happy. She wouldn't have to worry alone any longer. She hadn't even ever been sure what in fact to worry about. Now Melba could handle all that.

"Have you been to a doctor?" asked her mother suddenly.

Sharelle nodded. "He gave me vitamins."

"Have you seen Dr. Franklin?"

Sharelle shook her head.

So did Melba. "I'll make an appointment for you on Monday, and then we'd better see about getting you a gynecologist. I think my own died years ago."

"Mama, I—"

"Don't say one word!" Melba almost shouted. "Not one word. This is hard enough as it is. And it's going to get harder, let me tell you, miss!" She paused, lowering her voice and lowering her eyes. "Sharelle," she said softly, "I'm going to try to be good about this, good to you. I can't make any promises."

Sharelle nodded. "I know. I appreciate that."

"I just wanted to make sure you did," Melba said, the strength returning to her voice. "I'll try not to shout and scream, but you have to realize what a blow all this is. If you'd only tell me about the boy, Sharelle. Couldn't *he* help, too?"

Sharelle shook her head. "No, he couldn't. He's already married."

Melba's mouth fell open and she was about to let loose a stream of invective when she stopped herself and seemed to be counting. Then, "Boy, you sure know how to pick 'em!"

"I didn't, Mama," Sharelle said, deciding suddenly that since her mother was offering a gift of a kind, she should return the gesture. "He picked me."

"Then he's beneath contempt, is all I have to say," Melba said sharply.

Sharelle sat dead still. "It was Dallas, Mama," she said quietly.

"What? I don't believe you!"

Sharelle nodded. "It was. Believe me. I didn't want to."

"You mean your brother-in-law?" Melba shouted. "That's . . . that's almost incest, for God's sakes!"

"He wasn't that then," Sharelle explained. "It was before."

"Before the wedding?"

Sharelle nodded.

"Jesus!" Melba whispered under her breath. "What in the world possessed you?"

"Nothing," Sharelle said. "I never said yes. Or no."

"You don't mean he . . . he raped you?"

"Not exactly," Sharelle admitted. "I don't think you could say that. I mean, I guess I sort of knew what was happening."

"But you let it happen anyway?"

"It was something I needed just then, I guess."

Melba looked heavenward. "Promise me you'll never tell another living soul about this," she said then, urgently. "You've got to promise me, Sharelle."

"I do."

"I mean, think what this would do to your sister," Melba ran on. "It would kill her. And *she*'s carrying now, too. Ohmygod, if she ever knew! That son of a bitch!"

"Mama . . ."

"No, don't make excuses for him."

"I wasn't. I wanted to say something else."

"What, although I shudder even to ask."

"Thank you," Sharelle said gently. "I mean that. Thank you."

Melba looked at her daughter a second and then turned quickly away. "It's too soon to say that, Sharelle," she cautioned. "Wait."

"But—"

"No, just you wait, please!"

10

SHARELLE's first meeting with her ninth-grade counselor, Mr. Bernstein, did not start well. She was nervous, and afraid. True enough, school would be over in days, but she still feared he might get it into his head to take some drastic action that would unmask her before her classmates.

Sharelle stood just inside Mr. Bernstein's small office entry, waiting until the counselor put down his telephone and asked her to sit down. She studied him, feeling shaky but knowing she could get through the interview, knowing she *had* to: ever since Melba and she had had their heart-to-heart, Sharelle had focused unwaveringly on one idea—that, yes, she did want to finish school. That she did want, even with a child to care for, to go on to college if she could. If she didn't need this Mr. Bernstein's help, she would need another's.

She guessed the man was about thirty. His hair was permed and curly, which made guessing tough. He wore horn-rimmed glasses over blue eyes, and his gestures were swift and decisive. When he put down the receiver and looked up at her, he seemed at first puzzled. He reached for his desk calendar and looked quickly at it before nodding. "Hi," he said, smiling broadly. "Come in and sit down. We haven't really met before, have we?"

"No, sir," Sharelle said.

"That always makes me feel good," Mr. Bernstein said,

still grinning. "It means that whatever problems you might have, you feel pretty sure you can handle them. That's part of growing, I guess. Of accepting responsibility."

Sharelle nodded, uncertain what to say.

"So, now then," Mr. Bernstein ran on, "what kind of trauma are we dealing with today that suddenly seems bigger than it used to?"

Sharelle smiled in spite of herself, and relaxed. "I'm pregnant," she said without any warnup.

Mr. Bernstein's smile faded for a moment as he regarded her closely. "I'm sorry to hear that, Sharelle," he said. "I truly am."

"So am I," Sharelle told him. "So was I."

"Well," her counselor said, leaning back in his chair, swiveling just slightly. "Well."

Sharelle waited.

"What do you want to do, then?" asked Mr. Bernstein.

"How do you mean?"

"Well, you might have been dealt a tough hand, but there *are* choices still."

"Like what?"

"Well," Mr. Bernstein smiled easily again, "the first question to answer is whether you want to continue school."

"Yes, I do," Sharelle said firmly.

Mr. Bernstein nodded. "Good for you," he declared. He rifled a minute among folders on his desk and looked through one. "Good for you. Your marks are high, and your record's pretty impressive. I'd hate to see you throw that all away."

"So what do I do?" asked Sharelle.

"Leave it to me," Mr. Bernstein announced. Then he laughed. "Not entirely, of course," he added. "I mean, it's still you who have to work hard and will have to, probably harder than you ever thought you could. But it can be done. What *I* do is first of all ask a few questions, and

75

then, second, scout around on the telephone and find out which of our nursery programs has an opening." He looked carefully, kindly at her. "O.K.?" he asked.

Sharelle wasn't certain what to say, or what was at stake. She nodded. Mr. Bernstein searched for a form among the papers in his top desk drawer, pulled one out, and picked up his pen.

"Now," he began, "when is the baby due?"

"August."

He nodded. "Good. During vacation. Easier that way. Normally a school likes to transfer a student who's pregnant to a school with a pregnancy program, but in your case, since you've lasted so long, we're safe. O.K. Are you still seeing the father?"

"Pardon me?"

"Is the boy going to help you, be supportive? Are you going to try to live together? Marry?"

"Oh, no," Sharelle said quickly, shaking her head.

Mr. Bernstein nodded, unsurprised. "Your family knows about this, I imagine?"

"Yes, sir."

"Are *they* helping?"

"Yes, sir."

"Good. You need friends and kindness at a time like this. Now, I need the name of your physician, your family doctor or your gynecologist."

"I haven't got one, yet," Sharelle answered, a little embarrassed. "My mother's getting me one, today."

"All right. You can get back to me with that. Does your mother carry health insurance?"

"Yes, sir. I think so. She said so."

"When we meet again, Sharelle, could you bring me the name of the company and the plan?"

Sharelle nodded.

"Is your family now getting any kind of governmental assistance? Are they on Welfare?"

"No."

Mr. Bernstein nodded. "And this is still your address?" he asked, handing her a sheet of paper headed by Sharelle's name and address at the top. She nodded again.

"O.K.," Mr. Bernstein said then, smiling encouragingly. "The only thing you have to do now, Sharelle, is stay healthy and come back here, say, on Thursday. By then I should be able to tell you what school can handle you and your baby in a nursery program, and I'll try very hard to find room for you both somewhere not too far away from your home."

Sharelle guessed the interview was over. She felt relieved. Mr. Bernstein had made everything seem so easy for her. He seemed so willing to be helpful. Maybe it was just making him happy to be rid of a troublesome student with a problem. Sharelle thought for a second about this, and decided that was unjust. She liked the man.

She stood up. "By Thursday," she said almost proudly, "I'll have a doctor, too."

"Good. Give me his name then, and we can complete the forms and you can finish the year feeling confident that there is still a good, solid future ahead of you."

Sharelle nodded and turned to leave.

"Sharelle?"

She turned.

Mr. Bernstein stood at his desk, reaching out his hand to her. She took it. He held it a moment. "I am sorry about your having to come to me for this," he told her directly. "I wish we'd met to talk about something else. But still, you've a good record, and a good head. I know you can handle this."

Sharelle nodded, feeling grateful and on the edge of tears. She left his office.

She felt confident on Thursday as once again she waited for Mr. Bernstein to finish a telephone call. Her mother had discovered that her insurance policy at work did indeed cover her children, and would help to pay the hospital bills when the time came. She had arranged an appointment with a gynecologist who examined Sharelle and told her that basically she was sound and in good health and that there was no reason to imagine a bad time at delivery. Melba had promised not to say anything to Annette and Dallas until the coming event was so evident it could not be missed, but she had also, in a burst of rare enthusiasm for the project as a whole, gone out and bought Sharelle two maternity blouses and a pair of slacks with a waistband that expanded as required. Almost better, or more important, school would end for the year and Sharelle's secret had been discovered by no one there. Summer might be hot, but it was also an escape.

Mr. Bernstein motioned her into a chair as he spoke into the receiver. When his call was over, he looked up and smiled. "How are you feeling today?" he asked solicitously.

"Fine," Sharelle said. "O.K. Here's the things you asked me for." She opened her purse and brought out a sheet of paper on which were written the name of her doctor, her mother's insurance company and policy number. Mr. Bernstein took the information and copied it quickly onto a form. Sharelle waited, feeling calm.

"Now," Mr. Bernstein said, putting his pen in his coat pocket, "I scoured the district. There are three nursery centers in San Diego, all state-supported. The problem was edging you and little whatever his or her name is going to be into one." He grinned. "It seems you're not the only summer mother-to-be." Then he sobered. "Not that that's such happy news. It really hurts us when good students have these lapses."

Sharelle sat without moving. She felt his sympathy was real.

"The good news is that we *can* squeeze you in. The bad news is where."

Sharelle waited. She had no idea what to expect.

"This particular program's at a school you may have heard of," Mr. Bernstein told her. "But let me tell you, I

78

spent some time there a couple of years ago, and as far as I'm concerned, the kids there are top-notch and the teachers terrific. No matter what anyone says."

Sharelle still couldn't imagine where Mr. Bernstein was leading. After all, a school was a school, as long as she and the baby could get to it.

"One good thing is that the bus service there is wonderful. You can both be picked up each morning and brought home each day, rain or shine."

Sharelle nodded.

"Lincoln," Mr. Bernstein said.

"Abraham Lincoln High School?" Sharelle asked.

"Right," said her counselor. "But, Sharelle, don't make judgments yet. Believe me, I think you'll be happy there. I think you'll be surprised."

Sharelle was speechless. Not only was Lincoln clear across town, but she *had* heard of it, heard about it. It had been so far out of her mind when Mr. Bernstein was warming up with his bad news that the possibility of it, of having to go there, only now hit her.

Mr. Bernstein stood up and walked around his desk. Sharelle stood, but as though in shock. "They do wonderful work there, Sharelle," he told her, putting an arm around her shoulder. "Give them a chance. I promise you, if you really don't like it or find you can't handle it, that it's impossible to do good work there at the same time the baby is being taken care of, then all you have to do is call me and I'll do my damnedest to find you both another spot." He paused. "It's important to me, Sharelle, that we don't lose you. You have too much promise, you're too smart to stop school now. Give it a chance. Give *us* a chance, and yourself."

Sharelle nodded dumbly, standing at the door to the office.

"Just have the best summer you can, and deliver a healthy, happy kid," Mr. Bernstein said gently. "I won't forget you, Sharelle. I promise."

Sharelle had enough presence of mind to blink and say, "Thank you."

"And don't worry about anything," Mr. Bernstein said quickly. "The system will get in touch with you during the summer and tell you how everything works and what to expect. Just go home and relax and concentrate on happy thoughts. Having a baby can bring people great joy, no matter when."

Sharelle cleared her throat and realized how dry her lips were. She licked them. "I'll try," she said finally. "Thanks again."

And she walked down the hall towards her locker.

In despair.

It wasn't enough being taken advantage of. It wasn't enough having to have a baby alone. It wasn't enough that no one special loved her. Or that, despite Melba's good intentions, there was going to be nothing at all easy about summertime.

Now she was sentenced to a school where—the more she remembered the more she shuddered—there were riots and drug busts and violence and vandalism. She remembered hearing what kids said when they met someone who went to Lincoln. "No wonder you're so dumb!"

She opened her locker and stood there, facing into it, on the verge of tears.

She wanted the baby, but she wondered whether the baby would be so all-fired happy about being born into this kind of world.

PART
THREE

11

SHARELLE pulled her way slowly from the ocean of
anesthesia and for a reason she could not then, or ever
afterwards, recall, decided on "Renee." She was insistent,
almost tearful in her first conscious moments that the
name be spelled with two *e*'s, and this was as mysterious
to her as the name itself.

Melba snorted loudly and declared her daughter was
still "under" and for no one to listen. But Sharelle was
definite and demanding, and so her daughter became
Renee Patricia Marston.

Sharelle knew where the Patricia came from, and it
pleased her, made her smile to herself at night in her
hospital bed to know that she alone would carry that
knowledge always. ("To the grave" was how she mentally
phrased it, but then she shuddered and rejected the image
as bad luck on a happy day.)

In fact, as Sharelle held Renee in the front seat of
Melba's Camaro on the way to church and thought about
it, the entire experience had been happier than she had
imagined. The birth itself, befogged and misty, only
weakly recalled, seemed swift and nearly pain-free. Although Sharelle had decided she needn't do it over again
soon, she felt glad that when and if the time came to have
another child, she needn't be fearful. People around her
had been helpful and kind.

Even Melba, during the summer and the few weeks

before Renee's appearance as a living, breathing human being, had been considerate. Sharelle appreciated this and told her mother so often, joking a little about the strength it took to be patient with the increasingly rotund figure who came home from McDonald's absolutely swacked, all-in, exhausted, unable to move a limb or lift a finger. Every so often Melba would swing by the shop to pick up Sharelle and bring her home. Once or twice Melba had honked and when Sharelle was in the car had announced they were going out, just the "girls," for dinner. And they had. Melba would have two or three drinks; Sharelle soda water. Melba's mood lifted and she reminisced freely about having had Annette and Sharelle, what she had gone through, what she had thought, how the girls' father had behaved, what baby gifts the two had received, how they had taken their first steps, said their first words. On these occasions Melba would roll on and Sharelle was perfectly content to sit listening to her, rubbing her own abdomen, feeling whoever was in there kick and bounce around trying to get comfortable.

Melba had also taken to buying things for the back room that until now had been Sharelle's exclusively, but was rechristened the "nursery." Mother and child would not be separated immediately, but that was where Melba planned to put the bassinet and a crib, and picture books and clothing and toys. The playpen would certainly have to be downstairs or the baby would feel isolated and cut off, growing up to be angry and destructive. Along with the Disney decals and crib toys and stuffed animals, Melba was also picking up stray bits and pieces of psychological information, either recalled from her past or from her friends at work. All of this was passed on to Sharelle, not always calmly. For Melba was Melba, and she could not be expected to stay on an even keel indefinitely throughout the waiting period. There *were* little flare-ups, usually on mornings-after. But strangely, where once Melba would explode and then remain silent and pouting for half a day, now she made an effort to apologize quickly and to pull herself together again into what she imagined she should be.

Sharelle wondered whether Melba envisioned the birth of this child as another, perhaps final, chance to learn how to be a good parent. Sharelle was of the opinion that not everyone she knew who had children was good at it, Melba being the number-one example. What mattered most, she decided, was her mother's good will and willingness to help, no matter how badly executed. For without Melba and her house and her insurance and her sometimes dithery support, Sharelle would have had nothing. And the child would have had less.

Naturally, with Renee's erratic sleeping schedule, Sharelle was tired. As Melba drove, humming some long-forgotten but newly recollected hymn, Sharelle held Renee carefully in her arms—the child's warmth, its perfect helplessness, its wonderful clean, powdery smell all combining to make Sharelle almost feel like a baby herself. Everything about Renee made her try to remember what *she* had done, had been, at that age. And made her vow to remember everything she experienced now, as a mother, for her daughter.

One of those precious moments, Melba had insisted, would be an early christening, to which Sharelle and Renee now were being driven. Melba had arranged it all, declaring it to be a rite of the church, necessary as soon as possible, and also a celebration so she had planned a buffet lunch afterwards at home. Sharelle had been happy enough to go along with her mother's plans, up to the point where godparents had been proposed. Sharelle thought that her Uncle Jack as godfather was suitable, but she balked at Annette becoming godmother. She was already Renee's aunt and that should be enough. But Melba held forth loudly and long, and finally Sharelle gave in, hiding her fear that if Annette were at the ceremony, in all probability, so would Dallas be.

Actually, Sharelle was less disturbed by seeing Dallas over the font than she was by Annette's attitude. When her sister had found out Sharelle was expecting—and so far along—she had turned silently away, clearly feeling cheated. Melba had tried her best with Annette, pointing out the disgrace and uncertainty that surrounded Sharelle (as though this needed to be stressed) and comparing it to the joyful situation of Annette's own unborn child—legitimate, loved, able to carry its father's name.

Annette's silence persisted. She offered Sharelle neither congratulation nor advice. She ignored her whenever possible when visiting and made more than she needed to of how Dallas felt about the coming birth, what plans *he* was making, how excited and proud *he* was. Sharelle bit her tongue, feeling just every so often tempted to blow her sister out of the water.

But at church, when for the first time Dallas was seeing his child, Sharelle was soggy with perspiration although the day was clear and cool. Renee was wrapped in a white blanket and a white handwoven shawl. She was quiet. Her eyes were barely beginning to focus and recognize, and Sharelle longed for the day when she would see her daughter's first honest smile. From that moment on, the little girl would be committed, and Sharelle wanted that desperately.

Standing at the baptismal font with the Reverend Lee reading the service, Sharelle almost ignored everyone around her. The words of the service had managed to break into her consciousness, and their meanings, their weight and their promises made her blush with worry and nerves.

She had given no real thought to the service itself, not thinking much about it one way or another. But here she was, holding her very own child, and making promises for Renee that sounded impossible for anyone to keep, let alone Renee's mother.

She stared down at Renee's serene face as the Reverend

Lee read his instructions. "Dost thou, therefore, in the name of this Child, renounce the devil and all his works, the vain pomp and glory of the world, with all covetous desires of the same, and the sinful desires of the flesh, so that thou wilt not follow, nor be led by them?"

Sharelle looked to one side and read her response aloud from Melba's opened prayer book. "I renounce them all; and, by God's help, will endeavor not to follow, nor be led by them."

She did not concentrate so much on the sinful desires of the flesh as on the pomp and glory to be had in the world. She felt the question was a direct blow at what she could accomplish as a person herself, later, when Renee was older and capable of being looked after with less attention and worry. She knew she wanted to go out into the world and make something more of herself, for herself. She adored the baby in her arms, but there had to be something more for her in all the years ahead.

"Having now, in the name of this Child," read the Reverend Lee, "made these promises, wilt thou also on thy part take heed that this Child learn the Creed, the Lord's Prayer, and the Ten Commandments, and all other things which a Christian ought to know and believe to his soul's health?"

"I will, by God's help," answered Sharelle and Melba, Annette and Dallas, Jack and his wife, Barbara.

Sharelle smiled thoughtfully. That was a task she felt up to. It would be easy to incorporate those teachings into a child's life. Even Melba had been able to do as much when Sharelle was growing up.

"We receive this Child into the congregation of Christ's flock; and do sign her with the sign of the Cross, in token that hereafter she shall not be ashamed to confess the faith of Christ crucified, and to fight under his banner, against sin, the world, and the devil; and to continue Christ's faithful soldier and servant unto her life's end. Amen."

The group echoed somberly, "Amen."

Sharelle remained thoughtful after the ceremony as Melba insisted everyone pose with the baby on the church steps. Dallas, when his turn came to hold Renee, refused, saying that he'd rather wait for his own kid, thanks very much.

Sharelle wondered if he suspected. Dallas wasn't dumb. He could count. Maybe he suspected and wanted to protect Annette as everyone else did. Perhaps he would say something to her back at the house. Sharelle wasn't certain whether she would dread that exchange or welcome it. She could be big, she decided. If Dallas did say something, she would forgive him, set him free. After all, the child now was *hers*. He had one of his own coming soon enough. There was no reason to punish him or make him think she would take him to court for child support. All Sharelle wanted now was peace and ease.

There was a crowd at the house, and the noise was high and loud with laughter. Dallas was once again asked to hold the baby and this time he did, peering down into her face as Annette, over his shoulder, said, "Isn't she sweet?"

Dallas frowned. "All kids are sweet this size. Wait."

Sharelle smiled as she heard this. He didn't know. Good. She felt light-headed and terribly happy. *She* had a daughter, someone who loved her for herself, no matter what. The worst had passed.

She shook herself. Well, not quite. There was still Lincoln High tomorrow. She and Melba had made the trip across town a few weeks earlier to sign the appropriate forms and applications, and to see the nursery. She had met her new advisor and had rather liked him. He seemed to understand right away how nervous she was about the school, the nursery program, the prospect of hundreds of new faces and names to deal with, the daily bussing back and forth with clothes and books and formulae and food. He had advised her to have as much fun as she could, to study in her classes, to try to be as normal a schoolgirl as possible. That, after all, was what the program was designed for—to allow young people to continue their education simultaneously with helping them see into the future and preparing them for going out into the workaday world. Child care, child development was the top line, but immediately beneath it, and no less important, was picking up the tools and trades that would enable new mothers and fathers to go out after they graduated to find rewarding and suitable jobs in order to support their own new families.

He hadn't mentioned anything about going to college. Sharelle thought later that this was because he didn't yet understand that she still kept that particular candle glowing on the shelf above Renee's bassinet. And that she did not intend to have it blown out, by anyone.

12

━━━◼━━━

THE bus picked up Sharelle and Renee at ten minutes to seven in the morning. The drive was long, not because distances were so great but because of all the stops made from the ocean to Lincoln High, south of the city. The freeways were filled with commuters, all driving back and across, north and south, at seventy or seventy-five miles an hour. Sharelle's bus did a steady sixty on its stretches between stops.

She was surprised she was not nervous that first morning. She had dressed carefully, packing everything she could think Renee might need: her bottle, enough formula, Pampers, blanket, clean clothing. Maybe it was taking care of someone else, having all your attention centered on another person that kept you from trembling and worrying.

Sharelle had tried to be diligent about her homework. She skimmed the pamphlets and the texts that she and Melba had collected on the mid-summer visit to the center. She had taken all the charts she was to fill out as the course progressed and, at the top of each page, had written her own name and the baby's and had dated each in advance, too, specifying clearly when Renee would be six weeks old, then seven, eight, and so on. For immunization, for hand and eye coordination, for body position while sleeping, for limb strength that would progress from

Renee's holding up her head to rolling over, to beginning to get to her knees.

But concentration on all this had not been easy. There had been so much else to do, not just dealing with and learning about a new baby, but dealing with and relearning about the old baby upstairs.

Melba's change—her reversal—had not been immediate, but neither was it all that gradual. After the christening, and after the lunch Melba had arranged that day, Sharelle's mother seemed to decide that her own duties and responsibilities to the baby and its mother were at an end. There was no single moment that Sharelle could point to that told her this. She was simply aware, almost unconsciously, that she had suddenly become Cinderella to her mother's spoiled Stepsister.

Not that Melba wasn't pleasant most of the time. But "pleasant" wasn't much help to Sharelle who every day felt more sapped of energy, and for whom nighttime was not always a blessing. There were always late-night feedings and changings, bathing and diapering. There also was the house to keep up while Melba went to work, the shopping to see to, cooking, laundry, the yard. Melba had never been good about details, and Sharelle was used to pitching in but with Annette at her side. Now she was alone and the duties both sisters had shared fell only on Sharelle's shoulders.

The amazing thing was that no matter how peculiar Melba might be, or how tired Sharelle was, picking up Renee and talking to her, smelling her, just watching her, made Sharelle feel better, feel lighter and happier, gave her the energy to turn away finally and to start again worrying about what Melba would need at the end of the day.

As the bus turned off the freeway at 47th Street, Sharelle thought back to her summertime visit. Lincoln High empty had not seemed forbidding. It wasn't the prettiest

91

set of buildings Sharelle had ever seen, and the neighborhood in which it stood was also plain, too close to the freeway, surrounded by shopping areas and gas stations. The colors of the school—green and white—were not much in evidence, either. Lockers were painted red or green, the hallways were undecorated but broad. There was a sort of yard between the school's two main buildings, with crosswalks and trees (scraggly ones) where she had imagined kids gathered and fooled around during lunch hour. In fact, Lincoln was not very different-looking from any other school Sharelle remembered but for the cloud of newspaper articles that hung over its shape growing darker and heavier year by year with reports of gangs and drugs and violence.

The bus finally arrived outside the school and its passengers got out. Sharelle had not noticed that behind her on the bus had been another girl carrying a baby. She did now. The two smiled and started to walk alongside each other as they made their way past the scholastic classrooms to the pale russet outbuilding that housed the school nursery.

"How old is he?" Sharelle asked, carrying Renee against one shoulder.

"Seven months, Tuesday," said the girl. "Is this your first . . . are you new here?"

Sharelle nodded.

"Me, too. My name's Carmen," she offered. "And this is Christopher."

"Really?"

The girl nodded. "We didn't want him, you know, identified."

Sharelle looked sideways at Carmen. She was a pretty girl, a little overweight, with full dark hair and painted fingernails. She looked older than she must have been.

The two turned right and made their ways up a ramp and through a small cemented play yard to the doorway of the nursery. They paused before climbing the few steps up to it.

"I really didn't want to do this, you know," Carmen said quietly.

"What do you mean?" asked Sharelle. "Why not?"

Carmen shrugged. "I'm not so smart. I was never very good at school. I'd just as soon stay home with him."

"Then why come?" Sharelle wanted to know.

Carmen smiled. "His father."

"Is he in this school?"

Carmen shook her head. "But he thinks Christopher'll be smarter if he's around other kids his age. Meaning more people than just me."

"Maybe he's right," Sharelle judged. "Are you married?"

Carmen smiled again. It was a nice, shy smile, but also a little sad. "Lordy, no! We couldn't be."

"But why not? If he cares about you and the baby, why not?"

"He's in jail," Carmen said softly, looking away. "But don't tell anyone, please."

Sharelle promised she wouldn't.

A bell sounded far off in the two big academic buildings.

"Well, I guess it's time," Carmen allowed.

Sharelle adjusted Renee again and the backpack in which she carried the baby's things. For just a moment she thought she would rather stay outside talking with Carmen, finding out about the father of her baby, what he'd done to go to prison, where she lived, *how* she lived. But a lesson had been learned in the past months and Sharelle was determined never again to put anything off that needed to be done promptly. She started up the stairway ahead of Carmen and Christopher.

The room into which the two walked was large. In its center was a formation of tables and chairs. Around its edges were posters about child care, counting, doctor's visits. There were official notices, too, posted on pegboard, and pictures of animals—bright, funny, small, quizzical. There was a tiny trampoline at one end of the room, and shelves of books—mostly about raising children, about what to expect day by day—around on window ledges and in bookcases. A film projector was stationed on a rolling table and a screen for seeing films hung above a blackboard.

But there were no people. Carmen and Sharelle stood a moment, looking and listening, and then the sounds of gurgling babies and mothers' encouragements came to them and they followed these into a second, larger room which seemed filled with bending forms, squiggling little bodies, musical voices.

This area was divided in half. Just before Sharelle and Carmen was a carpeted, clean-smelling area around the edges of which, along the walls, were stationed perhaps a dozen cribs, each made up neatly and with a name-tag scotch-taped to one of the bars. "Scott." "Renee." "Charisma." "Jeremy." "Christopher." "Concepción."

The far side of the room was filled with tiny chairs and tables, walkers, play steps and gyms, bassinets, shelves of supplies with powder and creams and ointments, soap and water in a sink. A small stand-up kitchen was on the far wall, behind a counter.

The people in the room, apart from infants, were just like Sharelle and Carmen. None seemed older than fifteen, but for the supervisory staff: two wonderfully jovial-looking and patient-sounding grandmothers, or grandmother-types, who worked daily as aides and assistants to Ms. Cummins, who was finally spotted crawling out from under a crib perhaps fifteen feet away, her face bright with the effort and her plump arms and hands pink in the early-morning light. She looked up at the girls and smiled broadly.

"There you are, our two lost sheep. Four, really, isn't it?" And she laughed deeply. "Come in. Don't be bashful.

Introduce yourself around." She stood up, huffing a bit from her exertion and straightening her flowered dress. She wore wire-rimmed glasses that accented rather than hid her wide brown eyes, making them seem bigger and deeper than they perhaps were.

She reached out suddenly and took Christopher from Carmen's arms. "Now, this is Christopher's," she announced, stepping quickly to a crib on which his name hung. "You remember about your responsibilities, Carmen, don't you? About making the bed, changing its sheets every day, washing? We did go over all that when you came visiting?"

Carmen may have visited, but to Sharelle she looked as though she hadn't a thought in her head. She watched as her baby was put down in the crib and played with for a second. Then automatically and as though in a daze, she moved to the foot of the tiny bed and just stood there, looking at him.

Sharelle found the crib designated for Renee and put her down in it. As far as she could tell from just glancing around, Renee was probably the youngest child there. She was drowsy and quiet and accepted her new home-away-from-home docilely, falling asleep almost as quickly as Sharelle put her down on her stomach. She stored her backpack with Renee's belongings beneath the crib and straightened up, looking around. There were eleven other girls in the room, all busily primping their kids or cleaning them up or just holding them silently and rocking them. One or two of the girls there seemed to know each other from earlier semesters. They seemed to be friends. Sharelle ached a moment, and then thought brightly that she had already met someone new whose life and experiences sounded at first blush a whole lot worse than her own.

"Now, gang," Ms. Cummins crowed, standing in the center of the carpeted play area. The room quieted a little. Sharelle looked and tried to guess through the fat: late twenties, maybe, barely thirty. She noticed Ms. Cummins did not wear a wedding ring.

"Now," she said again after a moment, "you all know the way things work here. You spend this hour or one other each day with your children here, and lunch. That means you have five academic periods, and it means a lot more work than most students face. You'll have to keep up your grades. But you'll also have to be here, on schedule, rain or shine. This is not a place to dump your kids and then head off to the hills for a good time."

She looked severely around the room.

Then she smiled broadly. "You can call me Mattie," she invited. "I'm here because I want to be here. I'm crazy about kids. I know a little something about them. My degrees are all in child development and psychology." She raised her hands as though to ward off applause. There was none coming.

"Now, the program's nurse will be here once a week, so that if your children get colds or rashes or whatever, she can help you decide what to do. We'll also have people come out to talk to you from the Welfare office, from employment agencies, from the school district, about what happens to you next." She grinned like a conspirator. "We all know how you got here," she said. "What we need to do now is make certain you know what to do next, out there in the big world. Some of you have parents at home who are helping you, and some of you are on your own. We want to make having your first child as much fun for you as we can. We don't have many rules here," she added. " 'Rules are made to be broken,' " she intoned half-seriously.

"But there is one thing we under no circumstances tolerate. And that is hitting or spanking a child. If you're tired or angry, or your baby is acting up, give him or her to someone else to handle for a little. Take time off. Or go outside and cool down. Having a baby gets busier and more demanding as the child grows, and our nerves get shorter. We won't tolerate a big person taking out her anger or frustration on a little person. Is that understood?"

No one spoke.

"You'll all get lunch every day here, and so will your children. And they'll have whatever snacks are appropriate for them, in addition to whatever you bring from home. The clothing you bring is what they'll wear, and we want them clothed. We don't want naked bodies, and we don't want saggy diapers. Personal appearance is important, not just for the sense of well-being a child develops, but for your own selves, for your own pride. After all, these are your children. They're your little Xeroxes. They should be as neat and clean-looking as you are."

Sharelle stole a quick glance around. Most of the girls her age were dressed ordinarily, in jeans and blouses, or sweaters and cords. Only one girl wore a skirt. The babies, as far as she could see, were dressed to be presented to society: neatly pressed, flounced and beribboned. She thought that Ms. Cummins'—Mattie's—words were unnecessary. Idly she wondered if the girls felt any competition about this, about how well their babies looked. She shrugged inwardly. She and Renee had better things to worry about.

Mattie Cummins' voice changed then, and became less that of a cheerleader than a human being's. "One of the problems young mothers have," she said, "is that they so often feel isolated." She smiled. "Well, here's a chance to break that. Your classmates have all been in that boat. Circumstances may be different but the results are the same. You'll find sympathy and understanding here, especially if you yourselves offer it."

She turned and turned again, looking slowly at each girl with a playful sort of grin on her rotund features. "You should also know that not everyone in this program is a parent. This class is open to anyone who wants to work with and learn about children. Boys, too, if you can

97

feature that. So don't be surprised if the person you see powdering your baby when you get back from class is a male. It happens. It also happens some boys are terrific at all this."

She coughed, bringing up a pudgy fist to her mouth. "Two more things," she said. "If you can, if you're still seeing the father of your child, encourage him to spend time here, too. Whether or not he's here at Lincoln, we welcome him. It won't be easy to persuade him to come, maybe, but if you can, do. I think he'll enjoy it. I think he'll be proud, not just of his child, but of what *you're* doing.

"Second, we are not here to be judges. The reason this program exists is to help young people learn about and get a fair start in life. If for some reason one of you or another wants to leave, wants to pull out of the program for your own good reasons, then fine. We won't argue with you. We care. We'd like to know where you're going and why; we'd like to help, to talk things over and maybe offer a different point of view. But you're on your own, basically. These are your children, your responsibilities. What you think best is what we want to work with. So"— and she sighed finally, appearing to Sharelle as though she'd lost weight, as though her enthusiasms had filled her balloon shape but slowly seeped out and away—"if and when you come and go, know that we love you still, that we'll worry about you, and that if you want to come back, we'll welcome you."

13

AT ten on a Saturday morning the last person Sharelle expected on her doorstep was Monica Ruskin. "What are you doing here?" she asked, not all that gently.

Monica either did not hear Sharelle's tone or chose to ignore it. She stepped across the threshold and marched directly into the Marston parlor. "A whole summer goes by and not a word, not one word," Monica complained dramatically. "I have to hear about you from Marcella Douglas, of all people!"

Sharelle leaned against the wooden lintel at the room's edge, almost knocking over the carpet sweeper she'd been using. "Hear what?" she asked cannily.

Monica spun on her heels. "Come on, Sharelle," she said. "This is me, Monica, the girl who took you to the doctor's, remember?"

"You've lost weight," Sharelle said, hoping for no particular reason to keep Monica off the track as long as possible.

Monica smiled proudly. "I have," she admitted. "Almost fifteen pounds. Three more and I'll be perfect."

"For what?"

Monica shook her head. "Don't tease, Sharelle. I worked as hard this summer as you did."

Sharelle couldn't help herself. "I doubt it," she said.

"That's what I mean!" Monica cried out. "I mean, I *know*, Sharelle. Marcella Douglas *saw*. You know Marcie.

Nothing's secret, a direct echo chamber from ear to mouth."

"What did Marcie see?" Sharelle asked, pushing away from the wall.

"She saw *you*, my dear, carrying a small bundle, something that looked suspiciously like a baby, getting on a bus for Lincoln High, of all places!"

"How did she know I was going there?"

Monica shrugged. "Marcella's relentless. Now, where is it? Let me see!"

"*It* is upstairs sleeping."

"And is it . . . is it . . . yours?"

Sharelle nodded.

"But who?" Monica demanded. "Sharelle, you held out on me. I figured you quiet and shy, a little goony, even. Who got to you?"

"It doesn't matter," Sharelle said evenly.

"You mean you aren't telling, not even me?"

"Right. Come on, there's coffee in the kitchen."

"I thought you weren't supposed to drink coffee," Monica objected but following Sharelle.

"If you're pregnant," Sharelle said over her shoulder. "I'm not, not anymore."

"I just can't believe this!" Monica gushed. "Someone I know an actual mother!"

Sharelle smiled. "I was surprised, too," she said, going to the stove and reaching for the coffee pot.

"Sharelle!" Monica screamed. Sharelle jumped and turned around. Monica nearly knocked her against the gas burner as she rushed forward to throw her arms around Sharelle.

"For heaven's sakes," Sharelle said, finding Monica's embrace uncomfortable and wriggling free. "What are you doing?"

"I'm just so overwhelmed!" Monica said, stepping back and throwing her arms skyward. "I mean, honest to God, Sharelle, I never would have believed this, any of it."

"Well, believe it," Sharelle smiled. "And *try* to keep your voice down. Renee's asleep and my mother has her Saturday-morning symptoms."

"Renee!" Monica shrieked.

"Monica, shh!"

"Renee!" Monica repeated, sinking into a chair. "You had a girl!"

"You *are* quick," Sharelle said, pouring two cups of coffee.

"My dear, it's just too much for me," Monica shook her head.

"Then what are you doing here?" Sharelle asked sensibly. "I mean, you're welcome and all, but since you already know most of the answers, why bother with the questions?"

Monica stopped swooning. "Social intercourse," she announced seriously. "Good manners, form."

Sharelle laughed as she delivered Monica's cup of coffee. "My *dear*," she mimicked, "the summer has done wonders for your vocabulary."

"I worked on that, too," Monica admitted. "Did it hurt?" she asked, changing directions abruptly. "I mean, was it awful and bloody?"

"No," Sharelle said, sitting across from Monica. "I was mostly out anyway, so I couldn't tell. But I don't think so."

"But it must have hurt," Monica insisted. "I mean, they're called labor *pains*."

Sharelle nodded. "But you forget them. You want to, so you do. It's nothing terrible, anyway."

"*I* couldn't stand it."

"You will."

"No, I won't, not for years and years," Monica argued. She dropped her voice. "Besides, I've got something I can wear now."

"You do?"

Monica nodded. "Not that I'm planning to do anything

about it, you understand. It's just something, well, you know, better safe than sorry."

"You wearing it right now?" Sharelle asked.

"What for? This is Saturday *morning.* I'm not planning anything."

"But who knows?" Sharelle teased. "Suppose on the way home you get hit on by some gorgeous creature who wants you *now,* he can't wait, he's ripe and ready and it's your only chance."

"Common sense would prevail," Monica said calmly, sipping her coffee.

"You better hope so," Sharelle advised.

Monica put down her cup. "Seriously, are you sorry, Sharelle? I mean, so many changes, so many things you have to give up."

"Like what?" Sharelle asked, though already she knew the answers.

"Well, like dating, for one," Monica said soberly. "I mean, how many boys you think are going to be turned on by a baby?"

"It's me they take out, not Renee," Sharelle reasoned.

"You know what I mean," Monica persisted. "It's a responsibility, having to be home at a certain time, worrying, running on schedules."

Sharelle knew all about that, though her exact experience was limited. She had thought of all this more than once. "Well, if you want to know, just now I'm not exactly queen of *The Dating Game,* anyway."

Monica shook her head in wonderment. "I don't mean you were a dog, exactly, Sharelle, but you were always so shy, so quiet. You needed so much help. I mean, last year you—" Monica stopped as she heard Renee's tiny waking squeal.

"Come on," Sharelle said, pushing back her chair. "You wanted to see. You can."

"Oh, I don't know, maybe I should stay down here and . . ."

"Come on," Sharelle said again. "She won't throw up all over you."

Monica sighed and got to her feet. "Really," she said as she started up the back stairs after Sharelle, "I think you're just so brave!"

Sharelle laughed quietly. She stopped outside Renee's door and looked at Monica. "Not brave, Monica. Dumb, maybe. Unprepared."

Monica shook her head.

Sharelle walked into the nursery and bent down to lift Renee out of her crib.

"She's so small," Monica wailed. "I mean, is she all right?"

"She's fine," Sharelle said, carrying the baby a step across the room to lay her atop the bassinet. "Babies start small, Monica, in case no one ever told you."

Monica stared at Renee over Sharelle's shoulder. "What's her last name?" she asked, hoping to catch Sharelle off-guard.

"Marston," Sharelle answered firmly without looking up.

"You're so brave!" Monica said once more.

Sharelle started to change Renee. "So, how's school?" she asked, her fingers moving quickly: wiping, washing, powdering, pinning.

"My dear!" Monica sighed theatrically. "You wouldn't believe how everything's changed. I mean, just being in tenth grade is a whole new world."

"Better or worse?" Sharelle asked idly.

"Oh, better!" Monica said quickly. "I mean, the whole world's open to you. Of course, there are a lot of new responsibilities, too, but you feel so capable, really. There are so many new things you can get into. And the boys, Sharelle. The boys finally start to take you seriously."

Without meaning to, Sharelle tuned out. She adored Renee but hearing Monica begin to rhapsodize about boys and freedom and choices was too much. She wouldn't exchange the baby, but the idea that someone else's world was bursting open while her own was closing down, limited by the baby and Melba and all the real, adult responsibilities Sharelle felt (those Monica ran on about were make-believe, Sharelle thought) was more than Sharelle wanted to consider.

". . . allowance was raised, too, so I can actually make some intelligent selections. And I get to—" Monica stopped suddenly. "But why am I telling you all this? You're in tenth grade, too."

"True," Sharelle said flatly, annoyed at herself for being annoyed at Monica's mention of an allowance. After all, it was she who had offered to help pay household bills, thinking Melba would credit her with a sense of womanhood. She didn't.

"And now you're really going to Lincoln."

"We both are," Sharelle corrected.

"But it's so—so scrungy!" Monica protested. "I mean, it's so seamy!"

"Is it?"

"You know what I mean, Sharelle," Monica closed her eyes with exasperation. "You heard the same things I did. About riots and dope and rape and everything. They're animals over there!"

Sharelle laughed out loud in spite of herself. "We're animals over here, honey," she said. "You think I got this way from some nice easygoing polite All-American in the neighborhood?"

"How would I know? That's a state secret."

"Going to stay that way, too," Sharelle said, lifting Renee up into her arms. "Say hello to your auntie Monica, Renee."

"On no!" Monica backed away. "I'm too young for that!"

"Here, take her. She won't break."

"I couldn't! I wouldn't know how to. I mean, of course I do, but what if—?"

"Here, Monica, hold her," Sharelle insisted, thrusting Renee out. Monica was forced to accept the baby.

Monica stared down at the small face and form she held. "She can't be all right, Sharelle. She weighs hardly a thing."

"Monica, she's perfectly fine."

Monica shook her head doubtfully. "It's too soon to tell," she said almost whispering.

"Tell what?"

"Who she looks like."

"Not really," Sharelle replied. "She looks a little like me, and a little like my father."

"Your father!" Monica gasped. "Sharelle, how horrible! You mean your own . . ."

"No, I don't mean *my own father*," Sharelle said. "Honestly, Monica, where's your brain? You think my father could phone this in?"

"Well, you just said—"

"I know what I said. It's not surprising a baby looks like other members of its own family."

"No, I guess not."

"Here, I'll take her now," Sharelle said.

Sharelle reached out to the bassinet to pick up an extra diaper that she draped over her shoulder before lifting Renee up to it. "Come on, let's go downstairs," she said, putting a finger to her mouth to caution quiet.

Monica seemed to understand and left the room quickly. They settled again in the kitchen, Renee drowsily gurgling from Sharelle's lap.

Monica shook her head sympathetically. "To be locked up over there, Sharelle. God, my heart just aches for you."

"It's not so bad," Sharelle allowed.

"Are you kidding? Raping and shooting up in the johns and sit-ins and gang warfare! Not so bad? What could be worse?"

Sharelle jiggled Renee, making cooing sounds to her. "We'll survive."

"How can you be so cool?" Monica demanded. "The reputation of that school alone could destroy a building!"

Sharelle's face began to burn. "Still, it's probably what someone like me deserves, with an illegitimate kid and all."

"You don't have to get defensive," Monica pointed out quickly. "My God, the whole city knows, Sharelle. You don't have to prove anything to me."

"Look," Sharelle said firmly, "you came here because Marcie Douglas got one up on you and you're scoring her back. You don't really care about Renee or me, just about *knowing*. Well, I'm fine, and Renee's fine, and Lincoln's fine. It's been getting a bum rap since who knows when, since probably even before we were born." Sharelle took a big breath, thinking she should stop. She didn't.

"There are some good people there, Monica. People who really care. And the kids are just the same, really. Sure, one or two shuffle through the day a little strung out. But we saw that last year, too. It's nothing special. The only thing's different, really, is me. I just don't have time to think about me all the time, that's all."

"You saying that's what I do?" Monica straightened in her chair. "You saying I'm hung up on myself? Honest to God, Sharelle, for someone who never in the first place even—"

But Monica was stopped in mid-flight as a bathrobed and beslippered hunched form shuffled into the kitchen waving her arm weakly in greeting and headed directly for the coffee pot. Melba's eyes were almost closed, making it seem as though she were operating on automatic pilot. She was.

"Thank God!" she muttered, putting her hands around the still warm percolator.

The two girls watched, one fascinated and a little uneasy, the other amused and almost proud as her mother performed a mime in total and silent concentration.

Melba's hands went up to a cupboard above the sink to find a mug, brought it down to sinkboard level, reached out for the coffee pot and found it, poured, added milk from the refrigerator (pulling it open with her toes and easing it shut again with her hip), lit a cigarette and stuck it between her lips, making her squint even tighter, sidled over to the kitchen table for the sugar and a spoon, found both and managed with minimal spillage to dump two teaspoons-full into the mug, and then, saying not a word, carefully and slowly headed back the way she came, smoke trailing over her shoulders, her hands shaky but capable still of holding fast to the handle of the mug.

Monica said nothing about the performance. Instead, still annoyed and feeling unjustly accused of egotism, she finished her own coffee and made up a sudden, and transparent, excuse to leave.

Still holding the baby, Sharelle edged the front door closed after Monica left, realizing that Monica's Saturday morning social intercourse was not likely to be repeated. Fine with her, she decided. She liked the people at Lincoln better, the girls who had children, who knew what you were up against.

14

THERE had not been a lot of time to think about the newness of her daily life at Lincoln High. Sharelle had been a little timid at first. That was easy enough to admit. But having Renee nearby gave her more than confidence, it gave her purpose. She knew who she was. She was Renee's mother.

And so, with Renee in her arms, Sharelle did not feel alone or frightened. The girls who spent their one class hour of the day with her in the nursery, whom she saw again at lunch-time, were easy and understanding and patient and had sudden laughs that combined both sympathy and teasing. There was a lot to learn. About Renee, about the other small children, about what demands there were when working with them; about the rules and etiquette of handling some one else's child—for each hour spent in the nursery was regulated so that a mother spent time with others' babies, sometimes even more than with her own.

In the few weeks since Sharelle had transferred to Lincoln, she had diapered, powdered, bathed, dressed, played with, lifted, held and crooned to a dozen children not her own. They were of different ages and weights, some boys, some girls, all dressed beautifully and smelling of talcum and spit in equal parts, all bright-eyed and happy, it seemed, to be mauled and pawed by well-meaning nonmothers in the course, as well.

As for the presence of boys in the class, as promised or threatened by Mattie Cummins, Sharelle had yet to identify one boy who consistently came to class and seemed to care. There were boys dropping in from time to time but mostly to visit particular girls in the parenting program—girls who were parents, girls who weren't. The russet-walled nursery building and its cemented play yard seemed to give these romances a curious atmosphere, away from crowded halls and shouts and classroom bells and assignments, away from the Hornets' pep rallies and football practices, away from ninety-nine plus per cent of the competitive and inquisitive eyes of classmates. Ms. Cummins' attitude towards the guys who cut class to drop in to kill a little time was serene but firm; if they were in the nursery, they had to take care of a child every now and again, too, like anyone else. And the few boys who did, did it well and with good humor.

Sharelle heard Melba upstairs beginning to pull herself together, not yet vocalizing for real but humming a little refrain from "Rock of Ages." Melba's musical selections on weekends had a unique rhythm. Saturday mornings were pious; Saturday night she broke down and "got down" with Smokey Robinson or Charlie Pride of Kris Kristopherson, and Sunday morning, bleary but unbowed, brought her back to "Faith of Our Fathers."

Carrying Renee into the parlor and putting her on her back on a sofa, nestled against its inside backrest so she couldn't roll or fall, Sharelle straightened the room and in the kitchen rinsed out the coffee cups she and Monica had used. She wondered whether she should call up to Melba to offer to fix a breakfast of some sort but decided against it. If her mother wanted food, let her say so. Sharelle did not really mind helping Melba, but she was beginning to feel raw that Melba hardly ever spoke to her kindly or at all. Besides, if Melba were dressing, that meant there were errands to be run, people to see. Melba would go out and tackle her "chores"—undefined and unspecified to her daughter—return for a beauty rest around two, snack at six ("something to drink on") and be out of the house by eight.

The truce that seemed to have been instituted by her mother had at first been unnoticed by Sharelle. She was too busy getting Renee ready to go across town each morning, making formula, packing diapers and leggings and toys. She was too busy at night, rushing home to care for her child and then to straighten up around the house for Melba's return and dinner. She was too busy cleaning up the kitchen and doing the dishes and then going upstairs to work silently in the nursery on her homework assignments. She was too tired at ten o'clock even to notice that weeks passed before either she or her mother had remembered to wish each other a good night.

But then one day in mid-October, Sharelle had suddenly pulled herself upright from bending over a couch and fluffing its cushions to wonder aloud, "Hey, am I the only one around here who cares?"

She began to see her life anew.

If she didn't clean the house, keep it straight and tidy, no one else would.

If she didn't get dinner ready for her mother and for Renee, no one else would.

If she didn't cart the baby down to the nearby shopping center at least twice a week, no one else would order or buy what was needed for the family.

If she didn't use her own money, the money that was left from her summer's work at McDonald's, for household needs, they were never seen to.

She brought in the mail every afternoon, sorting bills from fliers or correspondence and putting them in Melba's room atop her pillow so they couldn't be missed.

She managed to scratch around for money to pay the delivery boy from the newspaper.

She raked the small yard on Saturday mornings and swept the walkway clear.

She never left for school without making certain a pot of coffee was warm on the stove for her mother.

She picked up her mother's dry cleaning on Saturdays and did her own and Renee's washing then, as well.

She leapt out of bed every night when Renee awoke and began crying for her late, or earliest, feeding, fearing all the time that Melba might be disturbed.

"Wait a *minu*te!" Sharelle had said aloud that day in the living room. She put aside the soft linen rag she used for polishing and purposely sank into a chair she had dusted and fluffed. "Well, hell!"

She had become a servant.

Her whole life was being run by two women, one nearing forty and frightened, and the other too young even to feel guilty.

Sharelle had stared into space, thinking back, trying to see how this had happened. Some of it was her fault. Putting aside the fact of Renee at all, Sharelle had tried to impress Melba with her willingness to help, had hoped that by quietly accepting as her own chores and duties around the house, her mother would come to see her as growing up and somehow worth more than before— someone with whom she could share time and events as a friend instead of merely a daughter hanging around.

That, after all, had been behind Sharelle's offer to donate a few dollars each week from her savings to the household. It made Sharelle herself feel more adult and responsible, and she hoped it would be noticed and appreciated by her mother, too. It wasn't. Melba had nodded silent agreement and nothing more was offered, not even a thank you. Well, Sharelle had thought at the time, there really wasn't any *need* to say thank you. But it would have been nice, just the same.

Sharelle made certain *she* thanked Melba whenever her mother lingered in the same room for more than thirty seconds. For a lot. After all, Melba had uncharacteristically softened and sentimentalized during the final weeks of Sharelle's pregnancy; she had been enthusiastic and doting about Renee up until the christening. There *had* been that one period of sharing and concern that, in Sharelle's mind at least, was finally more than role-playing.

But Melba had withdrawn again emotionally, thrown herself back into her old habits and pursuits. With Annette at home, jobs had been divided. Doing these things now alone wasn't especially new—what was new was the feeling of having to do them, Or Else. And the Or Else was what Sharelle feared to focus on. The Or Else seemed every day to hang above her head. The Or Else kept her uncomplaining on her knees in the kitchen, at the stove, carpet-sweeping, shopping, tending to and caring for.

But life was beginning to make Sharelle a little testy. After all, she had a child to raise, someone to worry over and educate. And what kind of environment was this house, anyway?

With Melba zipping in and out on various pretexts, coming in at all hours from "business conferences," dropping cigarette ashes over everything, leaving empty glasses to make rings on carefully polished table-tops, shedding clothes throughout the house on the assumption that someone would pick them up after her, not even bothering to pick up clothing that belonged to her "business colleagues" on the occasional sleep-over invitation ("It's such a long drive back, for heaven's sakes; I couldn't say no")—just what sort of house was this in which to raise a brand-new, clean, and untouched baby?

Sharelle and Annette had survived all this before, even though they were neither demonstrative nor emotionally terribly close, because the presence of one to the other had always been silently comforting. Their mother's habits and failings, as well as her enthusiasms, were well known and accepted for what they were. But how could Sharelle let them continue now when a new set of eyes and ears would soon enough begin to pick up and understand, would judge or laugh at what Sharelle herself all the years before had seen and heard?

What could she do? What could she *safely* do?

She could try to talk to her mother, to reason with her, to ask gently about some kind of realignment of daily duties. After all, while she and Renee were grateful, Melba still lived under the same roof and what harm could there be in agreeing to a few tiny changes in her routine? Not that Sharelle underestimated the amount of patience it took for her mother to stay even distantly even-tempered. Having visible proof of your age and history in front of you all the time could not be easy. Still, if Sharelle was growing, so too should Melba be. Not simply older, but wiser, more capable.

Perhaps that was the approach to take: growing together, becoming friends instead of relatives. Yes, Sharelle liked that idea. People did grow and change, understand and see more. If she could, and did, so could Melba.

Sharelle had smiled to herself that October day. There was another course available, subtle and not terribly risky. She could let some of the household chores go awhile, not be so neat, not be so attentive. It was an old trick but one that, at least in stories, worked. You simply didn't pick up after someone for a time and then one day that someone would wonder aloud how the house got to be so cluttered, what had happened, what had changed? The explanation would be simple and eye-opening, and the lesson learned easily and without anger.

Well, yes and no. Melba had never been overly fond of being criticized, even sideways.

Well, nuts! Sharelle had decided then. Take the gamble. Take the chance. You have a life to lead, too.

Sharelle had wrapped Renee up warmly that day and left the house— her cleaning unfinished, dishes still in the sink—in order to give the baby a change of air: Melba's cigarettes and their odor were everywhere—the curtains, the carpets, the towels. She had felt triumphant and determined. Sooner or later she knew Melba would see and understand the change.

As it turned out, it would be later rather than sooner, and long after Sharelle herself could stand the clutter and mess, and had returned to doing things all over again. Not so much for Melba, she reasoned, but for Renee, as an example.

The day of Monica's visit, all this came back to Sharelle and so, without offering her mother breakfast, Sharelle packed up Renee and put her in a second-hand baby carriage and trundled off down the walk towards a park that overlooked the Pacific.

Monica's clucking over the awfulness of Lincoln made Sharelle focus on her short time there. She had thought at first how much luckier she was than most of her new acquaintances. She was living at home; her mother was supportive, in a way. Now she wasn't so sure. She hardly had a moment to herself, and she certainly had no time to go out on dates. She wasn't at all certain Melba would baby-sit, and her own funds were so low she hated the idea of spending them on a sitter from the neighborhood.

Still, Sharelle had her dreams. That she kept them alive at all was a victory. Her own ambitions existed still in her imagination and now new ones were added, somewhat cloudier and less precise, for Renee. But listening with even half an ear to Monica made Sharelle see that what she wanted from life—not only a task she could enjoy and feel worthy doing, but also *fun*, for heaven's sakes—was day by day growing more difficult to remember, let alone achieve, under the weight of her school day and her duties at home.

Not every girl in her classes kept a dream alive. Some were simply less bright and eager. Some were permanently silenced by life, people who never raised a hand in class or ever seemed to have anything worth saying. Not in Sharelle's estimation, but in their own. Some seemed a little tougher than Sharelle herself thought necessary or admirable—like Paula Beale, whose son Jeffrey was nearly two and clearly sending his mother up a wall. Paula fought back, against Jeffrey, against Ms. Cummins, against the world. Sharelle wasn't certain she approved, although if that's what it took to get Paula going and to keep her in class at her baby's side, then fine.

There was tiny Carmen, shy and not terribly bright, who seemed to have had Christopher simply because her boyfriend (in jail—how could *he* worry about it?) wanted her to. Carmen was living in a hostel near downtown in a neighborhood that was half urban renewal and half beyond even that as a possibility. She and Christopher were probably the youngest members of the hostel, and certainly the soberest. Yet for all her avowed affection for the child's father, Carmen moved eternally in a sort of daze, as though if she fell someone would somehow miraculously appear at her side to break her fall and to lift her up.

And there was Michelle Sheeter who was as close to Punk as Sharelle could imagine with her fringe-dyed purple hair and safety pins in the ears, wearing overalls and no bra and usually sandals without socks no matter what the weather. Michelle just didn't care, she told one and all. She didn't really care about her baby, Flex, and she certainly didn't care about Flex's father with whom she had lived for a summer and a fall a year ago out at the beach. Michelle also didn't care about the Bomb, about politics, about money, about good diet for Flex, about drugs, sex, Medicare, cars, records, music, books, food, drink. Which was to say, Michelle cared in her way about all these things and long ago had apparently decided that they, and everything else Society offered or supported, were tainted by self-interest and selfishness. What was offered as good was bad, underhanded and mean-spirited and demeaning. Michelle just didn't care, she told one and all, and not caring meant that if every few years she "dropped" another kid, that too was Society's fault and responsibility. In her own skewered reasoning, Michelle announced that while birth control *might*, it could also kill. And though she didn't care about death, either, she wasn't in any hurry to look upon that dark face sooner than she had to.

There *were* other people in Sharelle's new life at Lincoln. There were two boys, as different as war from peace, and while what Sharelle had said to Monica was true—that she wasn't being rushed off her feet to bliss and rock 'n' roll—at least she had begun to experience what Melba had long ago forecast, attention. Good and bad, but attention all the same, no matter how you looked at it, and though Sharelle felt she was not free enough to do much about any of it, the mere fact it existed at all was definitely better than nothing.

15

IT was almost eleven when Barney Carnes finally showed up, dropped off in front of Sharelle's house by a team-mate. She heard the car stop outside, heard a door slam, heard Barney's approach along the walk. She waited for his knock, which seemed a long time coming. Sharelle had never before entertained a boy at home alone. Although they sat side-by-side in math class, Sharelle and Barney had never spent time outside of school together. Sharelle wondered if he were as nervous on his side of the front door as she was on hers. She doubted it. The knock came.

"Hi," Sharelle said, pulling open the door. "Are you a winner?"

"Always, baby," Barney said, standing on the threshold without making a move to cross it. He was at least three inches shorter than Sharelle and wore an ever-present piece of round, flat, squashed-down felt atop his tight curls that Sharelle had decided was his way of showing off, of drawing attention to himself among his taller friends.

"Well, come on in then," Sharelle said. "I saved dinner for you. I figured you'd be starving."

"Got a beer?" Barney asked, his compactly powerful body brushing past hers as he looked around the house.

"Sure," Sharelle said. "In the kitchen."

She led him through the living room and into the

kitchen which smelled of onions and chopped meat and home-made French fries. She opened the refrigerator door and reached in for one of what Melba called her life-savers. She handed this to Barney who, either showing off or nervous, spun the can around in the air, making quick catches and tosses and finally bounced it off a bicep into his hand. Sharelle grabbed the beer back from him and pulled it open at the sink. Its foam exploded over her fingers. She wiped the can off and handed it back to Barney. "Funny, but dumb," she decided.

Barney took a long swallow. "Twelve points," he said, grinning proudly. "Couldn't hold a good man, Sharelle. I made a net through 'em!"

"*Are* you hungry?"

"Sure. Hey, is that all you're going to say? I mean, I was a star out there. I could be anywhere I want tonight, and here I am, and all you want to know is if I'm hungry. Don't you want to *hear* about it?"

Sharelle smiled nicely. "I guess I do," she said. "You talk, I'll cook."

Sharelle did not go to football games. Or to movies. Or to a Jack-in-the-Box just to hang out with friends. She was nervous about asking Melba to stay with Renee, and Melba never thought to volunteer. Sharelle thought it best to save Melba's good will, what remained of it, for emergencies, though of what sort she wasn't certain and didn't want to imagine. Then there was the matter of money. Melba never suggested that Sharelle take some and go have a good time, and Sharelle herself was reluctant to ask. Her own funds were being exhausted. She gave Melba a few dollars weekly for expenses, but also too often had to have some for last-minute purchases or bills Melba had overlooked.

At the stove, she began heating up food as Barney paced the kitchen behind her, reliving Great Moments on the Gridiron. Sharelle was satisfied to listen with half an ear, cooking and setting the table, catching the sense of pride and accomplishment in Barney's voice, secretly wondering if the same sort of excitement would exist if he were telling his friends about *her*.

It was nice being noticed, being thought of as helpful and intelligent and not terrible-looking. From Barney's point of view, who knew? He was quick with his smile, and with his hands, Sharelle imagined, and not afraid of girls. He had probably been around a bit; if Sharelle believed everything he had told her, he practically ran the football squad's off-hour social life. She didn't. She was happy just to have someone want to give up a rowdy night out with the boys after a game, to come to her house just for *her*.

As Sharelle delivered a ceramic bowl full of French fries to the table, she and Barney seemed to bump into one another. Sharelle decided quickly to ignore the contact, even though Barney's hands—the backs of them— had rubbed across her chest.

They sat down to eat. Barney ate; Sharelle watched and listened amazed as his career of crashing, stomping, driving, scoring tumbled through the food in his mouth. He ate everything she placed before him nonstop, pausing hardly to breathe, talking all the time, taking quick looks up at her to see whether she was paying attention, whether she really understood the importance of what he was telling her.

"Nothin' can stop me, Sharelle. I'm fast. I make holes, I run through 'em, I *push!* That's what you need to get ahead, see? Drive! I mean, all I have to do is hang in there long enough to be noticed. Then maybe I get a scholarship to State and hey, baby, it's home free! A ticket to the big time!"

Sharelle did not doubt what Barney said. But for him to stay in school long enough to be noticed, even to stay on a team in order to be noticed, seemed to her questionable. If he couldn't add or write or remember—or *wouldn't* (because she felt Barney wasn't at all dumb)—

119

how could he expect to keep carrying the green-and-white colors of Lincoln onto any field at all?

"Then you'd better buy that ticket right now," she said, "and start *learning* the math we get in class instead of just leaning on me."

Barney scowled. "Hey, I don't care about that," he said sourly. "All I need is to be smart enough to make the right sounds, turn in the answers. *Your* answers, baby," he added, and smiled at her.

"Sooner or later, Barney, somebody's going to realize your work's getting better, and wonder about it. I mean, you just better stay eligible, is all."

Barney brushed aside her warning and patted the cap on his head with one hand while, with the other, he shoveled more food into his mouth. Sharelle began nodding at what he was saying to her about how he swiveled and pommeled and swung wide around his ends, and wondered whether inviting Barney to the house had been such a good idea after all. She hadn't given it much heavy thought, but she was fairly certain she didn't want to listen indefinitely to the life and times of the team's greatest halfback since Marcus Allen.

This was not to be. Barney finished everything on his plate, leaned back in his chair and wiped a paper napkin across his face, sighed and smiled, at ease. He and Sharelle looked at each other for a moment and then Barney stood up and moved away from his place to stand behind Sharelle's chair. "That was real fine, Sharelle," he said. "You keep me in class, and you care, and I like that."

Sharelle was about to turn around in her chair to say something—what it was going to be she forgot since suddenly Barney's hands were around her shoulders, moving swiftly down her front, resting but not resting on her breasts.

"What are you doing?" she said quickly, swinging out of her chair and turning to face him.

Barney grinned. "Giving you a little present," he said

confidently. "After all, you give me, so it's my turn. I mean, I play fair. I give as good as I get."

"You think so?" Sharelle asked sharply, forcing herself to stay calm. "What makes you so sure I'm hot to get what you got to give?"

Barney shrugged and held out his hands. "Hey, Sharelle, come *on*," he said sweetly. "Relax. Let's have a good time."

"I thought I was having a good time," Sharelle answered, moving away from him now to the other side of the table but keeping her eyes always on him.

"Not as good as we could have," Barney suggested, beginning to follow her.

"What *is* this?" Sharelle demanded. "What sort of person do you think I am?"

"Hey, it's not as though you haven't done it before," Barney told her, catching hold of her hand and forcing her to stay in one place.

"So what if I have?" Sharelle asked. "That doesn't mean I'm going to do it every time you think I should say thank you. I mean, what is this? I feed you and I'm supposed to be grateful?"

"Let's just think of it as dessert," Barney said then. "Just a good way to get to know each other."

Sharelle laughed despite her anger. "I thought people got to know each other first," she said. "I mean, I don't hardly imagine people sack out and then say, 'Hi, my name is So-and-so.'"

"That isn't what I mean and you know it, girl," Barney said, squeezing Sharelle's fingers.

Sharelle broke his grip and went to lean against the sinkboard, her arms crossed in front of her chest. "Tell me if I'm wrong, Barney, O.K.? But it suddenly got to me that all this attention just leads in one direction, up to one big moment. I'm supposed to fall all over myself for your hot bod, not so much because I feel anything but because I've 'done it' before and what the hell, what's the big deal? Right? I mean, is that right?"

Barney smiled crookedly. "You ain't *wrong*," he admitted.

"Suppose I didn't have a kid upstairs," Sharelle asked. "I suppose if the real actual evidence weren't around, you'd wait a little longer, maybe say hello first and *then* make your move?"

"Hey, Sharelle, *kid*," Barney explained, "we've already said hello. I mean, we see each other almost every day. We're not exactly strangers or anything."

"What are we supposed to be, then, friends?" Sharelle demanded.

Barney looked away. "Well, sure," he admitted. "I mean, you been good to me, helping me and all in class. I mean, I *like* you, Sharelle. Don't forget that."

"It would be a lot easier to remember if you took off that silly hat!"

"Easy there, you sound like my old lady."

"I'm happy to hear it," Sharelle said tartly. "You ever take that thing off?"

"Yeah," Barney said. "But what's that got to do with anything?"

Sharelle felt very calm very fast. "A lot," she said. "Tell you what. You think I'm easy to get, right? Well, you're wrong. But just to be fair, when you start thinking about coming round here without that dumb beanie on your head, I'll start thinking about being as grateful as you think I should be."

"That all it takes?" Barney asked, instantly putting his hand to the top of his head.

"Not now!" Sharelle said quickly. "I want a lot longer hello than the one I'm getting. Just because I made one mistake doesn't mean I liked it so much I have to do it over and over again. When something like that happens to me now, Barney, it's got to mean a lot more than you came in here offering."

"You sure?" Barney asked. "I'm real good."

Sharelle laughed kindly. "Hey, you probably are. If it

makes you feel any better, I'm *not*. I just happened to get hit on and didn't know as much as I should. But I know more now, and saying 'no' now is nothing I'm afraid to do. You want me, you earn me."

Barney's face clouded. "Jesus, you sound like an adult, for God's sakes!"

Sharelle laughed again and went across the room to give Barney a hug. She kissed him on the cheek without seeing or sensing that he flinched and pulled away slightly, his forehead still furrowed. "Thank you," she said. "Believe it or not, I think that's the nicest thing anyone's ever said to me."

Barney stepped out of her embrace. "I didn't come to play teenage romance with some wimp of a string bean," he told her angrily.

"What?"

"There are plenty of women around town who'd crawl a hundred yards *on their knees* to be where you are tonight!" Barney spouted.

Sharelle stepped back and looked at him a moment. She understood where his anger came from, and because she did, she herself couldn't really get angry. "Is 'no' such a terrible word?" she asked gently.

"You figure it out!" Barney steamed, moving out of the kitchen towards the parlor and the front door. "My time's too short to waste bargaining!"

The front door slammed behind Barney and Sharelle leaned still against the kitchen doorway, wondering with a surprising sense of amusement why she didn't feel that way about *her* time.

16

―――

WHAT makes you such an expert?" Paula Beale asked loudly, interrupting the more or less calm question-and-answer session that U. S. Howard was conducting.

He was the director of the Crisis Center at the Community Medical Center not far from Lincoln. Middle-aged, tall and stringy, with a crown of white hair roosting above his narrow mahogany face, he was loud and quick and more likely to joke than not, more likely to tell the truth straight out than not. Mattie Cummins invited him every semester to Lincoln. She thought he offered what some of her students needed: tough talk, good advice, sound judgments. And the students themselves, after an initial period of watching and listening and making up their own minds, were seduced, and gave U. S. Howard as good as he gave: straight, direct talk, no excuses.

U. S. Howard turned towards Paula Beale and looked directly at her. "You think your case is special?" he asked in turn.

"I'm not saying it is, it isn't," Paula told him flatly. "I just want to know how come you think you know all the answers."

"I don't," admitted Mr. Howard. He grinned suddenly and purposely looked away from Paula, almost dismissing her. "But I sure as hell know a lot more than you do."

There were a few cough-covered laughs around the

square table from girls secretly pleased to see Paula take a shot. But Paula fought back. "You spend every day with a two-year-old driving you bananas?" she insisted.

Mr. Howard turned back to face her. "Nope," he admitted easily. "That's just one of the answers I would have given you if you'd asked. I mean, how *not* to have a two-year-old driving you crazy."

'Fat lot of good that does now," Paula said under her breath.

"I know that." Mr. Howard sounded genuinely sympathetic. "And I can understand your anger, your frustration."

"Anger!" Paula shouted suddenly. "What anger? I'm just *tired!*"

There was another stir in the room but Mattie Cummins cleared her throat and the students quieted. "Not everything Mr. Howard has to say, Paula, is directed at you, dear. Remember, not everyone in class is a mother yet."

Paula Beale sank down in her chair and glowered around the square, but she said nothing more.

"Now," Mr. Howard picked up, "we were talking about the sorts of experiences we had that got us into this dilemma in the first place. Carmen, I think it was going to be your turn."

Carmen reddened slightly and put out both hands to finger the piece of cardboard on which her name was written in bright felt-tip printing. "Nothing special," she said quietly. "My boyfriend and I, we, well—it happened. And then . . ." She stopped and shrugged.

"Was he at all helpful?" asked Mr. Howard.

"How?" Carmen asked back.

"Did he suggest you might get married, or that he would help pay for the child? Did he suggest an abortion?"

Carmen shook her head vigorously. "Couldn't do that," she whispered. "That's against my religion."

"Well, did he help you in any other way?" Mr. Howard continued.

Carmen shook her head.

"What about your family? What did they feel?"

Carmen looked down at her hands. "They kicked me out."

Mr. Howard's face showed no surprise. He's probably heard everything before, Sharelle decided. In one way or another. He had already listened to one girl in the class say that she and a neighbor had heard about "it" and just wanted the experience. And so they had "it." Sharelle herself was amazed at how coolly the girl admitted this.

"I got on a bus," Carmen volunteered then.

"Where'd you start from?"

"Tucson," Carmen answered. "I didn't really know what I was going to do or anything. I just thought I better get out."

"What about him, your boyfriend?" asked Howard.

"He couldn't come," Carmen declared simply. Sharelle did not blame Carmen for being evasive.

Mr. Howard himself did not press. "That's a brave thing to do," he said gently, approvingly. "In a way, you should be proud of yourself."

"I'm not, especially," Carmen told him.

"You will be one day," Mr. Howard assured her.

"Hearts and flowers," Paula Beale muttered.

Mr. Howard heard her. "We need more of both," he said quickly. Then, before Paula could get a second wind and take aim at him, Mr. Howard moved along to the next girl, the next story.

"Michelle?"

"Huh?"

"Is there anything you'd like to tell us?"

"What difference would it make?" Michelle Sheeter wondered.

126

"I just like to know as much as I can about people I care for," Mr. Howard explained.

"Bull shit!" Paula Beale spat out.

"Paula!" Mattie Cummins called. "Please!"

"Well, it is!" Paula insisted. "This guy's a pro, that's all. Makes a living thinking he's doing good and all he does is go around and listen to people tell how bad their life is. I mean, he gets paid for that!"

"It's just a cop-out," Michelle Sheeter put in. "I mean, Society knocks you up and this guy thinks he can make it all right with a few words and maybe a piece of paper or something."

Mr. Howard cleared *his* throat. His voice seemed to grow stronger, less controlled and polite. To Sharelle he seemed to grow taller, too, and broader.

"You see Maggie over there?" he asked roughly, pointing to beautiful fourteen-year-old who sat quietly listening, whose name was Maggie Topshek. Sharelle had not yet had time to get to know this girl since she had just joined the class a few days before. Maggie was not pregnant and not a mother. What she was was dazzling, well-dressed, shy. She was the only girl in class who wore a skirt. Her hair was pulled back behind her ears and rolled in a bun, making her features and her eyes more startling and more grown-up than almost anyone else's.

"Now, it's my understanding that . . . Maggie there was sent to this class by her counselor. That man, or woman, knew exactly what he or she was doing. Bless you, Maggie, for agreeing to come. She's a target, Paula, to the boys around here, just as *you're* a lesson to her. No, Maggie, don't blush. I'm not singling you out. All I'm trying to say is that what we want to deal with here today—birth control, understanding our own sexuality, how other people use us—is something we all need to know about before we get in over our heads. It's what Paula, and Michelle, should have had a firmer grip on

127

earlier, and that might have kept them both out of here and happy longer."

"I had a firm grip, sweetie," Paula leered.

"You mean having a baby was all the same to you, one way or the other?" asked Mr. Howard angrily. "I don't believe that."

"Believe it," Michelle Sheeter said then. "It is. Or was. I mean, who cares? So you have a kid. So it's rough for a while. Life's like that, always trying to get you down. Sometimes you win, sometimes not. I mean, look, I wanted to get pregnant," Michelle said challengingly.

"Why?" Mr. Howard asked. "Knowing as much as you say you did, why?"

"It was a way to keep hold of Freddie," Michelle answered simply. "At the time, I thought he was worth it."

"So what happened?" Mr. Howard wanted to know.

Michelle shrugged. "He wasn't worth any more than anybody else," she said. "He was a shit. I accepted that. So I made a mistake. I'll probably make more. I'm not perfect."

"But who pays for that mistake?" demanded Mr. Howard.

"Nobody," Michelle said securely. "I mean, well, sure, I suppose everybody does in one way or another. But they're going to pay anyway, whether it's me who needs it or someone else. I mean, look at the way the world works. There's nothing anyone can do. You roll a little, and duck, and then get up and start all over again."

"You mean you're going to have more children?"

"Why not? It's no big deal," Michelle answered calmly. "Sure, it's not exactly heaven, but what is? Who cares?"

"I'm standing here trying to tell you *I* do!" Mr. Howard shouted at her. "And I'm not alone! The city cares, your families care, your friends. I'm trying to share some information so that society doesn't seem so cold-hearted, so distant from you. There *is* help out there if you're brave enough to look. That's all I'm doing. Showing you a hand that's open and that doesn't want anything in return. That's what the number on my card says: Come, I'll try to help."

Mr. Howard turned his bulk in a small, tight circle. Sharelle thought he was going to explode.

Instead he looked around the square and then took a deep, controlled breath. Without looking at anyone in particular then, he sighed and said tonelessly, "Otherwise, you're hookers and there's an end to it. Otherwise you take chances and ruin lives for the hell of it. And I don't happen to want to believe that."

"Believe it," Michelle Sheeter advised.

"No, don't!" Sharelle said suddenly, surprising herself and realizing suddenly she was isolated but positive about what she felt.

"Oh, come *on*," Michelle groaned. "You going to tell us having Renee made you a better person?"

"No," argued Sharelle. "I know it didn't. I just know having her wasn't the end of my life, that I didn't give a big shove and then roll over and give up. I'm not ready to let someone else pay for what I did, either."

"It takes loot, baby," Paula told her quickly.

Sharelle nodded. "But what Mr. Howard's saying is that if we care, we can find it. Not a lot, maybe, but some. Or else some kind of help if we need it to take its place."

"I did," Carmen offered shyly. "I mean, where we live and all."

"And that's a lot better than waiting till you're down and out and then peddling your ass," said Mr. Howard frankly. "That happens, too, you know it does. How does a girl get money quickly? How else?"

"How about a job?" suggested Mattie Cummins.

"You think we can *get* a job?" Michelle Sheeter demanded. "You think society's going to go out of its way to make room for *us?*"

"Besides, you need help even if you do get one," Paula

added. "How many places going to let you bring a baby along nine to five?"

"And what can we *do?*" asked Maggie Topshek then. Sharelle turned towards her to listen; suddenly Sharelle thought she heard an accent, maybe from the Caribbean. "We're not trained in anything," Maggie said. "You can't pretend you are. People find out."

"Hey," said Mr. Howard, now with a broad smile on his long face, "that's exactly what I'm talking about. You don't really know what's out there. You get scared. You run, or you give up a child to stay free. But there are things to do, places to go for help. That's all we're talking about here, that and learning how to stop and think about the consequences of some very short meetings."

"Who can take the place of your own family?" Carmen asked sadly.

"No one," answered Mr. Howard, "and I'm not suggesting we can. But there are two kinds of families. The one you belong to by blood, and the one you eventually choose. Your friends, people you can trust, people you care about. If only you'd look a little more carefully, you'd be able to see that."

"At this point," Paula Beale sighed, "it's all we can do to get up in the morning."

17

AT the end of the day U. S. Howard visited the parenting program, as Sharelle and Renee headed out of the nursery towards the bus stop and the waiting vehicle that would take them back across town, a tall, thoughtful boy named Kevin Simmons appeared beside them and walked a ways silently. He stopped a few feet from the bus and cleared his throat. He was direct. "I've seen you a lot," he said in a somber voice, only the slightest smile making his expression something more than glum.

Sharelle had stopped, too, holding Renee. She looked at him, waiting. Surely there was more than this flat statement coming?

Kevin nodded, now shy. "It would be good to go out some time, if you'd like to."

Sharelle smiled. "It's not easy," she said. "Though I appreciate the offer." She lifted Renee a bit in explanation. "I'm afraid I don't have a lot of time."

Kevin pulled a pair of sunglasses out of his pocket. "I didn't mean anything special," he said, looking sideways at Sharelle. "Just sort of spend some time, you know?"

Sharelle shifted Renee a little. "Maybe we could, some time," she said nicely.

"Nothing special," Kevin Simmons said, putting on his sunglasses, turning then and starting to walk away.

"Wait!" Sharelle called, catching up to him. "Why me?" she asked straightforwardly.

Kevin smiled then, a sweet pensive smile, and asked in turn, "You know why you like ice cream?"

Sharelle laughed. "I guess not," she admitted.

Kevin nodded and started off again.

Sharelle watched him go. She had seen him around, too. In English class. He was quiet, a year older than she, popular with his classmates. He spoke whenever he seemed certain of an answer and he was rarely wrong. But up until that particular afternoon, as far as Sharelle could recall, he had shown absolutely not one whit of interest in her, or in any girl she knew.

Life was full of surprises, she thought then, turning herself and ambling back across the parking lot towards the bus.

Sharelle was pleased that Kevin's invitation was not a one-time spur-of-the-moment thing. She considered carefully and decided that a Friday would be easier to arrange than a Saturday, for to Melba Saturday nights still rang in her ears like bells on New Year's Eve. Grudgingly —announcing she was tired anyway and it would be sensible for her to rest—Melba agreed to stay at home and put Renee to bed. Sharelle was edgy as she left the house, but she calmed herself by thinking she and Kevin would not be late and how much trouble could Melba get into in a few hours?

Kevin took Sharelle to San Diego State where there was a Friday night dance in the student center. He gallantly paid for both admissions and bought soft drinks. Sharelle enjoyed everything she saw—the people around her, some from high schools around the city, some freshmen or sophomores in college; the casual way people dressed and treated each other; the sensuousness of their dancing. She felt grown up and sophisticated and, for a little while, free.

Kevin Simmons was quiet, but could he dance! On the polished surface he was a revelation. He was lanky and looked as though he would be all corners and sharp angles. But once he caught the beat of the records blasting from the loud-speakers, his entire body began to melt, his trunk became rubbery and his arms sinuous, and Sharelle couldn't help noticing that people around them —girls and boys—watched him admiringly. So did she, with a new sense of curiosity about him. She had felt easy and comfortable with him from their first meeting. Now, watching him bend away from her and seeing his smile—suddenly released and free and inviting—she was proud to be with him.

The only tension between them that night came from Sharelle, about an hour after they'd arrived at State. Between the change of beats, the idea of Renee at home, tended or ignored by Melba, came to her and she felt increasingly uneasy. Kevin noticed and asked if she was all right.

"Not really," she admitted sadly. "I hate to spoil this, but I'm worried about Renee. I've never left her before."

"Then we'll leave," Kevin said easily. "No sweat."

Relief flooded Sharelle. "After one more dance," she decided.

They danced and Sharelle found herself involved in her patterns and new moves, free of worry and conscious that the weight she had felt so heavily was lifting and dissipating as the record faded and came to an end.

As Sharelle and Kevin drove up to the house, they saw nothing unsual. Lights were on. They could hear faintly the sound of Melba's big radio coming from the living room.

"Will I see you tomorrow?" Kevin asked as he opened Sharelle's door.

"I don't know. My mother rules here on weekends. You can call, but I can't promise."

"That's good enough," Kevin decided.

"You can come in, if you want," Sharelle offered. "You could have a soda or some coffee."

"O.K.," Kevin agreed, and then grinned. "In case the fox can't invade the henhouse tomorrow."

"You have a pretty fine picture of yourself." Sharelle laughed, starting up the walk. "Or a pretty low one of us hens."

Kevin smiled and said nothing, waiting for Sharelle to open her front door, which she did quickly since, with Melba at home, there had been no reason for it to be locked.

They walked into the small entryway as Sharelle called out, but not too loudly, "Melba? Mother? I'm back."

No voice came from the living room, or from the kitchen.

"Maybe she's upstairs," suggested Kevin.

"Probably," Sharelle agreed. "You go in the kitchen. I'll check Renee and be right back."

Kevin did as directed as Sharelle went quickly up the front stairway and wound her way back to the nursery. She peeked into the room, in which only a night-light glowed, and saw Renee asleep on her stomach, her fingers clenched tightly beneath her chin. The baby was well-covered and breathing deeply, so Sharelle half-closed the door again and turned, going back down the hall towards her mother's room. She knocked on its door. "Melba? You awake?"

There was no reply.

Puzzled, Sharelle pushed open the door. The room was empty but for lamplight and its usual confusion. Atop Melba's bed was her flowered dressing gown, the one she had been wearing when Sharelle and Kevin left the house.

The door to Melba's small bathroom was ajar. Sharelle walked into the room and went towards it. "Mother?"

she called softly so as not to startle her mother or wake Renee. "You in there?"

Melba was not. She was not, in fact, anywhere at all in the house.

"But the baby's O.K.," Kevin said reasonably.

"I don't care!" Sharelle told him angrily. "You just don't leave a three-month-old child by herself at night. Anything could happen. Suppose the house caught fire!"

"It didn't," Kevin reminded her soothingly. "And Renee's fine. Maybe your mother got an emergency call, went to help someone or something."

"Then she should have taken Renee with her," Sharelle said firmly.

Kevin shook his head. "*Then*, when you got back and there was no mother *and* no baby, you'd really get hysterical."

"I'm not hysterical now, Kevin Simmons. I'm furious!"

"Wait," he advised. "Maybe there's a good explanation. Give your mother the benefit of the doubt, as people say."

"I'm forever doing that!" Sharelle objected.

"Then one more time can't hurt," Kevin reasoned.

"You don't understand," Sharelle said quickly. "My mother thinks there will always be someone around to take care of her. I mean, she's hardly a role-model as a mother to begin with. And as a grandmother she isn't getting any better! Imagine, abandoning a baby like this! I'll tell you one thing. This is the first and last time she'll ever get away with it."

"Maybe that's it, then," Kevin offered. "Maybe she got carried away and just forgot. I mean, there Renee is, sound asleep upstairs. If you weren't used to caring for her, you'd hardly know she was around. Things like that can happen."

"They sure can, especially around here!"

From the driveway out front, they both heard the

purr of Melba's car. Sharelle looked at her watch. It was nearly eleven. How long had her mother been away? Who cared? The fact that she'd left Renee alone was what was criminal.

"You want me to stay?" Kevin wondered. "I mean, maybe a third person could—"

"No, thanks," Sharelle replied. "I don't want a third person around. You're right. It might keep us a little calmer, but I don't think this is a time to be calm."

"You're sure?"

"No, I'm not," Sharelle admitted. "I just think if you were here, Melba wouldn't take this seriously."

"O.K., then," Kevin said, putting down his can of soda and starting towards the front of the house. "You call me if you need me, O.K.?"

"O.K., but don't wait up. And Kevin? Thanks for the dancing. It was wonderful."

Kevin nodded and passed Melba in the entryway.

"You two back so soon?" Melba sang out, all sweetness and good cheer. "Why, when I was your age, it was only every place closed up that made us come home."

"Hello, Mrs. Marston," said Kevin politely. "Good night."

"Good night, sweetie," called Melba, turning prettily in a pirouette towards the living room and Sharelle. "You and he have a little argument?" she asked her daughter, moving then across the room towards a sideboard on which were bottles and glasses.

"No, we did not have a little argument," Sharelle mimicked angrily. "I wanted to wait till *you* got home."

But if Sharelle was alerting her mother to a coming storm, Melba still saw nothing but bright seas and skies. She danced a little as she filled a glass and then waltzed in and out of the kitchen, ice now tinkling in the glass she carried. "Have fun, sweetie?" she asked, sinking into a chair and flipping off her heels.

"Probably not as much as you did," Sharelle said,

standing absolutely still about six feet away. She was beginning to tremble with anger. Melba sipped from her glass.

"Well?" Sharelle finally challenged. "Where've you *been*?"

"Just down to Georgie-Ann's," Melba said dreamily. "She needed some help."

"Doing what, may I ask?"

"Well, you know, she's not very good with people. She got sort of nervous and wanted a real pro around."

"Moral support," Sharelle judged flatly.

"In a way," Melba agreed. "It's nice to be needed."

"You don't think you were needed here?" Sharelle nearly shouted.

Melba finally looked up directly at her daughter. The direction Sharelle was taking at last filtered through to her and she swung around in her chair and straightened a bit. "I was gone for maybe an hour, total, honey," she said. "Renee is just fine."

"She is?" Sharelle shot back. "Did you even bother to go upstairs to see? I mean, just now. Were you at all concerned or worried? Doesn't look like it to me."

"But Sharelle, you're already here. Why should I worry if your baby is O.K. or not if you're here."

"I *wasn't* here!" Sharelle did shout now. "You were. You were in charge. Are you out of your mind leaving a baby alone at this time of night? Anything could have happened!"

"But it didn't, did it?" Melba responded as she sipped again. "I just left for a few minutes, that's all. I used to leave you and Annette sometimes, just like this, doing an errand or whatever."

"An errand?" Sharelle echoed. "You just couldn't turn down a drink!"

"Sharelle, that's unkind."

"But it's true, isn't it? Georgie-Ann called you up and

said come on down, some of the guys are here, and that was all you needed to get tarted up and hit the road."

"Careful, Sharelle, you makin' me sound a little worse than I am."

"You couldn't prove it by me!" Sharelle defended.

Melba put down her drink and stood up. "I don't have to prove nothin' to you, missy!" she said positively. "I am your mother, and I deserve respect."

"You're half-right, anyway," Sharelle judged.

"You skatin' on some very thin ice, girl," Melba decided. "Your baby's just fine, thanks, I might remind you, to me to begin with."

"Hardly to begin with," Sharelle inserted.

"Don't get smart with me!" Melba reddened. "You know damn well what I mean. I mean, in case you forgot, without me you and that kid would be out on the street beggin'! It's me who's paid for the food and the clothes and the hospital and the doctors and God knows what all! You think at my age I want to get mixed up with another kid, another kid and diapers and shit and spit-up? I've got a life to lead, young woman, and you got yours. I did my best to try to help, and what do I get? Shoutin' and screamin' and callin' names! I won't have it, you hear me! That's enough. That's it, over and out, amen!"

"I am *not* calling you names," Sharelle said next. "What I'm trying to do is make you see what your responsibility was tonight, and how you——"

"I *know* what my responsibility is," Melba broke in. "You think I'd leave a good party like Georgie-Anne's this early if I didn't?"

"If you're so all-fired responsible, I'd like to know how you could leave a defenseless baby here all alone, just tell me that."

"I already did. It was just temporary, just for a few minutes. She was sound asleep and dry and comfortable, and I had nothing else to do."

"I thought you were so exhausted from your work," Sharelle reminded.

"Well, I was, but then I got a second wind," Melba said, picking up her drink again and draining it. "Which reminds me, speaking of work and all, this place is a junk heap. I don't see how you can complain about anything around here, missy, when all you do is let things fall and pile up and never ever even pick up or put away."

"Now don't you start, Mother," Sharelle warned. "Don't get me really mad."

Melba smiled a little at some thought she had. "It's true, Sharelle. This place is embarrassin'. I mean, how could I ask people to come *here* and have coffee or something. I just have to go out, the way things are."

"It doesn't occur to you, I suppose," Sharelle said, crossing her arms, "that you live here, that most of the mess is yours?"

"I'm neat as a pin," Melba answered.

"You're a slob," Sharelle muttered.

"What?"

"You heard me," Sharelle replied a little more strongly, anger again making her feel she was going to choke. "You're a slob, Melba, and you're damned lucky you always had Annette and me around to pick up after you. The last time you even wiped down a table-top we were too young to remember."

"Now listen here," Melba cried out, beginning to shake in fury, "I work like a horse all week and I earn the loot that keeps this place afloat, and I'm damned sure not going to worry about anything else. That's what *I* do, and what *you* do is take care of things at home. It's always been like that and it's going to stay that way, and if you're ungrateful and unhappy about it all, why you have only to say so, missy, and find yourself another family to complain about."

"If I had any sense, I would," Sharelle said quietly. "If I had any money, I'd be out of here like a shot."

"Well!" Melba decided. "Well, we can certainly take care of that little problem!" She walked unsteadily across the room to the hallway and the small chair there where she had dropped her purse. She began rummaging through the leather bag and muttering to herself. Finally, after a moment or so, she turned back into the parlor with a triumphant expression and her hand outstretched.

"You need money?" she shouted at the top of her lungs. "You got it!" And she threw a handful of dollar bills at Sharelle. "There! Now you can go somewheres else and play princess-not-good-enough until *they* throw you out!"

Melba turned and started up the front stairway. From its landing she turned and shouted back down at her daughter, "You think I don't know anything about responsibility? Well, you're holding it in your greedy little hands. I hope to God it makes you happy!"

Melba's bedroom door slammed and Sharelle sighed. She waited a moment, listening in case Melba should decide she had another bulletin to issue, should decide to come back downstairs and launch another attack. But the house seemed strangely quiet. At least Renee had not been awakened. That was something to be happy about.

Sharelle knelt down and began gathering up the dollar bills that lay crumpled on the carpet. She shook her head sadly and, despite her anger, smiled a little. You couldn't hardly outfox Melba, she told herself. In a one-to-one face-off, her mother was still the champ.

The next morning the strange stillness of the night before lingered. Sharelle was up with Renee early and had fed her and bathed her and put her in her carriage to play a while before taking her out for air and sunshine. While waiting for Melba to stagger down, Sharelle straightened the parlor and the kitchen, and made a pot of fresh coffee and a plastic pitcher full of orange juice. She smiled to think that if she smoked cigarettes, that's what she would have been doing, waiting for her mother, tapping her fingers on the kitchen table, smoking.

Melba made an appearance not long after Sharelle had organized the kitchen. She came slowly down stairs and peered around the frame of the kitchen door to see if anyone was about. Sharelle saw her and sat still, smiling, saying pleasantly, "Good morning."

"Hummm," was what Melba replied, shuffling in her slippers across the linoleum floor towards the stove.

Sharelle watched as her mother poured a cup full of coffee and then edged carefully to the table to put in cream and sugar. Melba stirred and then put down the spoon, starting to leave the kitchen. "Wait," Sharelle said gently.

Melba turned slowly around to look her way.

"I'm sorry about last night," Sharelle said. "I got a little carried away."

"You sure did," Melba said. To forgive was weakness, not divine.

"Well," Sharelle said, just a little annoyed at her mother's too-easy agreement, "I am sorry. I was worried about Renee, is all, and I sort of, well, just overdid it."

Melba nodded.

"Your money's on the table in there," Sharelle indicated with her chin towards the living room.

Melba nodded again and turned to make her way back upstairs.

Sharelle watched her go, almost angry at herself for appearing to be so weak-kneed and mealy. Well, what could she do? The great gesture of money in the air had amounted to fifteen bucks all together. Big deal. Not that Sharelle wanted to take the money and leave. She didn't. But had she done, what Melba's generosity had amounted to was very little indeed. Besides, Sharelle thought, it wasn't generosity; it was more guilt, a payoff.

Hearing her mother reach the landing of the stairway outside her room, Sharelle sighed. What was coming next? Melba hadn't promised not to go off in the middle of the night again if she wanted. She hadn't offered to help share the daily chores around the house. Talk about being stubborn!

Well, Sharelle decided, she could be just as stubborn. She would have to be more careful, especially about leaving Renee at home with her grandmother. But also about her own temper.

It still surprised her to discover she really did have a temper. She decided that the only reason for it was defense of the defenseless. If she hadn't been a mother, she probably wouldn't have said word one. Whatever Melba wanted to do, or not to do, was all the same to her. But not to Renee, not to her baby's welfare. And that's what counted. You could overlook a lot, you could take a lot of guff and bluster, you could stand almost anything if what you were doing at the same time was protecting and cherishing a tiny bundle of brightness and charm and love.

18

ONE afternoon in the middle of November, Sharelle's last class was let out early. Sharelle packed up her books and purse and wriggled into a warm cable-knit sweater she had been carrying all day, and headed down the stairs and out, across a no-longer-used driveway that separated the two main campus buildings from the nursery buildings. There was a wind off the ocean that managed to climb the hillside on which Lincoln stood and she shivered, huddled in towards herself and walked quickly across the cement play yard.

She heard the music as she pulled open the nursery door. Without yet seeing where it came from, whether it was live or recorded, she carefully closed the door behind her and stood a moment, concentrating on the sound. A guitar, certainly, and a voice. Other than that, silence.

Intrigued, Sharelle edged around a corner and peeked into the big playroom. There, seated facing her, guitar in hand, eyes seeing something glorious in an interior distance, was Patrick Fitzroy.

Sharelle was amazed, not simply to see him but to see him *here*. And with a guitar!

She pulled back out of sight and listened a bit, not really hearing Patrick's words, just adjusting to his presence, wondering instantly if he would remember who she was, how they'd met. She doubted it. If she wanted to say hello, she would have to take a big breath and do so, introducing herself. She knew instinctively he would be polite and courteous enough to pretend to remember who she was. She would probably never really know the truth.

And how would he feel when she introduced Renee?

She allowed herself to inch out from the wall, to stand in full view at the back of the room. Seated on cushions on the floor in front of Patrick were half a dozen mothers holding their children, and two elderly volunteers, also holding babies. Sharelle looked towards Renee's crib. Empty. Someone was holding her, too, though at first she could not see who. It didn't really matter.

Patrick's song ended and the few people in his audience applauded quietly. He said nothing, instead strumming the instrument, pushing back his blond hair, and beginning another song.

Sharelle smiled. He was unchanged. He was still the most arresting person she had ever seen or met. His hair was darker now, the summer season's sun having faded after all, but it was still long and still being brushed in moments of modesty or unease.

Two things hit Sharelle then. Patrick was not just fooling around on his instrument. He was actually playing it; his left hand moved up and down the neck of the guitar, selecting stops and chords, while his right hand's fingers pulled at the strings with a sure sense of almost professional purpose. This was real artistry, not thumping and strumming and hoping for the best, which is what Sharelle had seen others do. She admired this skill immediately, wondering how he found the time to learn, nearly awestruck at his ability.

The second thing she noticed, when it was almost too late, was the sound of his voice. He sang not loudly but sweetly, his voice high and clear, every word understandable and whole ideas stressed in phrases his listeners (the older ones, anyway) could grasp quickly and appreciate. She was so entranced by his natural tenor that she nearly forgot to listen to the words of the song, and she caught only its two final lines, which came to her as "The door's still open, the fire's alight,"

She pulled back again quickly. Something about the song, about the sound and the few words she had heard made her tearful.

She heard his listeners clap again and realized that what she had heard was the last of the recital. She coughed quietly and took a big breath, wiping her eyes. Gracious, what was the matter with her, anyway?

She stepped from the corner and put her books and purse down on a tiny, child-sized table. Straightening, she smiled, though Patrick was not looking in her direction, and went to collect Renee from the arms of Suzy Light, a sixteen-year-old nonparent in the program. Renee smiled up at her mother when she focused, and Sharelle was pleased and proud. Holding the baby, she turned towards Patrick.

"You probably don't remember me," she began shyly as Patrick stood up, holding the guitar in front of him. "You gave me a ride home once."

"Hey!" Patrick smiled, brushing back his hair. "Wait. I do. Sharelle. That's it. Sharelle . . . something. Do I get five points?"

Sharelle smiled happily. "Ten," she awarded. "What are you doing here?"

Patrick looked at her a moment steadily, clarifying his recollection. Then he started to pack up his guitar as he spoke. "I'm in the Emergency Medical Training course here," he said.

"But you graduated?" Sharelle said quietly, feeling her stomach suddenly uneasy as he looked at her.

He nodded. "But I'm not eighteen yet, you see. And I'm not going to the—going to college until February. So I thought it might be useful to stick around and learn something important."

"But what do you do?" Sharelle asked. "I mean, is that the crowd I see around here in white?"

Patrick nodded again, snapping his guitar case shut. "Terrific bunch of people," he said. "Really interested, dedicated. E.M.T. can really be useful, you know? I mean, you never know when someone might be ill or in trouble." He paused. "You were ill that night, weren't you?" he asked suddenly, looking at Renee. "Is she why?"

Sharelle nodded, unembarrassed.

"Well, congratulations!" Patrick said. "She's a beauty."

"I still don't understand," Sharelle said then.

"What?"

"What you're doing here."

"It's simple," Patrick said. "I come over every morning and take classes. I enrolled in parenting, too, because E.M.T. is just a morning program, and I stick around till the end of the day and play a little basketball with guys on the team here. I mean, it's good to know about—it could be important, knowing about babies and children."

"You seem to know what's coming," Sharelle judged. "I mean, where your life is going, what you need."

Patrick smiled. "I have hopes," he admitted, blushing.

The room behind them was clearing, mothers collecting their children and packing up belongings and starting out for home.

"I saw you one day last summer," Sharelle announced. "You were in a car with about half a dozen little kids. They seemed to be having a lot of fun."

"We were," Patrick told her. "I was a counselor at a day camp last summer. It was really rewarding."

He smiled broadly and Sharelle saw again the discolored front tooth. She looked up into his face and was shot through by his look, his blue eyes steadily gazing back at her, clear, expectant, open. A hollow opened up somewhere deep inside her and for a moment its emptiness was filled.

Sharelle coughed. "I bet you even know what you're going to do *next* summer," she said.

Patrick reached out behind him for his jacket. "Well, I hope. But I don't know. I'd like to work with the Indians in New Mexico, but I'm not sure I'll be accepted for the program."

"You will be," Sharelle told him then, certain she was right. And also certain that there was something in this boy she understood, though she didn't want to put a name to it yet. In a way, it would hurt. In a way, it would also make her proud.

"I've got to get to the gym," Patrick said then.

Sharelle nodded.

"See you," Patrick called out as he started for the doorway.

"See you," Sharelle echoed, watching him go.

For a moment, only half-knowing where she was or what she was doing, Sharelle began to collect Renee's things, still carrying the baby with her as she walked from crib to playpen to the shelves above the bassinet where babies were bathed and changed.

"He's a nice boy, isn't he?" Mattie Cummins asked, startling Sharelle into the present. She turned and saw Ms. Cummins holding Jeffrey Beale, Paula's son.

Sharelle nodded.

"I think he's the only boy we've had in here in a long time who really wanted to learn about children," Ms. Cummins continued, bouncing Jeffrey on her hip.

"I knew him before," Sharelle offered. "A little."

Ms. Cummins nodded, looking around the emptied room rather impatiently. "Sharelle," she said suddenly, "could I leave Jeffrey here with you for a few minutes? I've got to go to the office and I don't want him to wait for Paula all alone."

"Well, sure, I guess so," Sharelle said doubtfully. "The problem is the bus. I mean——"

147

"Don't you worry about that," Ms. Cummins reassured her. "I'll see you both get home."

She put Jeffrey down on the floor and grabbed her purse and a sweater that hung over the back of a chair. "I won't be long, I promise."

"O.K.," Sharelle agreed with a shrug.

Ms. Cummins walked in her rolling, off-kilter, almost runaway gait towards the doorway.

Sharelle looked at Jeffrey, who was looking up at her. "Well." She tried to smile. "Want to hear the radio, Jeffrey?"

The little boy nodded shyly, and then, the minute music came from the portable speaker that sat on a windowsill, began to dance in a circle in time to the music. Paul McCartney and Stevie Wonder.

Sharelle sat down, still holding Renee, and smiled at Jeffrey's movements, some of which threw him off-balance and threatened to make him fall. But each time he was tilting dangerously, or spinning out of control, he stopped, giggled, looked at Sharelle for encouragement, and started all over again.

Ten minutes passed and then twenty. Sharelle wondered what was keeping Paula Beale from coming to pick up her son. She had seen Paula that morning in class. She was unchanged, nervous, a chip on her shoulder, ready to fight at the first opportunity. Sharelle tried to recall if Paula were involved in anything extra-curricular that would occupy her beyond the end of the last class of the day.

The radio played on, taking a commercial break and then offering a news-break at the hour. Sharelle bounced Renee on her knee, keeping one eye on Jeffrey as he circulated around the room, reaching out and grabbing different toys, counters, books. He was chortling to himself contentedly and Sharelle suddenly wished that Renee could talk, too, even if just to say yes or no. That was a difference between the two children: one was on the very verge of being a real human being, the other was still just a warm-smelling, needy little bundle.

Half an hour had passed and, as if to mark it, Jeffrey pulled down a vase of flowers from the top of a low counter near the room's makeshift kitchen. Sharelle was startled and close to being angry with him. She cleaned up the water and petals and mopped up around the spill, carefully picking glass fragments out of the combination carpet-and-wood flooring. She looked at her watch.

Feeling she had been totally forgotten, Sharelle picked up Renee again and, taking Jeffrey's small hand in her own, marched out of the nursery and down to the academic building towards the principal's office.

She stood outside a locked door.

She looked up and down the hallway. The doors to the rooms of the counselors were also closed and, presumably, locked. She could hear kids shouting in the distance from the playing fields behind Lincoln. She felt all alone for a moment. Then she remembered Jeffrey.

She knew she could get home one way or another if she had to with Renee. But what was she going to do with Jeffrey? And where was his mother?

Maybe Ms. Cummins had gone back to the nursery. Sharelle tugged Jeffrey along, now feeling the constant drag of her own daughter's deadweight, and started for the nursery building.

There was no one inside.

There was an envelope stuck into a telephone on Ms. Cummins desk.

Sharelle went to the desk and picked it up, looking quickly at the address. "Parentting."

With premonition, Sharelle put the letter down again. After a moment, she picked it up and managed, around Renee's bottom, to pull its flap open. "I can't do it anymore," it began;

Please take good care of Jeffrey. He's a good kid and desserves more than me. I do, too. We both do. And this is the onely way we can get it.

Paula B.

19

U. S. Howard read Paula's note quickly, shook his head and sat down—overwhelming one of the small children's chairs set at a tiny round table—and then read the note a second time.

"This happens," he said to Sharelle without looking up at her. "Happens all the time."

"It does?" Sharelle asked, surprised.

Howard nodded. "A two-year-old can be a terrible thing, demanding, physical, hard to control."

Sharelle looked over her shoulder at Jeffrey, swinging happily from the bars on a mini-gym in the center of the play area. She doubted Jeffrey was all those things. He was too sweet.

As if reading Sharelle's mind, Mr. Howard said to her, "He's not yours. You don't live with him. It might be difficult to understand."

"I just didn't know what else to do, who else to call," Sharelle said then apologetically.

"You did the right thing," Howard reassured her, still in the fragile chair.

"I'm glad you were there," Sharelle went on. "I don't know what I would have done otherwise."

Howard smiled. "You'd have asked someone else to come."

"So what happens now?" Sharelle wanted to know. "I mean, about Jeffrey? Where will he go?"

"He'll come along with me," Mr. Howard said, standing at last and putting Paula Beale's note in his shirt pocket. "We're all geared up for this sort of thing."

"What do you mean?"

Howard reached out towards Renee and let her play with one of his long, tapered fingers. "There are county facilities for abandoned children," he said. "Jeffrey'll be fed and clothed and cared for until we can find his mother, or, if we don't, until we can find a foster home for him."

"But how long does all that take?" Sharelle asked.

"Depends," Mr. Howard said. "Sometimes we get lucky. Sometimes we find the girl and talk with her. Sometimes she changes her mind. Sometimes all she wanted was a vacation, which she's had, and she's ready to take the baby back. Especially if she finally understands she isn't alone, that there are people who care and can help. It's not easy being a single mother, even if you're in school and your baby's taken care of, like here. After all, a girl Paula's age has her whole life ahead of her. She may start to feel cheated. Sometimes, if she feels that way too strongly, she'll finally give the child up, permanently."

"You mean for adoption?" Sharelle wondered.

Howard nodded. "There are times when it's the best thing that can happen to a child. He gets a new set of parents, *two* parents, who really want him, who are thrilled to death to put up with the terrible twos and and threes and fours. It all depends on who it is and how long they've waited to have children of their own."

"But how do you know they won't leave Jeffrey, too, later?"

"We check a family pretty thoroughly," Howard explained. "But that doesn't happen often, unless there's sickness in the family. If someone applies, it's a good indication that he's serious. It's a long, boring process, adoption, to go through. Especially if you're going to change your mind later."

"But suppose you give Jeffrey away and Paula shows up?" asked Sharelle.

"That's tougher," Mr. Howard admitted. "If it's right quick, soon after she left, then we let her have him again. Other times, if a year or so passes, there's not much she can hope for. We go to court. Not against the mother, you know, but for the child. It's the child we're mostly concerned with in cases like this. What's best for him in the long run."

Sharelle nodded. The whole thing sounded almost mechanical to her. She supposed this was so because it happened often, but she had a hard time believing it happened as often as all that.

"Where do you suppose Paula is?" she asked.

Mr. Howard shook his head. "Who knows? Maybe she found a boy who wanted her but not Jeffrey. Maybe she just ran off to clear her head. Maybe something happened to her."

"You mean she's been hurt?"

"It happens sometimes. As I remember, she was a pretty-enough girl."

Sharelle nodded. Even through Paula's defensiveness, there was a simple sort of appeal about her. Her features were almost perfectly regular; her eyes were wide and expressive, her skin was clear. Sharelle shuddered at the thought she might have been harmed by someone on purpose.

"You know," Mr. Howard said then, "this can all be positive, too, when you think of it. Jeffrey may find himself a family better equipped to love him. Paula may straighten herself out. Sometimes a girl wakes up and realizes that she can't do for her child what she wants. That she hasn't the money or the patience or the understanding. Sometimes it's loneliness that gets her down.

Other times, it's a big family yelling at her and criticizing. There are all sorts of pressures on young people today. The world hasn't learned to treat you all any better over the years. The same mistakes keep being made, no matter how much we think we know, no matter how far science leads us."

Sharelle pondered this a minute. A girl would have to be desperate to give up her own child.

"Well, I'd better get under way," Mr. Howard said with a sigh. "What about you? You live around here?"

Sharelle shook her head. "I usually take the bus.'

"Too late for that, now," Mr. Howard estimated.

"I can call someone," Sharelle said, trying to sound confident, not wanting to put more weight on Mr. Howard's shoulders. "Someone can come get me."

"If you're sure," Mr. Howard said, reaching out his hands then. "Come on, Jeffrey. We're going for a ride."

Jeffrey swung upside down a moment more before he reacted and let himself down onto the rug beneath the gym handily. He was not shy. He walked to where Mr. Howard stood and waited patiently.

"Nice little kid," Mr. Howard said, smiling down at him.

"Wait," Sharelle said then, putting Renee down on her back on the carpet and beginning to collect what things she could identify as Jeffrey's. She handed the small bundle of clothing and toys to Mr. Howard. "He should have familiar things, shouldn't he?" she asked almost shyly.

Mr. Howard nodded.

"What shall I tell Paula if she shows up?" Sharelle wondered.

"Just that Jeffrey's fine, and that she should call me," Mr. Howard replied, taking Jeffrey's small hand in his own. It was not easy. Mr. Howard had to hunch down a bit as he started to leave the nursery.

Sharelle watched the pair a moment and then picked up Renee and carried her to a small table on which sat the nursery's telephone. Putting Renee in her lap, she dialed the number of the San Diego Paint and Home Repair Center.

Melba had already left for the day.

Sharelle sighed and dialed again. Maybe Melba *wouldn't* come all the way down to get her. What would she do then?

She listened to the telephone at home ringing. Once, twice, three times. On its fifth ring, it was picked up. "Hello?" said a man.

Sharelle was startled. "Who is this, please?"

"Who is this?" came the reply. "Who'd you want?"

It was Dallas.

"I want Melba, Dallas, It's Sharelle."

"She's not here. Where are you?"

"Has she been back?" Sharelle asked. "I mean, is she coming back?"

"I don't know. Where are you?"

Sharelle's eyes went towards the ceiling. What could she do? "I'm at school," she said. "Something's happened and I need a ride to get home."

There was a moment's silence on the line.

"I'll come down," Dallas said then.

"No, you don't have to," Sharelle inserted quickly. "I mean, if Melba's on her way, why should you go to the trouble?"

"I'm on my way," Dallas said quickly, hanging up.

The buzzing on the line startled Sharelle and for no reason she could understand immediately, she clung to Renee a moment before getting up and thinking about going outside.

She was almost out the door when she remembered Paula Beale and Jeffrey. She turned quickly, putting Renee down again, and on the blackboard in the bigger of the two rooms she wrote, "Paula—J's all right. Call Howard. Or me. Sharelle."

As she stood patiently outside school, holding Renee

and waiting for Dallas, Sharelle found herself thinking terrible thoughts. They didn't make sense, or come in a direct line from one another. It wasn't reasoning, what she was doing. She was simply standing with an echo chamber for a brain, as signals entered and bounced off its walls: A good thing for Jeffrey. Maybe a good thing for Paula. A good thing for everyone, for me? For Renee? Good for Melba, that's for sure. It's positive, Mr. Howard said. Happens all the time. A vacation. Family criticizing. A vacation. A single mother. Single. Money. No Money. A vacation. Dallas. Damn Dallas.

PART
FOUR

PART
FOUR

20

SHARELLE saw Dallas' car round the corner at about the same time she wished Renee was able to stand on her own. She had shifted the baby from arm to arm, shoulder to shoulder, for nearly half an hour, and she was exhausted and sore. She hitched Renee up once more as the car came to a halt near her at the curb and reminded herself to be thankful someone had been at home, even Dallas.

Dallas leaned across the front seat and opened Sharelle's door from inside. Sharelle edged in, seat first, head ducked and hand covering Renee's tiny head, and then closed the door.

"I'm awfully glad you were able to come," she said without really smiling or looking directly at Dallas. "Thank you."

Dallas said nothing. He shifted gears and started down the street.

"What made you come over anyway?" Sharelle asked then. "To the house, I mean."

Dallas stared straight ahead. "I wanted to talk to you."

"You did? What about?"

"Andrea."

Sharelle was uncertain in which direction Dallas' thoughts were headed. She'd hardly given any thought at all recently to Annette's baby daughter.

Andrea had been born nearly two months ago, healthy and round and bright-eyed. Then, within a very short time, Andrea had shown signs that all was not as it should be. She had trouble breathing. Sometimes she even started to change color, and Annette and Dallas would have to drive her back to the hospital to have her throat cleared. At first the diagnosis was pneumonia. But later the doctors were less certain. Annette and Dallas were concerned, naturally, and afraid to go out, afraid to leave the baby for fear she would stop breathing again and die.

Sharelle herself heard most of this rather than saw it. Melba was running herself ragged, unnecessarily, Sharelle thought, insofar as her grandmotherly feelings towards Renee weren't so very strong and why should she care more about Annette's baby who wasn't even around? But Melba also loved drama, Sharelle recognized, and watched almost with amusement as Melba moaned and sighed and worried theatrically about Andrea and Annette.

Not that Sharelle didn't care for Andrea. She was a sweet little thing and who could resist her? But Sharelle also had faith in the medical magic of the day and felt sure that Andrea would pull out of whatever this was and grow up just fine.

Naturally, both Annette and Sharelle had kept their babies apart. Since no one knew exactly what it was that clogged Andrea's windpipe, the idea that she might be contagious worried both mothers, who, not overly friendly, almost competitive, felt caution made more sense than forced family togetherness.

"How is she?" Sharelle asked.

"Back in the hospital," Dallas said in a flat tone.

"What for this time?"

"Same thing. Only now they want to operate."

"Well, good." Sharelle tried to be cheerfully encouraging. "That must mean they can fix whatever it is."

"It's dangerous."

Sharelle nodded. Any operation on a baby would be, she figured.

Dallas steered his car past the turnoff for the freeway and went a block more before turning onto a side street.

"What are you doing?" Sharelle demanded.

Dallas said nothing. He parked the car and turned off its ignition. Finally he turned towards her and smiled. Sharelle felt herself stiffen. The fatigue she'd felt disappeared and she was alert and ready, her hand on the door handle, her arm tight about Renee.

"You're prettier than you used to be," Dallas told her softly.

"I'm older, too," Sharelle said quickly. "And smarter."

Dallas grinned.

"What do you want?" Sharelle asked angrily. "Dallas, I'm tired. I want to go home."

He reached out his right hand and put it on Sharelle's thigh.

"Cut that out!" Sharelle warned him.

"I want to be friends, Sharelle," Dallas said soothingly.

"Terrific," Sharelle replied. "Friends it is. Just get your hand off me!"

"Don't be so tough," Dallas said.

Sharelle wanted to laugh. "What about *Andrea?*" she asked instead. "I thought that's what you wanted to talk about."

Dallas nodded. "In a way," he admitted. "But I also wanted to figure us out."

"There isn't any us, Dallas," Sharelle told him. "There's Renee and me, and there's you and Annette and Andrea. All different, all separate."

"Shouldn't be," Dallas said softly, his hand moving towards Sharelle's shoulder to stroke it.

"Dallas, I warned you. Now stop it!"

"Cool down, girl," Dallas said, his tone changing abruptly. No more gentleness. "After all, you been around now. You know a little about what a man wants."

"If I do, it's no thanks to you!" Sharelle said quickly.

161

"With you it was selfish and quick. I hope to God other men have more feelings."

"Hey, I was a little carried away," Dallas said, excusing himself. "But I wasn't wrong, you know. You were such a sweet little thing."

"Lay off, Dallas!"

"Sharelle, I want that baby."

"What baby?"

"Renee."

Sharelle stared at him. "What are you talking about?"

"You know," Dallas said gruffly. "Quit pretending."

"I don't know a thing," Sharelle defended, her worst nightmares suddenly facing her.

"Renee's my kid, isn't she?" Dallas asked, but it was more a flat statement than a question.

"What makes you so sure?" Sharelle asked in return.

"Come on, Sharelle, I know you. You're not the kind of kid who screws around for fun. It, she, has to be mine. There are things I can even see now."

"Such as?"

"Don't play cute, girl. That baby's mine, and I want her. If Andrea dies, Sharelle, I'll take her."

"Like hell you will!"

"Listen, sister," Dallas said, lowering his voice then, "Annette's going to be in deep trouble if Andrea dies. There's something else, too, something we haven't even told Melba. The doctor's don't know for sure whether Annette should have another kid, any more kids."

"Wait a minute," Sharelle interrupted. "Am I supposed to give up my child for you or for Annette? Which?"

"For Annette," Dallas answered.

Sharelle shook her head. "Never."

"Sharelle, I'm warning you," Dallas growled. "I'll take you into court, kid."

"And do what?"

"Prove whose kid that is."

Sharelle did laugh finally. It was nervous and abrupt.

"Oh sure, and tell the world you slept with your wife's sister? Not very likely, the way I see it."

"Grow up, Sharelle. The world's seen a lot worse things."

"You think your wife's going to be happy knowing all about this?" Sharelle asked. "I think that'd be pretty much the end of everything, don't you?"

Dallas shook his head. "She loves me, Sharelle."

"Beats me why," Sharelle inserted.

"Don't make any difference," Dallas continued. "If I want that kid, Annette'll take it. I wasn't fooling around after, you know. I wasn't married then."

"Thank you very much," Sharelle said. "That makes it just fine, just all right, doesn't it? A lot of thought for me, Dallas. Nice, really nice."

Dallas shrugged and turned the key in the ignition. "Don't make yourself sorry, Sharelle. I tried to be nice to you. I liked you. You don't need to have a baby, not at your age. You got a whole lifetime to have babies."

He wheeled the car around and started back for the freeway.

They rode for a while in silence.

"Dallas?"

"What?"

"Listen good. I'd give Renee away before I'll ever see you get your hands on her."

21

SHARELLE sensed the dark cloud over her head, waiting to fall on her shoulders, but she fought it. There were still good times.

She didn't try to identify these. If she had, she would have seen that the most carefree hours were those when Renee was in the nursery and Sharelle was free to be just another student at Lincoln. When the day ended and she had to change back into being Melba's daughter, she imagined she could hear the low rumble of thunder. Her only umbrella was a smiling determination not to be deluged.

Paula Beale did not return to Lincoln. She was not greatly missed during class, but Sharelle wished she would run into her. She had some questions she wanted answered, badly.

Kevin Simmons stayed nearby, waiting to be rediscovered or even to be depended upon. He was unfailingly sweet to Sharelle when they met or sat together. Twice he asked about the possibility of taking her to the movies, but Sharelle had learned her lesson about leaving Renee with Melba, and Kevin knew it. He tried to be a good listener and, though rarely asked, to give good advice. He seemed content.

Barney Carnes sidled back into Sharelle's life—without a real apology, but as close to one as he could imagine. "I think I'll stick around," he told her one day in a school hallway. "I mean, sometimes the timing's not so good, you know? I maybe scared you, coming on like that."

"You didn't," Sharelle said.

"Well, I might have," Barney insisted.

Sharelle had put her hand on Barney's arm. "I'm not changing the conditions."

"Hey, who asked?" Barney said brightly.

Sharelle looked at the top of Barney's head to see his cap. Barney remembered, but before he took it off, he looked quickly around, as though if he were seen giving in, it would seem to some treason. He pulled the hat off quickly and grinned.

Sharelle wasn't quite certain whether she was pleased by Barney's new approach or not. She was amused by him, and liked him in a way. She didn't want to think she had been so very wrong from the start. But still he seemed to see her as less than a person, more a trophy, despite the trophy's ability in math. She thought she would just wait and see what happened next.

What happened was that Barney insisted Sharelle see him on the field. Lincoln was due to go against its main rival, Morse. It was a Saturday night game, and though Sharelle explained over and over again why she couldn't leave the house to see the game, Barney was adamant. If she cared for him at all, this would be her last chance.

Sharelle did care. She also felt trapped. Until an idea came to her.

She had a little money left, enough to pay once for an honest-to-God baby-sitter from the neighborhood. She could leave home around six-thirty and, if she didn't go out with Barney afterwards, would be back again by eleven. It was up to him, she offered. She would come and watch, but she would not go out later. If that satisfied him, terrific. Otherwise, he could come by on Sunday. He could take her to church (she would bring Renee). They could all spend the day together.

Faced with this ultimatum, it was Barney who gave in.

165

As long as Sharelle was in the stands to cheer him on, he would bend.

Sharelle felt she was balanced precariously, treading a dangerous path. She hesitated until the last minute to tell Melba what she had planned. When she did, Melba was astonished.

"I can't believe you'd spend your own money for something like that when I'm around," she said, making her voice tremble a bit with hurt feelings.

"Mother, it's just easier this way. You won't be put out any and Renee will have someone here."

"What makes you want to give money to other people?" Melba asked slyly, not really looking at Sharelle, pouting just a bit. "I mean, it's not easy making ends meet, you know." Sharelle knew. "We could use that for food, or for the utilities."

Sharelle sighed. "Look, you have plans for tonight, don't you?"

Melba nodded. "Of course."

"Well, there you are," Sharelle said positively. "Wouldn't you rather go out than be stuck here with a baby?"

Melba didn't answer right away. She seemed to be considering. She rummaged through her arsenal of guilt and came up with her best-aimed shot. "Maybe it's because of Andrea," she said sorrowfully. "I feel so bad about what Annette's going through."

Sharelle said nothing. Hardly a day had passed when she hadn't replayed mentally the scene with Dallas, his threat. The medical bulletins Melba brought home about Andrea had become as important to Sharelle as they must have been to Annette.

"So what's staying around here got to do with that?" Sharelle asked.

"It's only my duty," Melba decided rather sorrowfully but with pride in her own vision.

166

"Mother, you said you had a date!"

"Well, I do. But what's to say he can't come over here and spend the evening? I mean, I can cook a little something. We can play cards or watch TV."

Sharelle couldn't help smiling. That kind of evening was the very last thing Melba usually wanted.

"You think I'll leave the baby again, don't you?" Melba asked then.

"No, of course not," Sharelle lied. "That never entered my mind. I was just trying to make arrangements on my own so you wouldn't be put out any."

"You're trying to make me feel awful, aren't you?" Melba asked, keeping her voice low and her eyes averted.

"I am not," Sharelle argued. "I'm just trying to run things as best I can."

"Well, let me help, then," Melba said.

Sharelle was not convinced. This was not the Melba of the past months. This sounded pretend to her. It was like the few weeks before Renee had been born when Melba had seemed to enjoy the role of doting grandmother-to-be, or mother-and-daughter-going-through-a-crisis-together. That mood had not lasted. Why should this?

"Mother, if I call this girl and cancel, you won't change your mind?"

"I wouldn't ever," Melba denied. "I'll even call my gentleman friend and make sure he doesn't mind spending time here."

"Do that," Sharelle commanded. "Do that first."

Melba did and smiled as she told Sharelle her friend would be grateful for a home-cooked meal and a little peace and quiet.

Outwardly shrugging but inwardly alert, Sharelle agreed to cancel her sitter.

She left the house at six-thirty, having arranged to meet Michelle Sheeter at the stadium. Melba was all dressed up in her version of a hostess gown, long and fluttery, strangely demure, waiting for her caller, promising Sharelle she would feed Renee promptly and put her to bed and would stay at home no matter what.

It was at half-time, with Lincoln leading Morse by six points—six points that Barney Carnes had rung up with a twenty-yard bullheaded rush through the line—when Sharelle caught sight of someone in the crowded stands below her. "Look!" She pointed excitedly. "Isn't that Paula?"

"Where?" Michelle asked, craning and on tiptoe, following Sharelle's pointing finger.

"There, down there," Sharelle demonstrated. "With that man in the plaid hat."

"Couldn't be," Michelle said. "He's too old for her."

"Forget that!" Sharelle said. "It's Paula. I know it is. I'm going down there."

Sharelle edged her way out of their row and almost fell down the cement steps towards where Paula Beale was standing, her shoulders encased by her escort's jacket. Sharelle felt suddenly shy, but she was determined. "Paula? Paula, it's me, Sharelle."

Paula looked over at her, a little hazily. "Oh, hi, Sharelle. How are you?"

"How are *you?*" Sharelle asked urgently, reaching out a hand to try to pull Paula a little away from her friend.

Paula allowed herself to be separated and stood in the crowded aisle.

"Come on," Sharelle suggested. "Let's go get a soda."

"I can't, honey," Paula said sweetly. "I'm with someone."

Sharelle wanted to shake her. "How could you, Paula?" she asked instead. "How could you leave Jeffrey like that?"

Paula's pleasantly blank face changed and a frown formed between her eyebrows. "Sharelle, leave me alone."

"No, I can't," Sharelle said. "Paula, you have to tell me. How could you just leave your own child that way?"

Paula sighed, seeming suddenly resigned. "Sharelle, I got tired of fighting. I'm only sixteen, for Pete's sakes. I've got a whole life ahead of me. Jeffrey's better off this way."

"How can you say that?" Sharelle asked, wide-eyed. "You're his mother!"

"I can say that," Paula replied angrily, "because for almost two years I had him every minute, every day. He was all I had to think about, to worry over. No one helped me, no one cared. You get tired of fighting for every little thing—for food and shelter and clothing and just a teeny bit of time to have some fun for yourself. A baby deserves more than that, I think. I tried. God, I tried. But it was mean, Sharelle. I never hit him or anything like that, but I wanted to. I really did. Sometimes I wished he'd be kidnapped or something so I wouldn't feel so guilty. But I did, all the time, and I hated that!"

"But there is help," Sharelle said, almost pleading. "You knew there was. All you had to do was ask."

Paula shook her head. "Help wouldn't have helped me any," she said. "I'd have been saddled with Jeffrey just because there was help, if you can see that. I didn't want help, Sharelle. I wanted out." Paula paused and then turned to look directly at Sharelle without blinking. "It was out this way, or out another," she said in a low voice. "This way took less guts."

Sharelle stared at Paula, understanding what she was being told but denying it at the same time.

A roar went up from the crowd around them as Lincoln's Hornets took the field for the second half.

Paula smiled nicely then and said, "See you, Sharelle," before she nudged her way through the few people between her and her escort. Sharelle continued to stare, now seeing that the man Paula was with *was* older—he looked to be about thirty at least, Sharelle thought—and even a little paunchy. But he also seemed proud of Paula and happy to be with her. Sharelle had an unkind thought about the pair but she pushed it away. That didn't matter.

She climbed back up to her own row and Michelle, still thinking.

"Well?" Michelle asked. "What'd you find out?"

Sharelle shrugged. "How come *you*'re still at Lincoln, Michelle?" she asked suddenly. "I mean, for someone who says she doesn't care about anything, why stay in school?"

Michelle smiled. "Why not? I can't get a job with a kid around my neck. What else is there to do?"

"But did you ever, I mean—don't you want to learn things?" Sharelle pressed insistently. "Wouldn't that help get a better job later?"

"Maybe, maybe not," Michelle replied. "The important thing was to get out of the house, to get free of my old man. Not that I'm not grateful in my way, you understand, at least for the roof. But if I hung around all day, or left the baby with him, the honeymoon'd be over in nothing flat."

Sharelle shook her head as the two teams lined up for the second-half kickoff.

How could people let life stop them this way? she wondered silently. Just because you had a baby didn't mean life was over, that you wouldn't have other chances. Paula and Michelle both seemed to have sighed and laid down to die. Paula's escape didn't amount to anything, wasn't leading her anywhere positive. She was her own person again, but not for any good reason that Sharelle could understand.

The job situation she *could* understand. In fact, she had returned to her boss at McDonald's to inquire about starting work there again. But the problem was still, always, what to do about Renee. There just weren't facilities for a working mother to be with her child, even if the child didn't need to be watched and tended all the time.

Sharelle had gone further. She had visited a local job fair one Saturday afternoon, Renee in her arms, and after wandering up and down aisles full of people and placards and pamphlets, had worked herself up to finally stopping at one booth to ask, directly, whether someone like her could get a job at that particular company. The answer had been simple and direct. Not with a child that age who needed care. The company simply didn't have room on its premises for day-care, and day-care was an expensive program to start.

Day-care centers Sharelle had heard of, and she had telephoned to four of them, asking about the rules and regulations of each. Each seemed to charge about the same fee per day, which wouldn't be so terrible if a woman were earning decent money. But Sharelle had no skills to sell, no special experience to market. Her salary would naturally be small, certainly for a while until she could learn enough to prove herself. And the fee for the day-care center was money she just didn't have, and wouldn't, for some time.

She recalled Mr. Howard's flat assertion that one way girls earned money was on their backs. The idea made her shudder. But living with Melba made her shudder as well. The threat of Dallas trying to take Renee made her shudder. How could one be worse than another?

She had persuaded Melba to hang on to Renee for a few hours one evening—pleading that she needed time at a library for a paper that was assigned—and had taken a bus downtown to Fifth Avenue. The evening had been cool and fairly quiet, the streets not particularly busy with traffic or bodies. She got off where she thought activity of this sort might begin and walked carefully south, watching, listening.

She saw cars cruising, saw them circle blocks, coming to rest at curbside, their motors running, their windows rolled down. Girls (women) sometimes approached the cars and bent down to talk to their drivers through their windows, often getting in and then being driven away, often not, just laughing, straightening, and returning to the shadows of a convenient doorway.

Sharelle walked through this tenderloin district, her eyes averted mostly but quick enough to see, to catch.

She wasn't exactly horrified by what was taking place, the bartering of body for money. She had expected this, after all. But she wondered at the girls who could accept what seemed to be just anyone at all. The money mattered, of course, but still—to just put aside all feelings of like and dislike, of desire or distaste, of right and wrong when you came down to it—this was something Sharelle felt ill-equipped to do. More, she didn't think she wanted to be able to treat life that lightheartedly. There were too many awful possibilities.

Besides, and here she even smiled to herself as she walked along the street, from what she saw she would have to invest a lot of money in the proper working uniforms—in wigs, high heels, leather shorts and halters, jewelry and makeup. Even in this business there seemed to be money you needed to begin properly.

She got back on the bus and thought all the way home, looking at what she'd seen as calmly as possible. Putting aside every real sensation she'd had as she walked the streets, most of which were negative and frightened, even if she had the guts, she was convinced that somehow Dallas would find out and this would make him even more anxious to snatch away Renee. She would be labeled an unfit mother or something. It wouldn't make any difference to anyone *why* she was on the streets. The mere fact of it would sentence her, and Renee.

She could take out an ad in one of the local papers. She'd heard of other people doing that. The purpose was the same, the manner a little less public. But this too meant putting aside all your hopes, all your inclinations to like someone or not. You answered the phone. What did you have to go on? The voice on the other end of the line. Who knew what that person was really like? At least on the street you had a chance to try to figure out firsthand what might go down.

As Sharelle walked back up her own street towards home, she laughed a little, feeling guilty about her own thought but taking pleasure in it, too. Besides, suppose Melba answered the phone. Sharelle would be out in the cold all over again. Melba would take the money and run.

As far as Sharelle could see, there was nothing to do but stay in Lincoln and learn, learn everything that was put before her. And hope. Hope that something would stand apart from all the miscellaneous information and catch her eye, make her want to specialize. For she knew that if ever she were to have success in the outside world, if ever there were to be a chance for Sharelle Marston to succeed, it would have to come from knowing more about something important than almost anyone else.

Still, her own resolve, her determination had been shaken by the attitudes of both Paula and Michelle. Couldn't they see what she saw? Couldn't they understand that having a child was, at its very worst, like having a handicap? That it was something you could work with if you wanted to, something you could overcome. If you couldn't walk, you rode, you wheeled. If you weren't free one hundred per cent, you were still free some times. There were ways around obstacles, solutions, answers.

The game continued and Sharelle attended with half a mind. Barney Carnes knocked his way through, bruising others who opposed him, to play the entire game, earning another eight points for Lincoln. But Sharelle's mind was turned inward and she really didn't come to until she heard people around her counting down the final seconds to victory.

When the game was over, Sharelle and Michelle pushed their way down the steps against the exiting crowd to where Barney and a few of his muddied buddies waited —all smiles and self-congratulations and high spirits.

The minute Barney looked up and saw Sharelle, he whipped off his helmet.

Sharelle laughed and leaned uncomfortably over a railing to hug him. "You were terrific!" she said.

"Change your mind?" Barney asked quickly with a big smile. "Not every night you get to go out with a hero, a hero who *takes off his hat*."

Sharelle laughed. "I can wait till tomorrow, when I get to see all of him better," she said. "Duty calls, kiddo."

Barney shook his head. "That's what you should have called Renee," he said, disappointed even though they had had this discussion before.

Michelle dropped Sharelle off not far from a bus stop in town and Sharelle rode home in silence, staring at her reflection in the dark glass of the window to her right.

She walked towards her house hearing laughter from within, and felt relieved. She had not really been worried about Renee that night. She had made up her mind to trust her mother. There was little else she could do. The lights from the parlor spilled out its windows and crisscrossed the walk and dissipated in the bushes that ran alongside.

She made a little extra noise on the narrow porch as she approached the front door. The laughter within continued and finally Sharelle sighed, not at all curious about Melba's caller, and pulled open the front door, calling out simultaneously, "I'm home!"

"Hi, sweetie!" Melba shouted from the living room. "We're in here!"

Sharelle took the few steps that led to the threshold of the room and looked in. "Everything O.K.?" she asked.

"Right as rain," Melba nodded. "This is Harvey Peck," she said then, indicating a man who sat beside her on a piano bench. Behind them was a card table set up on which the remains of an early dinner still lay.

"Hello," Sharelle said politely. "Nice to meet you."

"How was the game?" Harvey Peck inquired.

"Fine," Sharelle said, having seen what she more or less would have expected: her mother in a looser robe, her

174

hair mussed, her face a little puffy still. The moderately unexpected thing was Harvey Peck himself, for he seemed to be about ten years younger than Melba, tall and muscular, with an easy smile and a masculine confidence that Sharelle, even at ten feet, felt engulfing. "Renee any trouble?" she asked.

Melba shook her tousled curls. "Not a bit," she said happily.

"Good as gold," echoed Harvey Peck.

"You know she's started teething?" Melba asked suddenly.

Sharelle nodded.

"We just gave her a bottle," said Harvey then, and Melba and he exchanged quick amused glances.

"Harvey was just keeping me company till you got home," Melba explained unnecessarily.

"Well, good night, then," Sharelle said, not able to think of anything else that resembled small-talk.

"Nice to meet you, Sharelle," Harvey called out as Sharelle turned and started for the back stairway off the kitchen.

Sharelle nodded to herself, wondering as she climbed the steps what Melba would do without someone like herself around to help keep her attached to reality. The more Sharelle watched her mother, the more she thought Melba was somehow slipping back into her youth, getting cuter and more girlish and dreamier. Unhappiness, Sharelle decided. Aided, of course, by the occasional tiniest bit of liquid refreshment.

Sharelle eased open the door to the nursery. The nightlight glowed in the dark and she tiptoed across to her own single bed and put down her purse and her jacket. She could hear Renee's easy deep breathing in the small room. She snapped on the tiny bulb in her reading lamp and went to tuck Renee in. She bent over the child and smiled to see her relaxed features and her tiny hands bunched up into fists. Tension, at that age? Sharelle wondered, pulling the perfect fingers apart from one another gently. She felt under Renee, thinking she might be wet. She wasn't.

Sharelle straightened and sighed. Another milestone passed: finding Renee safely at home with her grandmother.

She felt beneath the baby again, an odd odor coming to her nostrils that made her doubt her first check. No, the baby was dry. She stood a moment, thinking, and then saw Renee's bottle. It was empty. Idly Sharelle picked it up.

She raised the clear glass to her nose and inhaled.

Beer.

For God's sweet sakes! Beer!

22

MR. Howard's office was plain and small. The walls, which were fashioned of bleary plastic, didn't even reach the ceiling. He had his own desk and chair, and a chair for visitors. Beyond this, an empty umbrella stand and an ashtray and telephone, all Sharelle saw was paper—paper stacked, paper scattered, paper ready for filing, files filled with folders and reports and pamphlets. The neon light that lit them both from above made her feel washed-out and thin.

"I appreciate what you're trying to do," Mr. Howard said thoughtfully. "And I think you're moving in the right directions. I'm just sorry things don't work as easily as all that."

"What do you mean?" Sharelle asked, still hopeful.

"Well, to begin with, unless you want to move out of your house, you can't really qualify for what we'd call Welfare. Your mother's been helping, after all. And her income is probably well above the level that Welfare would allow."

"You mean she's too rich?" Sharelle asked doubtfully.

Mr. Howard smiled. "Not too many people are *that* comfortable," he said. "But the government, and the state, have to make *some* rules. Many of them don't make a lot of sense. They're sort of what-the-hell, why-not-draw-the-line-here. But still they're what we have to deal with."

"I don't want to move," Sharelle said firmly. "I'm trying

to find some way of staying where we are and getting some help so we won't have to depend on my mother for everything." She paused and decided to be honest. The idea that she was sitting in Mr. Howard's office to begin with was hard enough. "My mother's not very comfortable having a baby around. She's sort of, well, flighty, I guess you'd say. She means well, but she's short of concentration." Sharelle smiled to herself and at Mr. Howard. She was using strange words to describe what Melba was and wasn't.

Mr. Howard nodded as though he understood the words beneath Sharelle's. She doubted it, but said nothing, and waited.

"There is a program," he began, "called Aid to Dependent Children."

Sharelle straightened. "Well," she smiled, "that's what *one* of us is anyway. Renee or me. How does it work?"

"Its really designed for people who work," Mr. Howard said. "For mothers who need financial aid to keep their families together, or to keep them at all."

"Well," Sharelle argued, "I *can't* work. No, I don't mean that. What I mean is I can, and I'd be glad to, but I want to stay in school, too. And getting a part-time job where I can bring Renee with me doesn't seem possible. I've asked around."

"Chances are you could qualify, though," Mr. Howard estimated, "since you're under age and enrolled in school in the parenting program. I'd guess we could get Sacramento to allow that."

Sharelle's heart beat a little faster.

"The way it would work is that the state would send your mother a check every month and then she would—"

"My mother?" Sharelle asked, alarmed. "Why her?"

"Well, the check goes to the adult in the family. Since you're still under age and living at home, it would only be natural to send the money to her and let her give it to you for your own needs."

Sharelle shook her head, destroyed. "It wouldn't work."

"Why not?" asked Mr. Howard.

"You have to know Melba, my mother," Sharelle told him. "I don't mean nothing disrespectful, but I doubt I'd see a nickle if she got the check."

Mr. Howard thought a moment. "Well, is there any one else, another family member, who would—?"

Sharelle shook her head. "My sister's married," she explained. "She's got her own house. My grandmother's not right in the head anymore."

Mr. Howard sighed and tried to think.

So did Sharelle.

"Well, listen," Mr. Howard said then, after a moment. His smile was broad and encouraging. "I may not know everything about the system you need. Why don't I send you to someone who's really involved. I mean, I'm used to dealing with a lot of things here, mostly unhappy things. But the Welfare office itself has some really fine people who deal every day with situations maybe not exactly like yours, but close enough."

Sharelle looked at Mr. Howard a little sadly.

"I don't want to disappoint you," he said then. "Or give you information that's out of date or just plain wrong. Listen, Sharelle, I'm not just passing you on. Really. This just isn't what I'm strongest in."

Sharelle shrugged. "You mean if I was drugged out or raped or beaten up or something it'd be easier?" She grinned.

Mr. Howard laughed. "I'm afraid that's exactly what I do mean. Not that I'm not flattered you came by here, that you shared some of this with me. I am. And you're right to do so. But there are other people who can do better by you than I can, I think. It's just a matter of getting to them."

Which is how, the next day, Sharelle found herself sitting in yet another office facing the same news and the same explanations. She had taken her lunch hour away

179

from school to get to the Welfare office to meet with Linda Sampson, and within moments she was regretting the visit.

"I'm afraid what Mr. Howard told you was accurate," Linda Sampson said with a sympathetic smile. She was about forty, Sharelle guessed, and a woman with whom Sharelle had felt immediate understanding despite the differences in their ages. Ms. Sampson was blond, had clear and very bright blue eyes, a quick smile. She was a little overweight and Sharelle guessed, from seeing the mason jar on her desk filled with M and M's, that the weight came from having recently stopped smoking. The most reassuring thing about her was her manner, which, ordinarily, Sharelle would have rejected. When Sharelle had come into Ms. Sampson's office, the older woman had risen from her desk and walked around to greet her, and had touched her physically, softly, companionably on her arm and shoulder. Sharelle had flinched, but Ms. Sampson had persisted and had guided her to a chair, all the while maintaining this bodily assurance. By the time Sharelle had been seated, without even noticing it, she was smiling.

"Well, if he's so right, what do I do now?" Sharelle asked flatly, neither hopefully nor in despair.

Ms. Sampson inhaled and leaned across the table to touch Sharelle's hand. "There are options," she said simply. "Perhaps we can find a way to take some of the pressure off."

"That would be nice, but what I need is money," Sharelle allowed.

"Let's try to do both," Ms. Sampson suggested.

Sharelle sat waiting.

"Now, you don't want to leave home?" Ms. Sampson recapitulated.

"I'd rather not," Sharelle said. "I don't want to stay in some spaced-out halfway house with Renee. I mean, what

I'm *trying* to do is make sure where we are is healthy and safe."

"And your home isn't?" Ms. Sampson was not judging, only curious and concerned. "Why not?"

Sharelle looked back at the older woman. She made no decision. She found her eyes filling. "It's my mother," she started. "She's sort of . . . of crazy, I guess. I mean, I never know what mood she's in or what she's likely to do. She's left Renee alone, when she was supposed to stay with her. She gives her beer whenever she wants her to be quiet. She . . ." Sharelle stopped, choking.

Ms. Sampson still had hold of Sharelle's hand.

Sharelle could not look up. "She's messy, too, you know? I mean, if I wasn't there, God knows what the house would look like, what kind of junk would lie around. And she keeps inviting people—" Sharelle stopped again and looked up quickly at Ms. Sampson, changing her approach. "She likes to party," she said simply.

Ms. Sampson nodded and then leaned back, away from Sharelle. She reached out for the Mason jar of candies and opened it. "Want some?" she offered.

Sharelle shook her head, trying to pull herself together.

"You know, Sharelle, you can tell me anything you want," Ms. Sampson said then. "I mean, sure I work for the Welfare office, but I'm also a therapist. I mean, I was trained in psychology, trained to listen, to try to sort things out, to help. I'm not saying I can do all those things with everyone, but if you ever feel the need just to unload, you know where I am."

Sharelle did not answer.

"I don't want you to think," Ms. Sampson hurried on, "that we're giving up on finding some state aid for you. We won't. But sometimes, well, I know how hard it is to be alone and yet to have the responsibility of a child. Sometimes you just get desperate and depressed and it seems no one cares."

"You do?" Sharelle asked timidly.

Ms. Sampson nodded her head. "I have a son," she told Sharelle. "Of course, it's easier now he's grown, but there were a lot of times when he was a baby when I thought all kinds of depressing things. When I think back, I still don't understand where the strength came from to keep going. But it was there. It's in you, too, Sharelle. I just bet it is."

"I'm not that sure," Sharelle said in a whisper.

"I wasn't sure, either," Ms. Sampson told her. Then she smiled brightly and reached out for Sharelle's hand again. "But I pulled through. Josh and I made it."

Sharelle looked up quickly. "Are you proud of him?" she asked directly, not really understanding why this mattered to her.

Ms. Sampson beamed. "Terribly," she answered.

Sharelle nodded and looked away.

Then, without having planned to, in the next few moments Sharelle shared her entire history with Linda Sampson, from the night on the beach with Dallas to her fights with Melba, from her first day at Lincoln to Paula's desertion of Jeffrey. She came to a halt once, swallowing hard and almost half-ashamed to have laid everything on someone else this way. She took a big breath. "One night I even went down to Fifth Avenue," she admitted, laughing with embarrassment. "I mean, I heard about other girls and all."

"What did you find out?" Ms. Sampson asked gently.

Sharelle laughed again, nervously. "I don't think *I* could do that," she said. "It may be easy for some people, but it sure wouldn't be for me. I'd feel . . . I'd feel pretty small."

"So you would," Linda Sampson agreed. "So do most of those girls."

"But it's a way, you know?" Sharelle asked.

Linda Sampson shook her head. "Not much of one," she said flatly. "Those kids don't have time for their kids, if they've got them, Sharelle. They're on their feet for hours every night, every afternoon. What kind of attention and care do you think they even have the strength to give when they get home?"

Sharelle shrugged. "I never thought of that," she admitted. "It was the money."

Ms. Sampson nodded quickly. "I know. It's always money," she said.

"Well," Sharelle said a little angrily, "it *is*. I mean, if I had any, I wouldn't be here in the first place."

Ms. Sampson nodded. "I know. I know. And we'll try to find some for you. The hard thing is to keep you at home and still qualify."

"My mother needs me!" Sharelle cried out suddenly, not caring that she was tearful again.

Ms. Sampson got up quickly, reaching back down into a drawer for a handful of Kleenex, and walked around the desk, handing this to Sharelle, patting her shoulder and saying softly, "I know. And you need her, too, don't you?"

Sharelle nodded, unable to speak, shaking as she tried to control her sobs. Then, out of nowhere, Sharelle gasped in shame, "I even thought about giving her up! I thought about that *before* Dallas threatened me!"

23

—————◼—————

SHARELLE heard a telephone ring. It sounded as though it came from across the street, or farther. She rolled over, opened one eye to squint at Renee's crib. Satisfied the baby had not been disturbed, she punched her pillow, checked her bedside alarm—just after midnight—and squinched in a ball to go back to sleep.

It seemed to her only seconds had passed. But as she felt Melba's hand shaking her shoulder, Sharelle opened her eyes to stare at the alarm: nearly twelve-thirty.

"Sharelle!" Melba whispered hoarsely.

"What?" Sharelle's voice was weak and almost dizzy-sounding.

"I'm going to the hospital."

Sharelle's vision cleared again. "What for? You sick?"

"No," Melba said, shaking her head with impatience. "It's Andrea. She's having another spell."

For a moment Sharelle said nothing. She could feel her pulse quicken. "What good can *you* do?" she asked.

"Annette called. She wants me there. I have to go."

"What about Dallas?" Sharelle wondered reasonably.

"He's taking them, silly," Melba said. "I just didn't want you to be alarmed."

Sharelle nodded to herself. Thanks a lot.

"I'll wake you when I get back," Melba said.

"No, don't," Sharelle replied. "If Andrea's O.K., don't. I have a heavy day tomorrow."

184

"You'd think you'd be more concerned about your own sister's child."

Sharelle looked up at her mother, and spoke very slowly, very distinctly. "I am. More than you know."

Melba nodded, pleased, and turned to leave the room. Renee was still asleep.

It took Sharelle some time to recompose herself. She lay on her back, recalling an article she'd read in some magazine about how to relax. Feet straight out, ankles loose; arms at your sides, palms up. She waited. She felt no less tense. She heard Melba's car grumble out of the drive and start off down the street. She concentrated on her breathing.

She tried not to think about Andrea.

Sleep must have come. She heard Melba's car on the dirt below. Sharelle smiled drowsily. If Melba had returned, that meant Andrea was still in there fighting. She pulled half of her pillow over her face, hoping Melba would come directly upstairs to her own room and go back to bed.

Sharelle's eyes snapped open. What she heard were not Melba's footsteps. These were heavier, cautious. Someone was in the house who wasn't blind-sure where he or she was going.

Sharelle sat up quickly and snapped on her bedside lamp. Across the room Renee lay curled in dreams.

Sharelle didn't feel brave. But she had to know. She swung her feet out of bed and reached out for her robe. As she slipped it over her shoulders, her bedroom door began to open. Oh, God!

"What are you doing!" Sharelle shrieked when she saw Dallas.

Dallas did not answer. His face was ashen and looked ten years older than it should. He stepped quickly into the room and in almost one continuous motion, reached into Renee's crib and picked her up. Renee made a snorkling sound but gave no cry.

185

Sharelle was out of bed like a flash, taking the short step towards Dallas, her arms seeking out her child. Her fingers grasped Renee's legs and she pulled. Renee woke up, fast. She let out a squeal that grew into a continuous cry. "Let me have her!" Sharelle shouted. "What do you think you're doing?"

"I warned you," Dallas said almost calmly. "I told you what I'd do."

Sharelle kept hold of whatever part of Renee she could, maintaining her pressure on the baby's limbs, worrying suddenly about hurting Renee. "Is Andrea dead?" she asked, despite her fright.

Dallas shook his head. "No, but it doesn't look good."

"Give me Renee!"

Dallas did not. "I'll take good care of her, Sharelle. You can see her if you want."

"Want!" Sharelle echoed at the top of her lungs. She pulled harder. Renee's cries escalated and rose up the scale. "That's my baby!" Sharelle shouted. "You don't have any right!"

Dallas looked sideways at Sharelle and then, managing still to hang on to Renee, he brought his left hand up and around very fast, and clipped Sharelle's cheek.

Sharelle fell back away, startled but not terribly hurt. One hand still clung to Renee who, by this time, was wide awake and screaming for all she was worth. With her other hand, almost reflexively, without thinking in advance about what she was doing, Sharelle grasped her bedside lamp and pulled it up and out of its socket. She swung it hard at Dallas' face.

The room was almost totally black. Dallas grunted and brought his hands up to his head where the lamp had been smashed. Renee started to slide from his arms and headed for the floor. Sharelle reached out and grabbed the baby's arms as she slithered down Dallas' front.

Sharelle clutched Renee up and pushed past Dallas.

186

Dallas swore and reached out for her, grabbing her shoulder, tearing her robe.

Sharelle pulled harder and left some of the cotton-quilting with Dallas as she ran down the hallway and started down the front stairs.

Dallas was quick behind her. "Sharelle!" he called. "Wait! You don't understand!"

Sharelle figured she understood pretty well, and kept on heading down the steps. She reached the bottom and turned, wondering where to go. She was afraid to stay in the house with Dallas. Renee was choking on her own fright and screaming still.

Inspired, Sharelle ran for the front door. Oh, baby, keep crying, she pleaded silently. Keep it up! Yell your little head off!

She pulled open the front door and ran out onto the lawn. The coldness of the November air hit her and instinctively she pulled Renee more closely to her. The baby yelled and yelled, and at about the same time Sharelle saw Dallas' figure on the stoop, she also saw a light come on in her neighbor's house.

Dallas took a few quick steps towards her and then dived at her legs. Sharelle sidestepped his flying body and, as he hit the ground, with her bare foot swung out at him and caught him in the side.

"That you, Sharelle?" Mrs. Eaton called out from her window. "You all right?"

"No!" Sharelle called out. "No! Help me!"

Dallas was turning on the ground, getting to his knees.

"Gracious!" Sharelle heard Mrs. Eaton gasp. "George! George! Get up! Get up!"

Sharelle decided not to stand and wait for Dallas' next attack. She kicked straight out at him, missing him but making Dallas fall back onto the ground, and then she ran wildly for her neighbor's house.

She heard Dallas' footsteps behind her, heard them

come closer as she ran straight through the narrow hedge that separated the Eatons' property from her mother's. She was gasping for air. Renee was shivering in her arms, making sounds Sharelle thought no child could ever make. She ran up the few steps towards the Eaton's door and just as she reached out for its handle, she felt Dallas' hand again on her shoulder.

Then a pajama-ed Mr. Eaton stood before her, the light from his hallway behind him.

Dallas' grip did not lessen. Instead, all three people seemed to realize simultaneously that they formed a picture, a set of statues stopped in mid-crisis. There was stillness and silence, but for Renee's whimpering.

"Get in here," Mr. Eaton said, opening his door and reaching out for Sharelle. Sharelle obeyed. She stood in the Eaton hallway and waited, she couldn't say for what. Mr. Eaton turned towards Dallas. "What's going on?" he demanded.

Dallas simply stared at Mr. Eaton, a man twice his age and also, twice his size.

"Well?" Eaton insisted. "What're you trying to do here to this poor girl?"

Dallas was motionless for another moment and then suddenly shrugged. He turned his face away but did not leave the porch.

"It's his daughter," Sharelle said quietly, surprised she could even think straight. "She's not very well."

"So what's he doing chasing after you and the baby here?" Mr. Eaton asked, his wife just coming down the steps behind him to listen.

But before Sharelle could answer, Dallas finally took a step, backwards, and then another. Soon he was off the porch and almost running for Melba's car.

Sharelle heard the Camaro turn over. She started to shake with relief and gratitude. Mrs. Eaton reached out to take Renee from her and Sharelle found that without the baby to hold, she had no strength to stand. She fell

188

directly down onto the wood floor in a heap and trembled uncontrollably, every muscle aching and twitching in spasms, lying there until Mr. Eaton slipped his arms beneath her knees and under her shoulders and lifted her up to carry her tenderly into his living room.

24

SHARELLE and Renee were on the school bus the next morning, even though Melba had tried to make Sharelle stay at home. Sharelle would not be moved. To stay there alone, with Dallas out roaming the streets somewhere—for he had not returned to the hospital, nor had he returned Melba's car—was taking too big a chance. Sharelle knew she would be safer at school, and although she was exhausted and Renee still frightened, that was where she intended to go. She would go to her classes, in a daze perhaps but nonetheless knowing her child was sleeping soundly and safely in the care of people who would protect her.

There was a harsh and persistent wind coming off the ocean and sweeping up the hill toward Lincoln as Sharelle's bus stopped. She looked out her window and sighed tiredly when she saw Barney Carnes standing nearby, obviously waiting for her. Sharelle hoisted Renee up onto her shoulder and marched down the bus's aisle.

Barney's approach was unchanged, as goal-oriented as before: to get Sharelle to come across. Sharelle usually smiled and laughed and tried to defuse him whenever they were together, but that morning she felt edgy and sharp and not at all inclined to be understanding. She got off the bus and stood a minute as Barney came forward, smiling cockily.

"Hey, Sharelle, you look delicious," he said, all smiles. He raised his hand to pat her shoulder.

Sharelle stepped quickly out from under his touch. "Not now, Barney. Not today."

"What's the matter, baby?" Barney asked, trying to put his arm around Sharelle's waist as she started to walk towards the nursery. "That time of month?"

Sharelle stopped short. This was too much. "Look, hero, lay off!" she said angrily. "My day doesn't just start and end with you, understand? Buzz off!"

Barney's smile faded and his forehead creased quickly. Sharelle was immediately sorry she had said what she heard herself saying, but the energy to apologize or correct anything just wasn't hers.

"You won't have to say that again!" Barney stormed. "I hear that once, maybe, but not ever, never twice!"

He strode away, swinging his arms angrily, and Sharelle watched. Well, all right, she thought, I'll take care of *that* some other time. But not now. Not now.

A bell sounded in the distance. Stragglers hurried past Sharelle and Renee. One waved at her.

"Wait!" Sharelle called out suddenly. "Kevin! Wait!"

He turned and ran back towards her, out of breath and grinning a little. Seeing him made Sharelle feel somehow lighter.

"Hi," he said, beaming down at her through steamed glasses. "I'm late."

"Is your car here?" Sharelle asked him.

"Sure. Why?"

"Will you cut with me?" Sharelle wondered, feeling instinctively that being with him would make her feel better, safer, and that if what she were asking was really wrong, he would tell her so.

He looked at her seriously, his breathing slowing. "Why?" he asked. "What for?"

"Will you?" Sharelle asked again. "Just will you, for me?"

Kevin seemed to think a moment and then, somber now, he nodded. "What's it all about?"

"I'll tell you," Sharelle promised. "Just get me out of here."

"But what happened to *his* baby?" Kevin asked as they drove back across town. They had no precise destination in mind. Sharelle had only insisted they leave school, that she didn't want to go to her own house. "Just take me somewhere, anywhere," she had said. Kevin was glad he had thought to fill his tank the day before.

"She's going to be all right, I think," Sharelle answered, Renee lying in her lap. "That's what drives me craziest," Sharelle continued after a minute. "That he would come try to steal Renee without even knowing whether Andrea was O.K. or not."

"You know why, though, don't you?" Kevin asked.

Sharelle shook her head. "The amazing thing is that I'm not angry, not anymore. I feel sort of sorry for him."

"I would too," Kevin allowed, though he sounded a little doubtful. "I mean, I would maybe if he hadn't done what he did to you to begin with."

Sharelle reached over and caressed Kevin's hand. "I didn't tell you about that because I wanted sympathy," she said quietly. Then she laughed, almost giddily. "I don't really know why I told you at all."

"I'm glad you did," Kevin said, taking a quick look at her.

He drove another moment or so. "Where the hell are we going, anyway?" he asked then.

Sharelle shrugged. "Anywhere warm," she decided.

"Well," Kevin said slowly, "about the best place I could think of is my house."

"But what about your parents?" Sharelle asked.

"Hey, we're talking eight o'clock in the morning here!" Kevin laughed. "They're at work. Besides, who cares? I mean, do you care?" He looked quickly over at her again, and Sharelle saw the implied question in his eyes, and the excitement. She laughed.

"It's what you said," she told him. "We're talking eight o'clock in the morning. That ain't a time for romance."

Kevin grinned. "You never know."

"I *know*," Sharelle said firmly. "Just as long as there's heat."

Kevin steered his car with one hand and with the other reached out for Sharelle's.

"Easy, big fella," she warned him. "I mean, I may still be a little hysterical or something, but I'm not bananas."

Kevin squeezed her hand and drove on.

His house was larger than Sharelle's, and prettier. There was a real lawn and a short curving driveway. Not that Sharelle was intimidated. She had just never thought to picture where he lived or how, or what his father did or anything personal like that. She held Renee in her arms and followed Kevin around to the back of the house to enter through a kitchen door.

"Stay here," Kevin said once they were inside the house. "I'll go turn on the heat."

He pulled open a door and Sharelle heard his footsteps going down to a basement. Almost dreamily she carried Renee through a dining room, across a hall, and past a small den to a living room in which there was a fireplace and a view, from the front windows, of the bay below. She heard the whir of a motor start below.

"Can we have a fire?" she asked when Kevin returned.

"Sure, if you want, but I turned the thermostat up to seventy-five. You won't really need it."

Sharelle grinned at him. "I know I won't. I'd just like it."

"Hey, if that's what you want," Kevin smiled back.

"You make the fire. I'll make some coffee."

"You find your way?"

"Sure," she said, putting a drowsy Renee down on the

carpet not far from the fireplace and tucking her blanket around her.

She could hear Kevin in the basement again looking for firewood, and his footsteps as he carried the short, stumpy logs up and through the house towards the living room. She had easily found a jar of decaffeinated coffee on a shelf and boiled water. She found mugs and called out to ask if Kevin wanted milk and sugar. By the time she put the two mugs down on a coffee table, Kevin's handiwork was ablaze and sending out waves of heat.

Renee had fallen asleep.

They sat on pillows in front of the fire, sipping their coffees.

"What are you going to do?" Kevin asked. "I mean, suppose something actually did happen to your niece, something awful. You can't just wait around for him to come at you both again."

"I don't know," Sharelle admitted. "I honestly don't. I just can't think right now."

"You'd better," Kevin advised wisely. "I mean, if that guy's crazy, you better have a plan."

Sharelle sighed, but said nothing.

After a moment, she looked up. "You know, it doesn't seem like morning to me."

"That's because you're wiped out," Kevin guessed.

"No, that's not it at all," Sharelle argued. "I think maybe I *am* bananas a little. Let's close the curtains."

Kevin's eyes brightened.

Sharelle saw this. "Look, I—" she started to say. Then she stopped and looked away. "I'm glad I'm here with you," she said softly. "I don't know what it means, but it feels right."

Kevin said nothing in reply. He waited.

"Let's put some music on," Sharelle suggested.

"What kind?"

Sharelle looked up at him and grinned. "Something we can dance to."

"At this hour?"

"Why not? You don't move so good when it's light out?"

"Don't bet on it," Kevin warned, getting up quickly and going around the room to close curtains and shades. Sharelle watched as he went then to a closet and pulled open its door, and saw a stereo receiver and stacks of records there.

She sipped at her coffee as Kevin rummaged through the slipcases to pull out for or five albums. She was warmer now, the coffee and the fire and the central heating all seeming to swarm around and inside her. She looked at her wrist-watch: a little after nine. This whole thing was silly, she thought, but she was pleased. She did feel good around Kevin. Maybe she *was* a little hysterical still. She had thoughts that didn't seem to be right just then, thoughts that she imagined people might have when all was right with the world and cares were few and solvable. She had acted instinctively. She wanted to get away. And here—and she smiled again to herself— here was a knight on horseback who was her champion.

She heard the first few beats of a record and looked quickly at Renee. But she need not have worried, for the baby was as exhausted as her mother. Also, Kevin quickly turned down the volume of the set and then came to stand before Sharelle. He reached down for his coffee mug and drained it. "Well?" He grinned at her. "I think something's a little whacko here, but you want to dance?"

They started slowly, almost dreamily. Their movements were a little tentative at first, in part because of the carpet underfoot, in part because neither really knew what the other was likely to do at any moment. The room was darker than it had been, but far from night-like. They had turned on no lamps for there was still enough light to see and almost to make shadows. They smiled at each other shyly, dancing a few feet apart, not yet dar-

195

ing, either of them, to actually watch what the other was doing.

Time began to slip past, and the room got warmer as they filled it with their motion and body heat. They began to smile openly at each other, and to admire the moves each other made. Once or twice they held hands and twirled, or dipped under an arm, but still they both seemed aware they were floating in an unknown uncharted sea.

Sharelle watched Kevin's body move and wondered about it, wondered about him, wondered at herself. She really was crazy, but she was also suddenly and wildly happy to see him, to sense the sinew and muscle under his shirt, in his arms. She tried to ask herself if she actually wanted him, wanted him in that special way, but the answer never really came to her because she was spinning then, and laughing and hanging on to Kevin's shoulders. Suddenly he was lifting her into the air, her face high above his own, and turning with her in place.

She felt she was going to fall, that he would drop her. She hung on tightly and laughed and once leaned down to kiss his forehead. And then she was on the carpet again, her stockinged feet beating and shuffling on the floor, her body swaying sensuously in a mirror of his.

There was no sense of time to what they did. There was pleasure and heat and affection and touching, but no sense of morning or night. Kevin's shirt was open and his torso gleaming with perspiration as he leaned back away from her and tantalized her with the rhythm of his body. Sharelle spun in circles by herself and, knowing she was doing so but ignoring the action, too, she unbuttoned her own blouse and pulled it from her jeans. She tossed it to the floor and kept right on dancing, seeing the surprise and delight in Kevin's face, feeling flushed and free and cool, too, in her bra, her own skin glistening some now and Kevin reaching out for her hands to draw her towards him. Sharelle gave herself into his care and let him encircle her, let his hands slide up and down her back, along her shoulders. They kissed, still moving.

The kiss went on. Sharelle pulled Kevin's shirt off his shoulders and then shuddered a little as his hands once again touched her.

The music came to a stop. Silence broke around them. They didn't hear.

Kevin heard Sharelle's encouraging sighs and moans. Sharelle heard his breathing, his murmurings of her beauty, of her worth. She wanted to call out to him that she needed him, but hearing this in her own mind made her stifle the cry. It was too much. It would be too soon. And yet he was making her feel so incredibly special, so desirable, so wanted. He had to know. He had to. *He* was beautiful!

Renee's cry went through them both like an icicle.

They lay still a moment, listening, eyes closed, lips touching. Sharelle sighed. Kevin moved to one side and Sharelle slid off the couch and knelt by the baby.

Kevin watched, still sitting on the couch, as Sharelle changed Renee and held her for a few moments, giving her enough milk to make the child drowsy and satisfied again.

Sharelle put Renee back down on the carpet and knelt there at her side, her head bowed, her eyes screwed tight, her shoulders beginning to tremble in silence.

Kevin went to her then and held her there before the fire. Sharelle leaned into him and wept, the shadows of the night before mingling with the brightness of this strange morning.

He held her as her tears stopped, as her body relaxed against his own, as they lay together there on the carpet, Sharelle suddenly and deeply and gratefully asleep and warm and cared for.

Kevin drove her back to Lincoln at noon.

25

THANKSGIVING was not a happy time. The two holiday dinners Sharelle attended were somber, disturbing, rooms full of missing people.

At the nursery on the Wednesday before the holiday, mothers and children, staff and nonparents gathered at noon for a quick forty-minute feast and celebration. The food was *almost* right: turkey and stuffing, cranberry sauce, broccoli, and ice cream. Hearty but somehow a little dingy-looking, Sharelle decided, on its simple plates set on small tables between plastic tableware and patterned paper napkins with pictures of pilgrims and autumn leaves and Indians on them.

The day itself was overcast, and the weather cast its shadow on everyone.

Sharelle and Renee had arrived as usual by bus, traveling with Carmen and Christopher at their sides. Carmen had seemed unusually quiet until the bus neared the campus and then she had turned quickly to Sharelle and had taken her hand, whispering in a rush, "I'm cutting out of here."

"What do you mean?"

"I'm leaving," Carmen said. "We're leaving. I've got a job."

"You do? How wonderful!" Sharelle enthused. "Where? What kind?"

Carmen blushed. "It's nothing special. I'm going to be a maid."

"A maid?"

Carmen nodded, looking away then and speaking from the corner of her mouth. "You know. Someone who cleans, who picks up."

Sharelle was silent a moment. "That doesn't sound so solid, Carmen. I mean, it's nothing much to bank on."

"It pays," Carmen said a little shortly. "And we get to live there. We get out of the hostel. We'll have our own room, even our own TV."

Sharelle was still doubtful. "Where is this?" she asked.

"Out in Mission Bay," Carmen said. "Really nice people. They've got two little kids of their own, they've got a dog, they even have three cars!"

Sharelle shifted Renee from one shoulder to the other. "Carmen," she said slowly, "it's going to be tough becoming something else later."

"What do you mean?"

"I mean it's hard changing jobs like that. Once a maid, that's what you'll always be. The only way you could ever change that would be if you got married or something. If you went back to school."

"I don't want to go back to school," Carmen said defensively. "I'm no good at it. I want to get away from school, Sharelle. I mean, that's what all this is about. Christopher can go for me. He can learn things. I just want out."

Sharelle didn't know what to say. It occurred to her she couldn't really argue successfully with Carmen. Maybe what she was doing was right for her. Who knew? Still, she felt saddened. She wished she had the strength to make everyone she cared for care about the *things* she did. She was still certain that education was the one and only road to change, to better times. You could still learn, even with a child hanging on every minute of every day.

"They're nice people," Carmen said, strengthening her own resolve. "They like Christopher."

Sharelle nodded.

"And Mr. Clarke is really good-looking," Carmen added with just a trace of a smile.

Sharelle looked quickly at her friend.

"Well, he is," Carmen insisted. "And so nice to me."

Alarms rang in Sharelle's mind. She let them go unattended. If this was what Carmen wanted to play at, fine. Carmen and Paula, both. A shadow crossed Sharelle's mind. Maybe Paula and Carmen knew something good Sharelle didn't. She rejected this idea. What she did had to suit her. What they did suited them. If they wanted to take those kinds of chances, if they wanted to risk gambling with their bodies and lives, that was up to them. Suddenly Sharelle was conscious that she hadn't seen the sun in the skies for maybe three days. She felt pushed down in her seat, almost breathless with being contained in the smallness of her world.

The bus stopped at Lincoln and people piled out, rushing across campus either towards classrooms or towards the nursery. Sharelle and Carmen ducked their heads against the wind and said nothing as they climbed up the steps of the nursery.

It was warmer inside, but there seemed an odd sort of silence hanging in the air. Sharelle and Carmen carried their children into the larger of the two rooms, into the room where their cribs were, and both simultaneously saw a visitor, and understood the reason for the heaviness in the air. Paula Beale.

Not Paula Beale as Sharelle had ever seen her, but changed, altered, mystically thin and angular, her clothes ill-matched and colorless, too big for her. Paula was spinning in the center of the room, holding up someone's child and crooning to it, over and over again in a kind of singsong soprano, "Bye baby bunting, bye baby bunting, bye baby . . ."

The few mothers in the room, apart from Carmen and Sharelle, stood in a sort of lopsided circle around Paula, watching her suspiciously, as though they were waiting for her to fall and let the baby fly into the air. Ms. Cummins was nowhere to be seen.

Paula spun faster and faster, and her singing became a blurred humming sound as the child she held slid down her arms until it was held only by its tiny hands. One or two of the girls in the room made a tentative motion to step forward and to stop the whirling, to catch hold of the baby's feet, but Paula was spinning so fast that it seemed more dangerous than not to step into the whirlwind.

Then suddenly Edie Southworth, one of the grandmotherly aides in the course, materialized, her enormous form and heavy arms and legs almost a blur as she seemed to spin alongside Paula, waiting for the right second to grab the child and to hip Paula to the floor. Which she did with lightning speed, rescuing the baby and sending Paula to her knees, then onto her back, where she lay looking up at the ceiling dizzily and laughing to herself.

Sharelle sighed with relief and put Renee in her crib, wondering even as she did whether she should leave the baby there when her next class began if Paula was still around. She would wait and see. It was clear that Paula was spaced out on something, that her revolving for them all was both outward and inward. She just hoped with a sure sort of futility that whatever cry Paula was sending for help could be answered by *someone*.

Paula rolled over on her side and propped her head on one of her hands and beamed out at her former classmates. "Where's Jeff?" she asked lazily. "Where's my little boy?"

No one spoke.

"Well, he's got to be here somewhere," she said a little more positively. "I mean, you don't just leave a kid and have him disappear, do you?"

Amy Pritchard seemed to be the only girl in the room

capable of going to Paula's aid. She was a short girl, less than five feet tall, a junior, and very bright—sunny, always. She lived with her own family whose support and understanding she had, and who helped her take care of her baby son, George. Her eyes were always playful, but she was capable too of sudden, intense sympathy. Sharelle admired her. She had her act together, she knew she was going to go to college, she knew she was not going to have another child for a very long time, indeed. A cheerful, sensible mother, not easily alarmed, she was able to make the people around her feel, even temporarily, they too could succeed at anything they wanted, just as she had, or would. She always dressed simply but neatly, sometimes with humorous little pins or brooches on her sweaters or blouses. Her skin was perfectly clear, its color a lovely, dark rosewood.

Amy knelt at Paula's side and helped her to sit up. "Hey, sweetie," she said softly to Paula, "take it easy now, take it easy. Everything's O.K."

"But where's Jeffrey?" Paula asked again, her voice now trembling a little with confusion.

"He's just fine," Amy told her, helping Paula to stand and edging her towards the tiny stand-up kitchen at the rear of the room. "He's just blossoming!" Amy said more enthusiastically. "You wouldn't believe it!"

"But—" Paula started again.

"Just relax, honey," Amy said soothingly. "Have a little coffee. Why not have a little coffee and just relax?"

Paula apparently saw nothing to keep her from doing this and sank, under the guiding embrace of Amy Pritchard, into one of the miniature chairs near the kitchen counter. Sharelle stepped forward finally and went behind the counter to pour Paula a cup of coffee, handing the styrofoam cup across to Amy, who bent down solicitously over Paula and held the cup for her to drink from.

"Where's Michelle?" Paula asked suddenly, her eyes focusing a little more clearly. "Where's Michelle?"

"Probably just a little sleepy today," Amy answered brightly. "She'll be here."

"You sure?" Paula demanded.

"Of course I'm sure," Amy said. "Who'd miss a party like this one?" And she looked up at Sharelle and winked. It was not a gesture made in humor as much as it was conspiracy.

Ms. Cummins came bustling through the side door just then, talking as she rolled into the room. "Well, here we are at Thanksgiving already. My, the years positively fly by, don't they? As a special treat for the holiday we're going to see a film today about car seats. You've no idea how important that can be to a small child, girls. You'll see. A baby can just be a flying object sometimes. It's terrible how seldom we realize this. And then afterwards—"

Ms. Cummins great gush stopped suddenly as she saw Paula collapsed in her chair. "Why, my goodness, look who's here," Ms. Cummins said to no one in particular. "Paula! Well, gracious, what a surprise!"

Sharelle watched from behind the counter. Ms. Cummins had long since apologized to her for forgetting to return the afternoon Paula left Jeffrey in the nursery. Sharelle had accepted that in the spirit it was offered, sincerely, with a new understanding of the woman as someone who cared, desperately, but who was also just the slightest bit scattered. Her instincts were good, but sometimes she forgot on whom they were trained.

Ms. Cummins seemed to remember that afternoon instantly and looked up at Sharelle, her eyes pleading to be excused once more for her dereliction of duty.

Sharelle watched and thought she saw Ms. Cummins take in the scene before her and understand it with amazing speed. The woman's smile never varied, her tone of voice soft and supportive, her words well and quickly chosen.

"Why, we've certainly missed you, Paula. And we've

so often wondered where you were and how you were. We care, you know, we really do. Now, why don't you just rest there a while and let me get class under way, and then you can tell me all about it. Just the part you want to," she added quickly. "Only that. Only if you want to."

Paula looked up at her former teacher and smiled meekly. "O.K.," she said slowly. "But let's wait for Michelle, too, O.K.?"

Ms. Cummins nodded her round head quickly. "Of course, dear, of course. I'm sure she'll be along any minute now."

But she wasn't. Michelle had not shown up even by lunchtime when the parenting program was to hold its Thanksgiving celebration.

Paula was still in the room, sitting without speaking, looking aimlessly around the room at one pair of mother-and-child or another, sometimes making tentative gestures to get up and go to join them, or starting to reach out her arms to the child in question and then pulling them back. Only Amy Pritchard was brave enough to put her own child into Paula's arms, which seemed both to delight Paula and to make her sad. She held the little boy and sang to him a song of her own design: "Thanksgiving, let's go, here we go to Mam's house, for turkey and mashed potatoes, for fun and games. Thanksgiving, let's go, here we go . . ." The tune was one-note almost, repetitive, but its crooning seemed to hypnotize little George. Amy spooned food into his mouth every so often, whenever Paula's posture shifted to let her get close enough.

"Sharelle," Ms. Cummins said in a low tone, taking her slightly off to one side, "have you seen Michelle today?"

"She didn't show up?"

Ms. Cummins shook her head. "I hate to let Paula go without seeing her. For some reason, she thinks Michelle will know where Jeffrey is."

"Why?"

"I can't honestly say, it's just a notion she has. I'm going to keep her here, Paula, till the end of the day. I've already called the Crisis Center, and arranged for her to be taken there when school's out. Really, she's better off with us here for a while. She's already beginning to feel more her old self."

Sharelle looked across the room at Paula to see whether this was true, and whether the change was visible. As far as she could see, Paula was just as dazed as before, only quieter. That in itself, she supposed, was a change for the better.

Amy and Paula stood together and carried George over to a bassinet to be changed.

"Maybe I should call her house," Sharelle suggested to Ms. Cummins.

"What a good idea," Ms. Cummins agreed. "I've meant to do that myself but I didn't think I should leave the room."

Sharelle nodded and carried Renee with her into the other room to Ms. Cummins' desk. She picked up the telephone receiver and dialed Michelle's home number. She waited, letting the phone ring, counting. It rang almost ten times. She started to put down the phone and then suddenly heard something. Her hand was already in motion, though, so she redialed. The phone was answered almost immediately.

"Hello?" It was Michelle's father.

"Oh, hi, Mr. Sheeter," Sharelle said cheerfully from her end. "Is Michelle there?"

"Who is this?" Mr. Sheeter asked.

"It's Sharelle Marston, Mr. Sheeter. From school."

"Well, that's where she is," Mr. Sheeter said impatiently.

"Pardon me?"

"She's at school," Mr. Sheeter repeated. "Where else you think she'd be?"

"Oh, well, I . . ." Sharelle said haltingly. "It was just that I must have missed her or something."

"Right," Mr. Sheeter said. "You'll find her. Keep looking."

He hung up his phone.

Sharelle stood a moment holding Renee. She replaced Ms. Cummins' receiver on its cradle and hesitated before walking back to report the conversation.

Out of nowhere she remembered a feeling, a hope she'd had that day when she'd awakened. Since the Thanksgiving celebration at school was for the whole program, she'd hoped to see Patrick Fitzroy there. She'd kept her eyes open daily as she walked through Lincoln's hallways, hoping to see him in the distance or to bump into him outside a class. But she hadn't. Their schedules apparently were miles apart. But she had hoped, thinking even as she dressed Renee for school, that somehow the holiday would mean more to her if she could see Patrick even for a second, or, better, to talk with him just for the shortest time. She wanted to ask him about his medical course, what it meant, how it worked, where it could lead.

And she wanted to ask him something else, too. She wasn't at all sure how she would approach the subject, but she felt he would help her when the time came. She'd had an idea about him, about what he chose to do, why and how, and she wondered if she was right. She hoped so. He would be the only person in her whole life who had ever even imagined being that way. If she was right about it, then—and she smiled to herself to think this—then he was everything Monica Ruskin had ever imagined and a huge amount more.

Michelle Sheeter did not turn up for the rest of the day. By the time Renee and Sharelle were preparing to go home, to take the bus back across town, a car had come from the Crisis Center and two very gentle men had helped Paula out of the nursery and into its back seat. Paula had seemed perfectly willing to be led away like that. Sharelle had stood at the top of the steps watching until the trio disappeared around the corner of the building, feeling both relieved and hopeful that Paula might get help, and also inexpressibly sad that she needed it so badly.

Thanksgiving dinner the next day at Dallas and Annette's was not a great deal more cheerful. Dallas had sought and finally found a long-distance assignment that kept him on the road for the entire four-day weekend. In fact, Sharelle had not seen him at all since the night he had arrived so suddenly at Melba's and tried to grab Renee. She had imagined what she might say to him when next they did meet, but every time she had thought they would be face to face, and had prepared herself not to be nervous or angry, Dallas had found one excuse or another to absent himself from the family scene.

Andrea had pulled through once again, and was at home where Annette doted and worried and hung over her almost all the time watching for signs that anything might be wrong. Melba and Sharelle with Renee had driven over to Annette's apartment around three on Thanksgiving afternoon, carrying with them all the food and drink for a late-afternoon feast. Annette's attitude towards Renee was still somewhat distant but finally a little softer around its edges, a little more forgiving towards Sharelle herself. This made Sharelle angry more than relieved. She felt Annette was still criticizing her, and she was occasionally so stung by her older sister's gestures and words that she was tempted to lay her out, to load her up with the real information about everything and let *her* handle it. Still, Sharelle managed to maintain a sort of distant courtesy and interest in Annette, and a genuine concern for little Andrea, who was thin and weak-looking, and whose cries, whenever she had the strength to cry at all, sounded so forlorn and frail.

Melba rattled and rolled through the afternoon and early evening, seeming to try to fill the space left vacant by Dallas' desertion. Her voice bounced off Annette's walls and became, in time, like background music to Sharelle. Very little of anything Melba said applied to her or Renee, and so she ignored almost everything Melba thought worth commenting on. Which was nearly everything. In her strenuous effort to cover Dallas' absence, Melba managed to focus with increasing bleariness on national politics, on the weather, on winter fashions, on Sea World's latest acquisition, on Balboa Park and its good-looking joggers whom she passed each day on the way home from work. She imagined herself in a jersey running suit bouncing alongside the men, making friends. Both Sharelle and Annette exchanged smiles when they listened to this. It was a moment almost out of their past, when together they were united in surviving Melba's enthusiasms.

In fact, twice during that day Annette seemed to want to catch Sharelle's attention and to tell her something. What it was Sharelle could not imagine because every time things quieted down and Annette motioned with her head that Sharelle should follow her into the kitchen, Melba would come back to life and put the needle down on the outer rim and the noise issued from her larynx once again. And just when Melba finally seemed to have run down and Annette had motioned again to Sharelle, the doorbell rang. It was Melba's brother Jack and his wife with their own two kids. And that was the end of any time or silence the two sisters might have fashioned into a conference.

But seeing her Uncle Jack brought a hopeful and exciting idea to Sharelle's mind and she promised herself that she would take the first opportunity she had to speak to him alone.

26

MATTIE Cummins' face on the morning following the holiday weekend was pale and set. Around her, mothers and children settled in to cribs and chairs and playpens. No one was aware at first that Ms. Cummins was standing absolutely still, waiting, motionless. She neither cleared her throat nor clapped her hands.

But when the first few moments of adjustment ended, and the girls in the room looked up expectantly to learn whether the hour would begin in the nursery itself or in the classroom next door, the strain on their teacher's face was evident and plain.

"I have something to tell you," Ms. Cummins began. "It's not happy news."

There was no buzz of guesswork or worry. Just silence.

"You'll remember we missed Michelle at the end of last week," Ms. Cummins continued after a second. "She didn't show up at all on Wednesday, not even for our party."

A few heads nodded, Sharelle's included. She had not given a lot of thought to Michelle's absence. The holiday and her own problems had been too heavy.

"This morning I received a telephone call," Ms. Cummins announced. She inhaled hugely and her eyes seemed to fill with tears, although they were pointed towards a window. "Michelle, it seems, was pregnant again," she said flatly. "We can only guess what her thoughts were. In any case," and here she stopped and shook her head sadly, "she must have been feeling pretty hopeless because she took some pills."

No one breathed. They were waiting.

"She's going to be all right," Ms. Cummins said a little more brightly then. "But the child she was carrying died."

An almost inaudible moan came from someone in the group. Sharelle looked around. It could have come from the hearts of any of them there.

Ms. Cummins stood without speaking, seeming to have run out of steam.

Sharelle straightened Renee's clothing, wondering who the boy was with Michelle, what he would be thinking. What Michelle had really wanted to do. Was it over and out, the end of the line, or was it simply a way to be rid of one more problem Michelle could blame on someone else?

Sharelle shook her head thoughtfully. She had always thought Michelle smarter than this. For someone as verbal as she was about life and Society and who cares, Michelle must still have, underneath, been hoping. Otherwise how could anyone explain her pregnancy? She knew about birth control, about pills and condoms. If you believed what she said, she could have written an encyclopedia about various ways and means of having your cake and eating it. Someone had gotten to her, Sharelle decided, and wondered again why Michelle hadn't said anything to her. Not that they were such close friends, but Sharelle had thought they were friends at least, and capable of talking to each other when it mattered.

"What about Flex?" asked Amy Pritchard suddenly, remembering Michelle's son. "Where is he?"

Ms. Cummins smiled a little. "He's being taken care of for a while," she said. "Michelle's family have rallied round a bit, which is good. She'll need that."

"She'll need Flex," Amy Pritchard said firmly. "She'll also need us, I bet."

Ms. Cummins nodded her head encouragingly. "She will, you're absolutely right," she said. "Of course, she won't come back here tomorrow, or even the next day. But if we make it clear to her we need her, that she's loved and respected, that we even understand what's happened—although that's very hard, I know—maybe we can bring her back into the fold, her and Flex both, and help heal the scars."

"She won't want to come back," Sharelle said aloud.

"Probably not," Ms. Cummins agreed. "But I think if you talk to her, if we visit her—not all together, just one at a time over the next few weeks—well, maybe we can influence her a bit, show her we care, show her there's a place for her."

"Christmas is an awful time, anyway," Maggie Topchek stated.

There seemed to be general agreement around the circle about that. Sharelle nodded, too, and yet was struck by the idea that all the people there, but for the adults, should really be feeling differently, they were so young still, there was so much ahead of them, a hundred Christmas mornings at least.

For the rest of the day, most of the students in Sharelle's parenting program seemed thoughtful, distant, withdrawn. She couldn't tell what thoughts and ideas ran round the brains of her friends and classmates, but she assumed most were her own. The surprise of learning that the two most vocal, strongest-seeming girls in the program had folded . . . Paula and Michelle, each for different reasons to be sure, but collapsed nonetheless without seeming regard for anyone else, their children included. One could imagine that their actions came directly from having children in the first place, from the burden of being not only young but mothers when what they had probably been prepared to be at their ages was happy and flying and pretty and romantic.

Sharelle compared the anger and struggle of the two with someone like Amy Pritchard. Amy had one enormous advantage: her family gave her support and confidence, worked with her, shared her weights and burdens, allowed her to plan to be as normal as she could be under the circumstances. And with this behind her, Amy was able to be the young woman she wanted: helpful, courteous, happy, able to cope, a good mother whose dreams and ambitions lived and even grew as the days passed.

Sharelle admired Amy's attitudes, and her disposition, and although she knew their personal situations were different, she hoped that she would be able to be what Amy had become: well-adjusted, confident, forward-looking, instinctively concerned for others. It was Amy who had first wondered about Michelle's return to the parenting program, and who first wanted to visit her. Sharelle decided she would try to get Amy to let her come along, less for Michelle's sake than to watch Amy in action, to see and listen to her reasoning and her concern.

The day passed quickly enough. Sharelle caught sight of Kevin Simmons in the hallway and later, in class, though they had little more time than to nod hello, she smiled warmly at him and he at her. She began to feel as though something between them had been decided. It was a nice feeling, one she didn't want very badly to label, afraid to put too much stock in anticipation, in dreaming about ideas and events lest when and if those pictures in her mind became true, they would somehow not match up to the realities before her. Still, the idea of having Kevin near by, even mentally, gave her pleasure, if not strength. There was somone who cared, in whose arms she had lain, who had folded his strength around her weakness and in so doing had almost been able to transfer his own sense of right and wrong, of value or waste, to her. They had not discussed any of this. It had all just happened. It had happened the way Sharelle had thought all along something like this *should* happen.

So that, at the end of the day when she found Barney Carnes waiting outside the nursery for her and Renee, Sharelle was able to smile at him genuinely, almost tolerantly, and to accept his offer of a ride home.

She had teased and nudged Barney back from his farewell snit the morning after Dallas had tried to grab Renee. She had explained to him how low and exhausted she had been, though not telling him the details of why she felt that way, and had even flirted a little to raise his spirits and his interest once again. Sharelle decided that Barney was a romantic. Strange for a boy like him and something of which he himself might not even be aware. As for herself, she *did* enjoy the sorts of daydreams Barney had about himself and her, and she really couldn't imagine any harm coming from letting him fantasize from time to time. No matter how Barney phrased his needs, sometimes crudely, it was still nice to be wanted.

Barney seemed almost hyper that afternoon, plainly excited by something secretive, and instead of being angry at Sharelle for having missed yet another football game at Thanksgiving time, he was actually glowing with good humor and high spirits. Furthermore, and Sharelle could not help but notice this, he did not wear his tiny hat atop his curls with her. It stuck out of the back pocket of his jeans, still ready to be whipped out and up, but with her it was doffed and almost forgotten —though Sharelle smiled to see him nervously bring his hand to the top of his head and pat the curls to make sure they were still there.

"We're on the way, baby," Barney said as he steered his car onto the freeway heading north. "We did our job and, by God, it worked!"

"What worked?" Sharelle asked, tightening the seat belt around her midriff and around Renee's tiny waist.

"I did!" he nearly shouted. "I worked my tail off and, boy, did it pay off!"

Sharelle waited for more. She did not have to coax him.

"I got early admission, Sharelle!" Barney crowed proudly. "I *know* what's coming next!"

"What?" Sharelle asked, surprised a little but believing him and happy for him.

"I'm going to State," Barney announced keenly. "I got a football scholarship, Sharelle. I can go next year if I want to; I can start a whole year early."

"I don't get it," Sharelle said, puzzled. "How can you? You're only a junior."

Barney nodded quickly. "Yeah, but when talent's for sale, you buy or you pass. Who can afford to pass me up?"

Sharelle laughed.

"Don't you see what this means?" Barney asked then. "I get into college, I run myself ragged for a few more years, and then I jump out, into the pros. Sharelle, it's all downhill, baby. We've made it!"

Sharelle looked out the window as their car sped by a trailer. She didn't want to pour cold water on Barney's excitement, but she didn't want him going off half-cocked, either. "Suppose you don't pass this year," she said quietly. "I mean, suppose you can't stay eligible?"

"Hey, what do you mean?" Barney asked, surprised. " 'Course I can. With you helping, and me just sitting like some kind of quiet brain, paying attention and pretending to listen, I got it made. *We* got it made, Sharelle. Hell, you know about scholarships. You get money and clothes, and maybe even a car. You stay healthy and play good, you can have anything you want in the whole world."

"No, I understand all that," Sharelle said seriously. "What I'm talking about is your education, Barney. I mean, not every teacher is going to look the other way just so you can get your brains battered out. Sooner or later someone's bound to figure it out, and then what? Suppose it doesn't happen at Lincoln. I mean, I can see people here would be happy for you and want you to succeed and do everything they could to send you on. I can see that. But suppose someone at State doesn't feel the same way?" She paused to breathe. "You're going to have to do some work on your own, Barney. Really. I believe that."

Barney grinned sideways and looked at her. "Aw, come on, Sharelle," he said seductively. "I've got you on my side."

Sharelle nodded. "Of course, and I'm happy for you, I really am. But you just better start working a little on your own, Barney. From now on, I mean. I'll help you if I can, but sooner or later it's your own legs got to carry you, not mine."

The car turned off the freeway and headed up the hill towards Sharelle's house. Barney guided the car to a quiet stop along the curb and switched off the ignition, turning then to face his passengers.

"Sharelle, you and me is a team," he said then hopefully, his eyes alight and his hand on her shoulder. "We could be really solid together. You could go to State, too, and we could live together if we wanted. We could even get married later. And all the time you'd be right there beside me, helping keep me straight, explaining things, cheering me on. It could be something special, babe."

Sharelle couldn't help smiling. She wondered if this was her first proposal of marriage. It didn't sound like one, but what else was Barney talking about?

"You know we'd be good together, really tight," Barney continued, stroking her shoulder gently. "You know I'd make you happy, girl. There'd be such a smile on your face your friends and neighbors would just have to know why."

Sharelle laughed.

"What's funny?" Barney asked, his tone just a little tentative, a little hurt.

Sharelle shook her head. "I don't know," she said. "It's just all the pictures I'm getting."

"Well, they're great, aren't they?" Barney asked enthusiastically. "I mean, I told you, I give as good as I get. That's a promise, Sharelle. I don't disappoint people."

Sharelle looked over at him and took his hand down from her shoulder. She held it. *Now* she understood the harm in letting someone dream. "I'd bet you don't," she said softly. "But Barney, I never imagined myself in a spot where I *would* be disappointed. With you, I mean."

Barney's face showed his confusion.

Sharelle squeezed his hand. "I like you a lot," she said slowly. "You know that."

Barney nodded. "And look, no hat!" he said eagerly, stroking the top of his head. "That's what you wanted, Sharelle."

"And you look terrific, too," Sharelle said agreeably. "You're a dynamite man, Barney," she added. "You're fast and funny and you know what you want and where you're going. The thing is, I don't think I see myself going in the same direction as you, along the same road."

"Well, of course not," Barney said quickly. "It takes a little time to get used to the idea."

"No, that's not quite what I mean," Sharelle said thoughtfully. "What I'm trying to say is that as *I* see it, Barney, the kind of life you're talking about doesn't really have a lot of room for Renee and me in it. I know you're ambitious for *yourself*. That's what's going to make it all work for you, if your luck holds. But the way I see it, all you want from me is support. You want me to help you

216

get through. You want me in the stands. You want me to be and do whatever you think will help you. Someone who really cares for you *would* do those things, I know it. And I *do* care. But I've got plans, too, Barney. Good ones, I think. I don't see how the two sets fit."

"Boy, you really get to me, Sharelle," Barney said. "I'm offering you something really special, and you're telling me it's nothing much."

"No, that's not what I'm doing," Sharelle defended calmly. "It's just that the way you see the two of us, and the way I could even begin to do that, are so far apart. Barney, I don't want to just tag along, sitting in the stands cheering, cooking and keeping you happy at night."

"Well, what in hell do you want?" Barney demanded. "I don't see anything so terrible about what I want."

"There isn't," Sharelle agreed. She wondered if she should just tell him how she felt, deep down, instead of trying so hard to be gentle. And how did she feel? she asked herself quickly, trying in a secret way to take her own emotional pulse. She liked Barney. He was cute and funny and had a good body and a lot of drive and ambition. But it was all for himself, every ounce of it. It was nearsighted. There wasn't anything in Barney's mind but Barney. He didn't exactly dismiss Renee, but he seemed to be trying to pretend she didn't exist. As for Sharelle herself, the way she understood him, he hardly saw her personally either. She could fill a role in his life. She could help. She would fill out the picture he had, or thought he wanted. But then so could almost anyone else she knew.

"Look," she said after a moment. "I'm on your side, Barney. You know I am."

"Well, then!" Barney said happily, sighing. "It's all decided."

"No, it's not," Sharelle said quickly. "I'm on your side,

like I said. But I can be on your side and try to help as best as I can and at the same time stay true to what I want, too. If you'll let me."

"I don't get you," Barney admitted.

Sharelle sighed. "Barney, do you love me?"

He stared at her.

"Well?"

"Well, I don't know," he said. "I mean, I never said it to anyone."

"Have you ever even thought about it?"

Barney shrugged. "Maybe. It's the saying that's tough."

Sharelle smiled and raised his hand to her lips and kissed it quickly, opening the door of the car. "It wouldn't be tough if it were right," she said sweetly to him. "Believe me, the time will come when it will come out easy and smooth and it will even feel good to say it. But that time isn't now."

Sharelle edged her way from the front seat and hoisted Renee up into her arms.

"Sharelle! Hey!" Barney called out, leaning across the front seat.

She waited.

"Do you love me?" he asked. "I mean, maybe if you did and said so, maybe I could, too."

Sharelle laughed softly.

"Well?" Barney's tone had pain in it, and Sharelle heard this.

"Yes," she said almost in a whisper. "I do, in a way. But not the way you need, Barney. Not that much."

Barney stared up at her without an expression on his face.

She patted his hand as it lay on the window-ledge of the door. "Besides," she teased gently, "the way I understand it, you pros get followed by groupies everywhere you go. I mean, you don't need *me*, Barney. You're going to have all of it you need, and it's all free and no fuss, no muss, no bother. You don't need Renee and me hanging around to worry about. You're too hot, too on fire for us just now."

"But—" Barney started to protest.

Sharelle shook her head. "We're friends, Barney. I love you as a friend. I'll help all I can. I'll cheer and I'll be glad for you. And Renee will, too, when she's old enough to understand how special you are."

"Oh, hey, Sharelle, look . . ."

"No, don't say anything more, please," Sharelle asked. "Let's stay this way, O.K.? It's better. It's good as it is. You can put your hat back on and dazzle the girls some-where else." She smiled. "At least I'll be ahead of all of them. *I* know there's something good and kind and sweet underneath that grungy lid."

27

THAT night Melba did not show up for dinner. She had not called, nor was there a note in the hall as she sometimes left. Sharelle made dinner for herself and then, suddenly remembering, decided that this was an opportunity to be grabbed. She bundled Renee up in warmer clothing, for there was a damp night chill in the air over the hillside, and left the house, walking quickly and determinedly towards the house of her mother's brother, her uncle, Jack.

She realized as she neared his neighborhood that she should have telephoned ahead, just to make sure that he would be home, that he had time to see her. But she felt she had walked more than halfway by now, and since that was the case, she might as well just carry on and hope.

She walked up to the porch of Jack's house, aware there were lights inside and hearing his two children playing somewhere near the back of the house. She rang the doorbell, shifting Renee from hip to hip, and waiting. She rang again, and this time heard footsteps on the other side of the door.

"Well, Sharelle!" Uncle Jack said, looking out into the shadows and identifying her, reaching out a hand to pull her into the warmth and light of the hallway behind him. "Come on in, sweetie," he said, closing the door behind her. "What a surprise."

Sharelle nodded and smiled, uncertain whether to start so quickly, without any warm-up.

"Barbara's off at one of her classes," Jack explained, guiding Sharelle into the living room. "Tonight I think it's the history of women in the West, or something. She's batty for history, you know. That leaves me baby-sitting, poor old me." He laughed. "Actually," he said, guiding Sharelle and Renee onto a couch and taking an easy chair opposite, "I don't have enough time with the kids as it is. I really sort of like playing mother once in a while."

Sharelle smiled. "Barbara's pretty lucky, I guess," she said.

"That's what I keep telling her, honey," Uncle Jack said with a laugh. "She says I'm a dime a dozen."

"She doesn't?" Sharelle was almost shocked. But her uncle laughed and shook his head. "Only teasing," he admitted. "Now, what brings you over, you and Renee? Lonely? Where's your mother?"

Sharelle shook her head. "I don't know. It doesn't matter." She corrected herself quickly. "What I mean is that it's O.K., wherever she is. I really just came over because . . . because I wanted to talk to *you*."

Jack looked a moment at her and then smiled. "Hey, I'm flattered," he said. "You got boy troubles?"

Sharelle smiled. "No, not that I know, anyway. It's . . . it's Melba I want to talk about."

"Oh."

Sharelle nodded. "You know my mother," she said with a sad sort of little grimace. "I'm not saying she isn't swell and everything," Sharelle hurried on. "Or that I'm not, *we*'re not grateful for what she's done."

Jack nodded his head. "But . . ." he led her on.

"But, well," Sharelle shrugged. "It's getting pretty heavy, Uncle Jack. I'm going to have to make some decisions pretty soon and I don't want to. I mean, I *can* and I know it's me who has to make them. I accept the responsibility. I do. I mean, Renee's my problem, not Melba's."

Jack got out of his chair and reached across the space to take Renee in his arms and to send her ceilingward. "Way up high!" he sang out, and Renee giggled and squirmed in his arms. He held her and then sat back down in his chair, the baby on his lap.

"I'm afraid of Mother," Sharelle suddenly blurted.

Jack looked up quickly.

"I am," Sharelle said. "This isn't the way she wants to live, you know. She's a good-time girl, a fun lady. She doesn't want me and Renee hanging round her neck all the time."

"Melba doesn't feel that way, I'm sure," Jack said, trying to assure his niece. "She's just a little, well, a little skitzy, that's all. Flighty. She's always been interested in having fun. She doesn't mean harm to anyone."

"I *know* that," Sharelle agreed. "But she's not much good at anything else, really, is she? I mean, she works and everything, and does pretty well there. But she's not very comfortable around us, about helping or sharing or anything, I mean. And I don't ask all that much, really, Uncle Jack, I don't."

"No, I'm sure you don't, honey," Jack said nicely, still bouncing Renee about.

"I went to Grandma," Sharelle said then. "I thought maybe living with her would be better. But she's not strong or anything. I mean, I don't think she'd know one way or the other if we were there. She doesn't seem to remember things too well. I couldn't ever leave Renee with her and feel safe about it, you know?"

"I don't blame you there," Jack said. "She's a sweet, wonderful woman, but time's getting to her. Gets to us all sooner or later."

"I talked to a woman in the Welfare office, too," Sharelle admitted next. "I thought maybe we could get on some kind of program so I wouldn't be so dependent on Melba. But there's a hitch. The checks would have to go to Mother first, as the adult family member. I'm not sure Melba would pass the money on. I'm not even sure she would be all that happy being identified that way, you know, mother of a person on Welfare."

Jack looked thoughtfully at Sharelle and said nothing. She imagined he was trying hard to see where all this was leading. She imagined he knew.

"The thing is," Sharelle went on, "we *do* qualify, Renee and me. We *could* get help. But the rules are there and there's no way around them that I can see—'cept for one, maybe."

Sharelle felt certain Jack knew where this was headed, but he still remained silent, absentmindedly playing horsey with Renee.

"Of course, the thing is," Sharelle said next, "Melba really needs us. I mean, she's sometimes not quite in control, if you know what I mean. Most of the time I feel older than she is, even, silly as that sounds. I mean, it's she who needs to be looked after, cleaned up after, fed. Renee and I could do all that on our own and probably get by. Of course, I'd still want to stay in school. I mean, that's about the most important thing there is left, getting a good education, trying to gear up so I can get a good job later and take care of Renee by myself, *without* any help."

Sharelle felt herself beginning to get angry. Even a moron could tell what she was trying to say. Why was Jack just sitting there, not helping, not making this easier?

"This woman at Welfare, Ms. Sampson, well, she and I have tried to look everywhere, figuring this thing out."

Sharelle was burning with shame, and also with resentment. He was actually going to make her beg!

"The money would come to you, you see," she tried to explain calmly, fidgeting on the couch, watching Renee's face instead of looking directly up at her uncle's. "As head of the household, *you'd* get the check every month, and anything Renee and I didn't use would go to you and

Aunt Barbara. I mean, it couldn't do any harm to have a little extra, could it? And I promise Renee and I would be like ghosts, you'd hardly know we were around. I could even sit with the kids if you wanted. And I wouldn't bring boys in or anything, I'd play by all the rules you wanted. It would really be fine, you know, having other kids around, too, for Renee. And they'd get on, I know they would. So, what with the extra money and all, I sort of—"

Jack raised his hand and made Sharelle stop speaking. She sighed. At least she hadn't come straight out and gotten on her knees.

"Sharelle, I can't let you go on," Jack said finally. "This is between you and your mother. There's no place in it for me, or Barbara, or any of us here."

"But, Uncle Jack—" Sharelle started.

He shook his head.

"No, really," Sharelle continued, unstoppable. "You'd hardly know the difference. And with the money and all . . . you *know* our house, Uncle Jack! You know my mother! I've got to do something!"

"Sharelle!" Jack called out sternly. "Stop. Just stop. Now, listen to me. I told your mother the same thing the night she came rolling in here going crazy because you were pregnant. I told her there were some things a family had to go through together. That was one of them. And this is another."

"But you're our family, too!" Sharelle objected. "I mean, how much trouble could it be . . . ?"

"As a matter of fact, Sharelle," Jack said then, his voice noticeably cooler, "it would be a lot of trouble. This isn't a big house, as you know. There aren't any extra bedrooms, or even a den for you and Renee. Someone would have to move in with someone else. There *would* be a strain, Barbara'd feel it and so would I, and so would you, honey, believe me. You wouldn't have a home, and our home wouldn't be our own any longer, and there'd be a lot of hard feelings after a while."

"Not from *us*," Sharelle said. "Oh, Uncle Jack, we'd be so grateful, you wouldn't believe how grateful. And I could do lots of things around here for you, for Aunt Barbara. I could—"

"You could, but you won't," Jack said sternly.

"But . . . ?"

"No, I don't see this happening," Jack said decisively. "I don't have a lot of money, Sharelle. I don't make enough to carry the extra weight. And the little I'd clear after you and Renee had what you needed wouldn't hardly make a difference. I'm sorry, baby, but this is your problem. It's been that from the beginning." He paused. "I have a lot of admiration for you, Sharelle. Really. I know you can work this out without Barbara and me. If this were an emergency, then, well maybe we'd feel differently. But as it is—"

"You don't know at all how Aunt Barbara'd feel!" Sharelle said loudly.

Jack shook his head. "Yes, I do. I think I do. I think she'd agree with me, Sharelle. But don't you go trying to get round me that way."

"I'm not trying to get round you," Sharelle defended. "But can't you see this *is* an emergency? You think I'd come to you if it wasn't important?"

"I can see it's important," Jack admitted. "And I can see how you might imagine there's something our family could do to help. What about Annette and Dallas? Can't they do something?"

"No."

"But, Sharelle, have you even . . . ?"

"No, and I'm not going to. I can't," Sharelle said flatly.

"Well, then, it seems to me, Sharelle, there's a certain amount of pigheadedness in the air. It seems to me we're not your last chance, then, are we? You just can't bring yourself to go over there and ask them, ask members of your own family to—"

"But you're a member of our family!"

"I have a family here of my own, Sharelle," Jack said. "You can hear some of them if you listen real good. My first responsibility's to them."

Sharelle sank back against the cushions of the couch.

"Look, honey," Jack said, getting up and carrying Renee over to her. Sharelle reached up and took her daughter. "The end of the world's a long way off, and Barbara and I just can't—"

Sharelle was on her feet quickly and moving towards the front door. "The end of my world's already in view, damn it!" she shouted. She pulled open the front door and then turned. "Thanks a lot," she said angrily. "You sure helped me see how close it is!"

28

THE day before Christmas break, Sharelle was called from her last class and sent down to a counselor's office. She walked the halls rather slowly, trying to figure out why she had been summoned. She had asked for no guidance; she had, to her mind, done nothing wrong or rowdy. Perhaps it had something to do with Renee, or with the parenting program. But even here Sharelle could not imagine what it would be. Renee was healthy and certainly no more noisy or troublesome than any other child in the nursery. Her own participation had been full; she had followed directions, accepted her responsibilities, cut only one morning's classes all year.

Whatever it was, really, it could also be a mistake.

Buoyed by this idea, she knocked on the paneled door and pulled it open, stepping into the first-floor office which was small and mostly unadorned. A man rose from behind a desk and smiled broadly at her.

Sharelle looked at him and thought she should be able to recognize him. His features were familiar, as were his blue eyes behind horn-rims. He wasn't as old as the counselors she'd seen around Lincoln lately. It had to be someone else, someone she might have met at—

"You don't remember me?" the man asked with an unwavering smile. "I'm Mr. Bernstein. The man who sent you here, remember?"

Sharelle smiled herself, grateful she had not had to guess, and, truth to tell, now pleased to see him.

"I told you I wouldn't forget you, Sharelle," Mr. Bernstein said, motioning her to take the chair opposite his own. "This is just the first time I could get away and across town to check up on things. How are you?"

"I'm fine," Sharelle said, sitting primly before him.

"And your baby?"

"Renee. She's fine. She's healthy."

"That's terrific!" Mr. Bernstein enthused easily. "How do you like the program here? How do you like Lincoln itself?"

Sharelle crossed her legs, feeling she could speak to Mr. Bernstein as directly as she chose, that he *was* interested.

"It's not what I expected." She smiled. "I mean, I *was* a little worried, a little scared. But once I got here, I don't know. The kids made it easy for me. It's probably just like any other school."

"That's what I told you, remember?" asked Mr. Bernstein, pleased. "If you just gave the place a chance."

"Well, I didn't have a lot of choice, did I?" Sharelle asked with a short laugh.

"Not too much," Bernstein replied. "Still, it takes a certain something to face down life and make the best of it. I thought you had that, Sharelle. I'm glad I'm not going to be disappointed."

"The year's not over," Sharelle warned half-seriously.

"I'm not going to worry," Mr. Bernstein reassured her. "I think you can do it. I know you can. Tell me, about the program, how do you feel? Are there things you'd like to see changed or added?"

"Really?" Sharelle asked in return.

"Of course, really," Mr. Bernstein told her. "The only feedback we get is what we ask for. People your age have a certain tendency to hold back, to volunteer information only when pressed. Not that you're being pressed. I just thought someone with your ability and insight might have a few suggestions to make."

Sharelle was pleased and she smiled and straightened in her chair. "It's tough, you know?" she asked. "I mean, not everybody in class has the same interests, the same brainpower. It's not a class where you have some heavy thinking or anything. It's fairly helpful. But if I were going to make one change, I think it would be in the career part. I mean, we don't really get enough information there."

"Of what kind?"

"Well, jobs, for heaven's sakes," Sharelle said. "I mean, we know, we're *told* all the time how tough it is to find a job, especially when you have a child to care for. But no one's coming out to tell us where we can go, what we could do, how we could balance both. No one's offering anything concrete, you know?"

"But you're still in classes," Mr. Bernstein explained. "How could you possibly stay here, work a job, and take care of a child all at the same time?"

"We can!" Sharelle said positively. "I know we can. *I* could. A lot of the girls could. And that's the biggest problem we have, you know. Getting money. Earning money. Feeling we *can* learn to keep living an ordinary sort of life."

"But realistically, Sharelle, I think the administration feels you kids have more than enough on your plates already. Not that we couldn't get visiting speakers and more films, but in the long run, you're all still here, in school, and people who hire like to feel their employees are dependable, on call whenever they're needed."

"Then how about a part of the program being an outside part?" Sharelle suggested. "Not that Ms. Cummins isn't good, or fun to be with. But why not figure out some kind of class where we would be here half a day say, and the other half be at some job, our kids with us or even still here, being taken care of. It's the money that makes most of the girls unhappy. Not the money, so much. The lack of it."

"Is that true in your case, Sharelle?" Mr. Bernstein asked directly.

Sharelle stared straight back at him. "Yes, it is."

Mr. Bernstein coughed into his hand. "Well, what about Welfare programs, Aid to Dependent Children, MediCal, that sort of thing? There are those resources, after all."

"Sure," Sharelle agreed. "I know about those. The trouble there is that the money doesn't come to the person who needs it most, me, or some other mother. It goes to the adult who heads the household. Sometimes," she looked down, "sometimes that's not the best way."

Mr. Bernstein looked searchingly at her. Sharelle turned her eyes away.

"See," she said slowly, "that's what hurts us all most. Here we are, mothers, adults. I mean, you look at us with our kids and that's what you see. But we don't feel so grown-up. We don't have the . . . the resources to make us feel that good. To our families, we're still kids. And when we can't get out, get away from them, that's the way we're treated. It gets to you, you know? Not having anything of your own except a baby. And that's what I'd change in this class, if you want to know. I thought the class was to be divided into two sections: how to learn about caring for your baby, learning about how she'll grow and what she'll go through, how to handle all that. But the second part, the part that I figure is more important, was supposed to help teach us how to go about getting a job, making a home, accepting our responsibilities *afterwards*. That's what we're not getting enough of. If we can't get a program like some of the others here—I mean, there are kids who come to Lincoln for half-days to study something in particular that isn't at their own school—it's not so unusual that way—if we can't learn how to make money, then at least help us understand what we *can* do about that, where we can go."

"So," Mr. Bernstein said, leaning back in his chair, "you feel the program only delivers half what it promises."

"That's about it," Sharelle said flatly. "I'm grateful for what's here. So are we all. But we'd like it a whole lot more if we knew what we could do about life, instead of just how to diaper it."

Mr. Bernstein picked up a pencil and tapped it against his front teeth, swinging a little in his chair. "How are *you*, Sharelle?" he asked suddenly. "How do *you* feel about life?"

Sharelle smiled a little sadly. "I'm hanging in," she said. "It's not easy, but I'm still hanging in."

Mr. Bernstein nodded. "Is there any problem in particular that gets to you?"

Sharelle laughed and heard herself do it. "I'm sorry," she said hastily. "That sounded awful. Sure. There are things. I mean, I'd like to get out from under, too, away from my mom. But there just isn't any way, any place. Not yet, that I see, anyway."

"What about state agencies?" Mr. Bernstein asked.

"I've made the rounds," Sharelle told him. "I even have my own case worker now, a Ms. Sampson. She's very nice, but she's caught between the same rocks I am. There are rules. There are qualifications. At least she's someone I can gripe to. That makes me feel good. Well, not good, because I don't like to do that, but at least better, you know? Looser. I can stand it longer if I can spout off once in a while."

"You're not sorry you came to Lincoln, though?"

Sharelle shook her head. How could she tell him she was sorry about something else, though, every so often? How could she tell him that in her dreams, she still saw herself alone and breezy and studying like mad for some clouded role in which she wore white? It would sound horrible, unnatural. But it was true, just the same.

"Well, then." Mr. Bernstein sighed not unhappily. "I'm glad we caught up this way. And I don't see why we can't look at the syllabus for next term and try to build in some of the ideas you mentioned. They seem perfectly reasonable to me, perfectly, and valuable, too."

Sharelle nodded. She smiled. She did not feel pleased necessarily, but she sensed that Mr. Bernstein *wanted* her to feel that way.

"Your grades are still good, Sharelle," he said then. "Top-notch. I hope you're still thinking about college?"

Sharelle nodded that she was. All the time. And thinking how far away all those dreams still seemed, no matter how she stoked that particular fire and blew on it to keep it alive.

Mr. Bernstein nodded, too, and stood up. "I'm glad we caught up," he said again. "Call me any time, Sharelle. I want you to. If you want to talk, or feel like changing, or whatever. I'm on your side, you know."

Sharelle understood she was to stand and leave. She smiled and shook hands with the counselor, thinking how easy it was and how often people said the same thing. They just had no idea what that would really mean. She wasn't angry or resentful, not really, and not at them, or at Mr. Bernstein. It was just too easy to make motions, make sounds and smile, but without really understanding, without really being committed it was all just for form, just to make *them* feel better.

"It was nice of you to come," Sharelle said. "I didn't really think you ever would."

"I told you I would, didn't I?" Mr. Bernstein asked dramatically, his arms wide. "I keep my promises."

Sharelle nodded and smiled and turned to leave the office.

"Merry Christmas, Sharelle!" Mr. Bernstein called out after her.

Sharelle half-turned in the doorway. "You, too," she

said now rather dispiritedly, and closed the door behind her.

She walked along the hallway slowly. She didn't feel like going back to class, and Ms. Johnson wouldn't mind. She still had her pass; she was legal. She might as well go to the nursery and start to bundle up Renee. There was sun that afternoon, but the weather forecast called for winds and rain squalls later.

She walked out of the administration corridor and took a right, leaving the building and crossing up to the nursery area. She could hear laughter as she approached. It did not lighten her heart.

She went through the classroom on the way to the nursery, putting down her own sweater and books on the square table there. She stood a moment at the threshold of the nursery room, looking in.

At the far end of the room, near the small stand-up kitchen, was a group of mothers and children, busily getting ready to leave when the bell rang.

On the mat before her was Patrick Fitzroy, lying on his back, his arms and legs extended above him, and Flex Sheeter balancing precariously but happily on the soles of Patrick's feet, his tiny hands held firmly in Patrick's. Patrick was making airplane sounds, and letting his knees bend suddenly and then straighten to make it seem to the baby that there was real motion, real movement. Flex giggled and giggled with that high, out-of-control laughter that Sharelle had learned to love hearing from Renee when she was being tickled or pleased in a special way. The sound was a high roll, and it always made Sharelle feel tears in her throat.

Sharelle was startled to see Patrick. Not that she'd forgotten him, but it had been so long it seemed since they had last talked. All the questions she'd been forming in her mind for their next encounter surfaced and she felt suddenly shy, as though to ask would somehow break apart whatever slight bond the two of them had. She stood watching, seeing how happy the pair of them were —Patrick glowed with pleasure and surprise, testing the baby, reassuring him, talking to him even as he bounced him and spun him and made him dip and rise. Flex—in the program while Michelle, his mother, recovered from her suicide attempt because Amy Pritchard insisted that it would be better for the baby, and that she herself would watch out for him, and take responsibility—clearly trusted Patrick, gave himself over to the delights of flight and sudden surprising sound effects, feeling secure in Patrick's hands.

Sharelle glanced quickly at Renee's crib and saw she was napping still. She took a few steps into the room and then stretched out beside Patrick, saying, "Hi, stranger."

"Hey!" Patrick greeted her. "How *are* you?" The way he said this made it seem he really wanted to know.

"Fine," Sharelle answered. "You haven't been around much."

"I know," Patrick said, still balancing Flex above him. "That E.M.T. course is a killer. I've been doing emergency ambulance duty, not to mention the hours working in the hospital emergency department. It makes you feel so good, Sharelle, even though you're totally wiped out when the day's over."

Sharelle nodded slightly. "You're really crazy about kids, aren't you?" she asked.

Patrick grinned. The discolored tooth gleamed dully. "Yep," he said. "I am. All of them. Every last one."

"You'll make a good father," Sharelle guessed, knowing even as she said this that if her instincts were right, that would never happen.

"Hey," Patrick said, looking over at her quickly before returning his attention to Flex above him, "with kids like this, who wouldn't be?"

"Up we go!" Amy Pritchard yelled suddenly as she scooped Flex off Patrick's feet. "Time to head for home."

Flex's face clouded over and it looked as though he would let out a thunderous shout of disappointment. But Amy bounced him in the air as she carried him to his crib and began dressing him for the ride home, and his attention seemed appeased by the motion.

Patrick and Sharelle lay on the mat, a few feet apart, each with a hand beneath his head. Sharelle studied his face, and Patrick just smiled easily at her. "How's Renee?" he asked finally.

"Good," Sharelle answered, and then gulped to herself. "Patrick, you've never had sex, have you?"

He did not flinch or blink or even get red in the face. "No," he answered simply, still looking directly into Sharelle's eyes.

"You're going to be a minister, aren't you?" Sharelle asked then. "A priest?"

Patrick did redden at this, as though the idea were too great to conceive. "I want to," he said. "I hope I can be."

"But why?" Sharelle asked. "Why? You have so much, you give so much."

Patrick's blush lessened a bit. "Because I've been so lucky, maybe," he said. "It's what I want to do with my life. It's what God seems to want, too. At least, I hope so."

"But why couldn't you have sex?" Sharelle asked, feeling on dangerous ground. Patrick was answering her directly, being open and honest, but he was still a boy and boys weren't all that keen to be put on the spot this way. "I mean, if it's something you have to give up, wouldn't you rather know what it is you're missing?"

Patrick grinned slightly. "No," he said. "Not that I couldn't if I wanted, and still hope to enter the priesthood. But it cheapens me a little in God's eyes, I think. I want to offer everything I have, Sharelle, not just what I'm done with. I want to serve with *every* blessing I have. I like to think it makes me more valuable in God's eyes, and makes Him more valuable in mine, that I'm dedicating everything I was born with to Him."

Sharelle wasn't sure she understood as well as she wanted to. "Can you really bring people to God?" she asked timidly.

"I don't know," he replied. "I've thought about that. I don't even know that that's my job. I can help people. I can show them how God wants them to live, but they have to find Christ themselves. I can't do that for them."

A tiny voice inside Sharelle called out, Help me! Show *me!* Take me with you! And then she remembered seeing Patrick with his carload of campers the summer before and watching them all drive away and feeling the same. She smiled to herself.

"What's funny?" Patrick asked her.

"Nothing," Sharelle said quickly. "I was just thinking it sounded as though I was trying to hustle you into bed."

"No, you weren't," Patrick said seriously, sitting up. "You were interested and honest. And you asked what you wanted to know. That's all."

"And you answered," Sharelle said, a slight question in her tone.

"I always would, Sharelle," Patrick told her. "I'm not anything special, you know. There are millions of people better than I am, smarter, more committed even. I'm just trying to do the best I can."

Sharelle nodded. "Your best is so good," she said quietly.

Patrick smiled and reached out to touch her on the shoulder. "So is yours," he said quietly. Then he got to his feet and reached back down for Sharelle's hands to draw her up, too.

"Not too many people know what you want to do, do they?" Sharelle asked.

Patrick shook his head. "It's hard enough dealing with my own expectations and feelings, without having to carry other people's, too. Suppose I'm wrong. Suppose God doesn't want me? Then what will people think?"

"But do you really care?"

"In a way," Patrick admitted. "In a way. The people

who do know, you see, my family, for instance, a few friends, they look at this as though it's *their* chance, too. I don't want to disappoint them. Not them, or God."

Sharelle understood this clearly, almost painfully. It was a thought she herself had had: if Patrick could do what he wanted, if he *could* be a priest and care for and love everyone, then in a way so would she be doing the same thing.

"Renee's named after you," she said shyly then.

"What? How could she be?"

"Her middle name," Sharelle explained. "It's Patricia. I know it's silly and childish and everything, but when I met you, I guess . . . I don't know, I had a feeling."

Patrick held both her hands. "I'm honored," he said seriously. "Thank you."

Sharelle shook her head and felt red in the face. "It will just remind me," she said in a whisper.

"It will be good for me to remember, too," Patrick said. They looked at each other a moment.

"When do you go to . . . when do you start—?"

"The seminary? Next year, just after Christmas, now. It's been moved up."

"I'm glad I know you," Sharelle told Patrick directly. "I want the best for you, always."

He ducked his head and ran a hand through his blond hair before returning her intensity. "Thank you," he said.

"You won't disappoint *any*one," Sharelle said positively.

Patrick looked at her, and she thought she saw moisture in his eyes. Then he grinned suddenly. "Only the basketball team, if I don't hustle." He reached down for his jacket and books and then straightened, smiling at her. "Have a good Christmas," he said, starting to move away. "See you."

Sharelle watched him leave the nursery, wondering whether she had embarrassed him terribly or if his departure simply covered confusion at her own declaration of affection.

Then she wondered why she hadn't thought to talk to him about Melba, and about Dallas and Uncle Jack, about Andrea and Renee and the future, bleak as it seemed.

And she realized she couldn't. She couldn't put that weight on him, not now, not so soon. Not when he was carrying the hopes of so many other people with him every day of his life. It would be too much.

She went to Renee's crib and started to wrap her warmly against the weather outside. Then suddenly she straightened up and looked out the window. It had come to her so quickly, so certainly.

She loved Patrick.

And Patrick loved her.

It was a special kind of love, not just physical but something broad and grand that included everything and everyone. For a second she wondered whether it wasn't this kind of love that God, or Christ, felt, for everyone left on earth, everyone coming onto earth. She wanted to go after Patrick, to ask, to find out. She knew she wouldn't. But if she was right, if what she felt was true, then no matter what happened to her, to her and Renee, they didn't have to feel alone.

29

SHARELLE shopped for Christmas gifts with great care and caution, trying to select things that would actually mean something to her friends and family, and that cost as little as possible, yet looked rather more glamorous. Her own savings account was exhausted.

Finding things for Renee and for Andrea had been simple enough. Anything small, glittery, colorful, and not dangerous were her standards. The stores in San Diego were bursting with just such notions and toys, and it took Sharelle a very little time to make up her mind. For Annette and Dallas (one gift for the pair) she hunted for something that might fit their apartment, something useful, and settled at last on a cut-glass lazy Susan that she imagined had been brought in from over the border in Mexico. Her Uncle Jack and Aunt Barbara were difficult —emotionally. After Jack's rebuff, Sharelle really didn't feel like buying them anything at all. But caution prevailed. Jack had said no on a direct approach. But Sharelle wanted badly to believe that if there were a real, honest-to-God emergency in her life, or in Renee's, then Jack would relent and help them. It was a sort of insurance policy she was taking out, hoping she wouldn't have to cash it in but feeling there was some hope of help if she did. She finally selected a framed painting she found at a swap meet that pictured a woman on horseback against a wild and rugged countryside. After all, Aunt Barbara was studying the West. Who knew? This might someday be valuable.

Her mother was an altogether different problem.

Sharelle canvassed stores and shopping malls for days before Christmas Eve, searching, weighing, deciding. The things she saw she *knew* Melba would appreciate were too expensive. Everything else was useful in a way Melba would never have recognized or wanted to learn. There were hundreds of different gadgets and containers for the kitchen, but Melba had little time to think about food, or prepare it. There were devotional statues that might match one of her church-going moods, but Sharelle could hardly ever anticipate these, and to have a reminder on a wall daily of devotion and piety seemed to Sharelle as though Melba might think her daughter was waving a red flag and criticizing.

In time, Sharelle opted to concentrate on clothing. Melba could never have enough of that. But here, too, the problem was one of expense. The kinds of outfits her mother favored were highly colored, a little glitzy, rather daringly cut and styled. The accessories that might go with such attire were glaring and cheap-looking, Sharelle thought, and not inexpensive, either. It seemed as though these days it cost more to wrap a package properly than to box it to begin with.

Sharelle felt certain that something sensible and useful and everyday was something Melba would overlook and hate in time. Therefore whatever she selected had to have some status attached to it, even though that meant paying more than for something just as good without a label. But Melba would respond to the label, Sharelle was certain, and having decided this, it was all a matter of finding something signed by someone whose name Melba would recognize that Sharelle could afford.

Finally, at five-thirty on Christmas Eve, pressed by the urgency and the hour of the event, Sharelle picked out a silk neck scarf signed by Yves Saint-Laurent.

She shuddered when she handed the saleswoman money for the item, and told her not to giftwrap it, fearing suddenly that the store might charge extra for the service.

Outside on the street again, Sharelle felt pleased and relieved. That she was now bankrupt she put out of her mind. She was certain the scarf would please her mother and, for all intents and purposes, all she and Renee had to do now was get through Christmas Day—a visit at church, lunch at Dallas and Annette, and home to safety and her own bed. Presents would be opened at Annette's house, a new annual event where before the three women had opened everything at Melba's on Christmas Eve. Sharelle would just have to hold her breath for a few hours, and then life would return to normal, more or less, a state she fidgeted in but one she felt at least she could handle.

She and Kevin Simmons had exchanged tokens the last afternoon of school before the holiday recess. She had given him a book about popular music of the Sixties, and he had given her a tiny silver cross, free-form, on a thin silver chain. Sharelle had put it on immediately and would not remove it, day or night, even when bathing.

She had also given Barney Carnes a gift: a new hat, deep blue, with a card that read, "For the changes ahead. Love, Sharelle." He had been embarrassed and had nothing to give her in return, but to Sharelle that mattered less than that he know she still thought of him gently.

Light was growing dim as she bussed back across San Diego towards her own neighborhood. She was a little uneasy about Renee, for while Melba had seemed happy enough to stay with her—especially after being told it was that or no present the next day—it was clear to Sharelle that her mother had begun celebrating Christmas at her office. Melba's spirits were high and her ideas bounced off walls and crashed into each other in a rush of good humor and memories. Sharelle actually was glad to get out of the house, pleased despite her own mood to see Christmas lights and displays outside other people's homes and in the store windows. California was not a good place to be at Christmas and Sharelle hoped that someday she and Renee would be someplace where there might be a chill in the air, leafless trees, and maybe even snow falling or left over in drifts along the roadways.

She heard Melba's big radio from the parlor booming out carols as she approached the house. You had to give Melba credit. When she celebrated, everyone knew.

She opened the door quietly, inundated by "Joy to the World!", and stood a moment holding her packages, listening.

Then, over the sound of the hymn, she clearly heard Melba say, "Cut that out, damn it! You want something to cry about, here! Now that's something worth crying over!"

Renee's cries, which Sharelle had not at first heard, escalated into an all-out scream of surprise and anger and pain.

Sharelle dropped her parcels where she stood and rushed into the living room.

Renee was still rolling on the carpet, Melba standing over her.

"What are you doing?" Sharelle shouted, rushing to the baby and picking her up out of the way of Melba's size-four high heels.

"Jesus, what a kid," Melba said sourly. "All she does is cry and whine. How a kid ever got into our family who behaves that way I'm sure I don't know."

"Like hell you don't!" Sharelle said, cradling Renee in her arms and trying to hush her. "She's not your child, Mother. You can't just hit her whenever you feel like it."

Melba grinned. "I didn't *hit* her, honey. I just gave her a little shove with my toe. It's her goddamned teeth, All she does is complain."

"You kicked her?" Sharelle was astonished, and furious. "You kicked your own granddaughter for something she couldn't even help?"

"You weren't here," Melba said, turning away. "You didn't have to hear it for hours and hours."

Sharelle took a big breath. Renee was still trembling. She walked to where her mother stood looking out a front window and, putting her hand on Melba's shoulder, she forced her to turn around.

"Listen to me, Mother. Listen and just shut up! I don't want to hear a word out of you!" She inhaled again and before Melba could high-horse a reply, went on. "You do not hit a child who isn't yours, ever! You do not hit my child, is that clear? Never! Never, never! I'm her mother and if she needs to be punished or anything, then I'm the one who does it, not you. Understand? Is that perfectly clear?"

Sharelle's protest was too long. It gave Melba time to ignore and rearm.

"Oh, honey," she smiled sweetly, inhaling on her cigarette, "you're just a baby yourself. You don't know nothin' about birthin' babies!" And she started to giggle, pleased she remembered a scene from *Gone with the Wind*.

"This is not funny!" Sharelle shouted at her mother.

"It sure as hell isn't!" Melba shouted back. "I don't need some dumb bunny of a kid telling me what I can and cannot do in my own house, baby or not!"

"I am not telling you what you can do," Sharelle objected. "All I'm trying to get across to you is—"

"No, don't even bother!" Melba shouted. "I know damned well what you're doing! You've been walking around here ever since that baby got here, looking at me, judging me, figuring out I wasn't hardly good enough even to stay under the same roof!"

"Mother, I wasn't," Sharelle said futilely.

"Don't tell me!" Melba continued, pleased at herself for getting up steam so quickly. "For your information, madam, I know more about babies than you'll ever forget. I forgot more than you'll ever learn! I know what's good

243

for a kid and what's not, believe you me. You think I'd let you or Annette run me ragged the way this kid is you? No discipline, that's what, just hog-wild is what! That kid of yours isn't anything so special, let me tell you. And it's never too early to learn that other people are in the room, in the world, and that there are rules and rules and rules." Melba seemed to have lost her place for a second.

She found it. "You're not even good at being a mother!" she sneered. "Do I be you, I'd have taken Dallas' offer and been damned glad to get out from under. You don't think Renee would be a lot better off with Annette? You're plumb-wrong. At least she has some common sense. At least she has a man around to help her, to draw the lines."

"The same one I might have had!" Sharelle screamed. "If you can bring your brain to remember back that far!"

"Oh, don't try to make me feel sorry for you, Sharelle. Hell, for all I know, you led Dallas right into it. Wouldn't doubt it one bit. You were just jealous, a snotty little kid, a slut. You got exactly what you deserved!"

"You don't really believe that?" Sharelle asked breathlessly.

"Maybe I do, maybe I don't," Melba teased. "Point is, some man walks in here and wants to take this damned kid off your hands and you don't even think about it."

"Mother, how could I? That's not fair. This is my child. She belongs with me!"

"She'd be one hell of a lot better off with someone else, even Dallas, as far as I can see. All she is is trouble. She runs this place. Well, she's not running me, not anymore!"

"The point is, you're not going to hit her or kick her or—"

"The point is I'm tired of pussyfooting around here in my own house, having to worry about *her* all the time. I don't work my fingers to the bone so I can come home and tiptoe, nosiree! Not anymore!"

"Babies do that," Sharelle argued weakly. "*They* don't know. They think the world revolves around them."

"Well, it doesn't!" snapped Melba. "At least not under this roof!" She took a big breath. "And you're not much better, eyeing me all the time, criticizing my friends, the things I do! Jesus, between the pair of you, it's a wonder I even manage to get up in the morning. I might as well stay in bed. It's the only safe place I got!"

Sharelle's face clouded and darkened and Melba saw it. She wasn't going to wait around. The idea was to keep slugging.

Melba turned quickly and ran through the kitchen and up the back stairway, leaving Sharelle furious and frustrated in the living room. Renee had stopped crying, but she was still nervous and jumped at each loud bang from above. Within seconds, it seemed, Melba was tramping down the steps again, laden with what Sharelle could see were Renee's toys and clothing.

"What do you think you're doing?" Sharelle shouted at her mother, rushing towards the kitchen, carrying the baby.

"Just you watch what I'm doing!" Melba challenged, dumping everything in her arms into the sink. She turned and ran back up the steps once more. Sharelle stood immobilized, not knowing what to expect, not even beginning to guess what was in her mother's mind.

Melba was back down in a flash, carrying more of the baby's things: a blanket, a stuffed bear, a plastic set of colored geometrical shapes that had hung above Renee's crib. She dumped these atop everything else in the sink and then bent down, reaching into the sinkboard below.

"Mother, what on earth?" Sharelle started to protest. Then, "No! You can't!"

"Oh, yes I can!" Melba sang out triumphantly. "Once and for all. It's just that easy." And as she spoke she sprinkled what was in the sink with lighter fluid, her arm making a circular motion over the pile. The fumes rose into the air around her. "Yes, I can, and I'm going to!" she declared firmly. "I don't need this, Sharelle. I don't need to live this way! I don't know you now and I don't need to know your baby! I want to live—me! I've got things I can do, places to go. I'm not going to be put in prison by a snip of a girl thinks she's better than me, smarter than me, knows more. Nosiree. What I know about the world would make your hair curl, and I'm through with all that now, every bit of it."

Before Sharelle could grab her mother's arm, Melba had dropped her lighted cigarette atop the pile in the sink and within a fraction of a second, the porcelain seemed ablaze.

"Mother!" Sharelle screamed, reaching out for Melba and drawing her swiftly back away from the fire.

"That's what I can do," Melba announced proudly. "I run this show, and don't you ever forget it for one little minute!"

Sharelle hardly heard what Melba was saying. Her horror at seeing Renee's things incinerated was less now than her own sense of real danger. The curtains above the sink had started smoking, and would burst into flames any second. She grabbed Melba's hand and dragged her out of the kitchen. Then, still holding Renee, she ran back into the kitchen—coughing, her eyes already beginning to water from the smoke—and reached out reflexively to try to turn on the taps. She couldn't reach them over the flames. She looked frantically around and spotted a long-handled spatula on the table behind her. She picked it up and then, unable even to shield her face because she held Renee, she thrust it through the fire in the direction of one of the tap handles. She pushed. She heard the water start. She pushed the other. That, too, opened.

Still burdened with Renee, Sharelle dropped the spatula and ran upstairs as quickly as she could to her bathroom. She ran water in the sink there and soaked every towel she could find. She hurried back downstairs, water trailing behind her, and threw the towels, one by one, into the sink, hoping this would help smother the flames. It did. Now, for the curtains. She remembered.

She shifted the baby and bent down to pull open the cupboard below the sink to find a wash pail. She hoisted it quickly and tried to steady it beneath one of the running taps. It seemed to take forever to fill, and as she stood there terrified, her eyes never left the thin runner of flame that crawled up the kitchen curtains towards the ceiling.

She couldn't wait too long. She pulled the bucket away from the sink and threw its contents upwards and at the curtains. They sizzled but they also still smoked, still glowed. Jesus! She shoved the pail again atop Renee's smoldering and ruined things in the sink and waited, counting, pleading with the tap to find extra pressure, to *hurry!*

She threw the second pailful up, holding her breath. It did seem to make a difference. Suddenly she remembered reading somewhere that the one thing you weren't supposed to do with a fire in your own home was try to put it out. Well, too late to worry about that. She refilled the bucket and threw a third and then a fourth shower against the curtains and the windows and the wall. There was water all over the room, all over the floor. In the sink, whatever Melba had dragged downstairs was totally charred, ruined, and stinking.

But the smoke died. And the fire.

Sharelle dropped the pail on the floor with a sigh, rubbing her eyes, knowing they were bloodshot. She couldn't imagine what she herself must look like, or even Renee, who seemed instinctively to realize that if she cried and yelled, she'd be breathing more smoke and odors. She had remained virtually silent, carried and hustled up and down, back and forth like a rag doll under a child's arm.

Sharelle turned finally to walk back into the parlor. Melba was standing in the precise position she had been,

247

looking back over Sharelle's shoulder at the damaged kitchen. Sharelle said nothing.

Melba smiled weakly and tried to reach out to take Renee from Sharelle, but Sharelle gripped her daughter tightly and sidestepped her mother's gesture, walking straight out of the house, not bothering to look for her coat or to wrap Renee up in anything.

Without knowing in advance where she was going, Sharelle walked down the darkened street. She did not hear the sounds of carols from her neighbors' houses. She was hardly aware of traffic as she and Renee crossed streets.

She had been in the building before, sitting in almost the same pew, staring ahead apparently without seeing or recognizing anything around her.

Now, instead of just a few women working around the altar, whole committees seemed engaged in brightening the church, in placing flowers and clothes and objects of silver and gold, lighting candles, preparing for midnight services.

Sharelle sat on a velvet cushion, holding her child, and looked above the communion table.

Someone watching might have thought she was lost in daydreams, or perhaps even devoutly trying to address her Savior.

What she was doing was thinking. Hard.

PART
FIVE

30

LINDA Sampson rose quickly from her chair and came to the door of her small office, her arm outstretched, pulling Sharelle into the tiny space quickly and excitedly.

"I think I'm onto something," she told Sharelle with pleasure. "It just never occurred to me till now, and I can't see how we could have missed this chance."

Sharelle docilely sat before Ms. Sampson's desk and waited, not terrifically hopeful but willing to listen. Her mind was already fixed, no matter what Ms. Sampson came up with.

"Now," said the older woman, still smiling broadly, "what about your father?"

"What do you mean?" asked Sharelle, puzzled.

"You never told me anything about him," Ms. Sampson said. "I mean, for example, the simplest fact. Is he dead or alive?"

"I don't know," Sharelle admitted. "Honestly, I don't. I mean, my mother never talks about him."

"Well, here's the thing," Ms. Sampson ran forward. "If by chance he isn't living, then we might be able to find some money in death benefits."

"I don't get it," Sharelle said.

"Well, if he's dead, then his survivors could apply for Social Security. Head of the household dies, leaves family behind, family needs to survive. It's that simple."

Sharelle thought a minute, and then remembered how Aid to Dependent Children worked. "Well, maybe," she allowed. "If we could find out and be sure. But I have a question."

"Yes?"

"Well, it seems to me that if he *were* dead, and I sort of hope he isn't," Sharelle told her counselor, "wouldn't my mother have to apply? And wouldn't *she* get any money, not me?"

"Well, yes," Ms. Sampson said slowly. "But—"

"No, you don't understand," Sharelle went on. "The problem with my applying for Aid to Dependent Children wasn't that I was proud. It was just that the money from there would have to go to an adult. And in my house that's Melba. I mean, you see what I mean?"

Ms. Sampson's hope and good humor seemed to drain from her eyes. "Well, yes, of course, I see that. But perhaps if we spoke to your mother, if we explained *why* we were investigating this . . . this possibility, perhaps we could get her to agree to endorse the checks over to you."

Sharelle smiled wryly. "You really think so?"

"Isn't it worth a try?" Ms. Sampson asked encouragingly.

Sharelle was doubtful. She said nothing.

"Sharelle?"

"What?"

"What's on your mind?"

Sharelle shrugged and then stopped herself. That kind of answer was childish. "I don't want to ask Melba for anything," she said plainly. "I don't want to have to search and scrounge around anymore."

Ms. Sampson sat back in her chair and regarded Sharelle seriously. "Is something wrong, honey?" she asked gently. "Is there something going on you haven't told me about?"

"No, there isn't anything going on, anything that hasn't *been* going on," Sharelle amended. "I just think I can do more for Renee than this."

"Well, of course you can, we all can. It's just a matter of finding our way through the forest to a clearing."

"No, it's a little worse than that," Sharelle sighed.

How do you mean?"

"I think Renee should have more of a chance in life," Sharelle said bluntly. "More than she has with me, more than she would have around Melba."

Ms. Sampson's breathing seemed to have stopped. There was no sound in the office.

Sharelle looked directly across the desk. "I want to have her adopted," she announced, her voice steady, her glance unwavering.

Ms. Sampson sat motionless for a moment. "Oh, Sharelle," she finally said, and shook her head sadly.

"It's not such a terrible thing," Sharelle said, her hands tightly pressed together in her lap. "If it means she'll grow up happy and loved and *normal,* then that makes it all worth it."

Ms. Sampson was still stunned. The two women looked at each other, Sharelle determined, Ms. Sampson at a loss.

"Will you help me?" Sharelle asked finally to break the tension.

Ms. Sampson blinked quickly. "Are you so certain?" she asked. "Are you so positive you can really do this and be happy?"

Sharelle smiled sadly. "No, not at all," she confessed. "I'm just tired, tired and sort of lost. I don't see any other way. I can't get out from under, but there's no reason to see Renee buried, too." And she told Ms. Sampson about how she spent her Christmas Eve, and why, and how she ordered her thoughts to come to her decision.

"The thing is," Sharelle explained, "it's not that I wouldn't miss her. Probably all my life I'd feel a piece of me was missing. But there just isn't any other direction I can turn. What I need to know now, from you, is whether I can choose the people—the kind of people—Renee should have."

"I don't know," Ms. Sampson said frankly. "This really isn't what I'm strongest in. Let me call Bert Bekin. He's the man on the spot here, he's the one who works with cases like this."

"But I want *you*," Sharelle said quickly. "I mean, I feel . . . see, you have a child, you'd be able to understand. A man, well, I don't know. It just doesn't seem to me he could . . ."

Ms. Sampson smiled sympathetically. "This one can," she told Sharelle. "I think you'll like him."

"Well, O.K.," Sharelle allowed, "but can you stay with me? I mean, if I do this, can you stay all the way through?"

Ms. Sampson nodded. "If you really feel that way, of course I will." She picked up her telephone and dialed an extension somewhere else in the building. Sharelle listened attentively.

"Bert? Linda, upstairs. Could you stop by? I think there's someone who could really benefit from talking to you. What? Well, it seems that way. This doesn't sound like anything impromptu." She nodded into the receiver. "We'll be right here. Thanks." She put down the receiver.

"What did he want to know?" Sharelle asked.

"He wondered if this might not be a case of financial need, rather than a conscious decision," Ms. Sampson told her. "I don't get the feeling that you can be moved very much on this, Sharelle."

"Good," Sharelle said. "I don't think I can. It's not that I don't feel awful in a way. I mean, I know what people might say and all. But if I just remember all the time *why*, I think I'll be O.K."

"Sharelle, isn't there *anyone* you know who could help?" Ms. Sampson implored then. "I just hate to see this happen to someone I admire."

Sharelle shook her head, though she was pleased in a way, too. "I guess you'd have to explain 'help,'" she said. "I mean, there are one or two people I can talk to, like yourself. There might even be someone who would . . . who would make a sacrifice for me and Renee. I don't want that."

Suddenly tears filled Sharelle's eyes and she turned her head away. She cleared her throat and took a quick swipe at her eyes with the back of her hand. "I'm sorry," she said quietly. "I promised I wouldn't cry. I've done enough crying."

"For heaven's sakes," Ms. Sampson comforted her, "I couldn't think of a better time to let go, if you want."

"I don't want," Sharelle said, sounding once again strong. "I just can't let that happen. Not and take care of Renee the way she deserves."

A gentle knock on the office door made both women turn. The door opened and in walked a man of medium height with curls and walnut skin and freckles. "Hi," he said, clearing off a corner of Ms. Sampson's crowded desk and then perching there. "Here I am."

"Sharelle, this is Bert Bekin," said Ms. Sampson. "He's in charge of the county adoption services."

"Hello," Sharelle said.

Bert nodded and smiled.

"Sharelle has decided she'd like to have her daughter adopted," Linda Sampson said.

Bert nodded and looked critically at Sharelle. "Why?" he asked straightforwardly.

Sharelle was a little startled. "What difference does *that* make?" she asked in return.

"It makes my job easier," said Bekin. "It'll make placing the child more successful. Also, sometimes people walk in and want to do this, and then change their minds. Not that I blame them, God knows. But if the reasons are good, the adoption'll be less traumatic, less emotional, although I guess that's pretty hard to believe, especially now, at first."

Sharelle nodded.

"Well?" pressed Bekin.

Sharelle inhaled. "I can't do what she needs," she said at last. "I can't give her what she needs."

"Like what?" asked Bekin, again directly.

Sharelle stared back up at him. "I can give her love," she said, feeling a little defensive. "But what I can't do is make sure the house she grows up in is warm and safe and loving. I can't buy her the stuff she needs. I won't be able to earn enough to keep her and keep myself, too. At least not for a while. I just think it's better to do this now, when she's a baby, than do it later when I'm really dragged, really down, you know?"

Bert Bekin nodded and finally his smile returned. "You seem fairly cool about all this," he estimated.

Sharelle nodded. "I thought it over," she told him. "I tried to imagine everything I could."

"Did you tell her," Bert turned to Linda Sampson, "that we have facilities so that she can think about all this a little longer?"

"No, I didn't," Ms. Sampson said.

"What do you mean?" Sharelle asked.

"Well, we have foster home care for children," Bert answered. "If the mother wants, we can place a baby in a foster home for as long as three months while she thinks it over, while she considers and, in a way, sort of experiences what it would be like without her child. Sometimes it's a good cooling-off thing, sometimes a girl decides she really doesn't want her child to be taken away. That's what the program's designed for. To sort out people who are down temporarily, at their rope's end, but who *can* climb back up again if they get a little time, from those who genuinely are convinced that adoption is what's best."

"Oh," said Sharelle.

"You don't have to do that if you don't want to," Bert told her. "It's just an option."

Sharelle nodded. "Can I ask a question?" she wanted to know.

"Sure," said Bekin.

"Can I—would I have a chance to, well, to sort of direct where Renee goes? I mean, help pick out the new parents?"

"Of course, if you want," Bert told her quickly. Then he frowned. "But you won't know the couple's name or where they actually live, Sharelle. You can find out general things about them, if you want, but the specifics we keep private. You can understand why."

Sharelle nodded. "That's O.K.," she said. "All I want to know is the kind of family she's going to have. I have some ideas, you see. I mean, I want to make sure she doesn't end up with the same thing she's leaving."

Bert turned again to Linda Sampson. "Are we sure there's nothing we can do?" he asked. "I mean, as far as your end is concerned?"

"Believe me," Ms. Sampson replied, "we scoured the regulations, we've tried to bend the rules. It's not so much there isn't aid. The trouble is . . . well, Sharelle, you won't mind if I tell him?"

Sharelle shook her head.

"It's the home front," Ms. Sampson said then. "Sharelle's concerned about raising a child in a certain environment just now. Her mother seems to have some rather severe problems."

Bert Bekin did not press for further explanation. "If you feel, Linda, this is good, then as far as I'm concerned, it's full speed ahead. I respect your opinion."

Sharelle looked at Ms. Sampson and held her breath.

"I'm not happy," Ms. Sampson admitted. "I don't like to see this happen." She looked at Sharelle. "I wish I could find a solution that made Sharelle feel better about herself, about life. But it doesn't seem I can." She stopped a moment and thought. "Also," she said next, "I think Sharelle's convinced that what she's doing here would really and truly benefit her child. I don't think I could imagine anything more unselfish, even though I don't necessarily approve."

There was a moment's silence. Ms. Sampson put her hand up to the back of her neck and stroked her hair up from her nape. "I don't know what Sharelle's requirements are," she said then, "but I'm almost certain they're worthwhile and solid. The only way I'd come down on this would be if Sharelle herself felt she could cope at some point and wanted to stop everything. Otherwise, well, I guess we have to agree that she's adult and mature enough to understand what this means."

Bert Bekin stared at Sharelle. Sharelle felt she was shaking all over, from her head to her fingertips.

"Well, let's get the paperwork out of the way, then," Bert said, edging off the desk corner. "You want to come with me, Sharelle? Down to my office? We can fill out whatever we need there, and you can think about what you want to do while we're trying to find the right combinations."

Sharelle nodded. "Can Ms. Sampson come, too?" she asked weakly.

"Sure," said Bert. "If she's got time."

"I've got the time," Linda Sampson said positively, standing up.

"That's it, then," Bert decided.

"Sharelle?" asked Ms. Sampson. Sharelle looked up, and saw both people standing near her, waiting.

No one moved for an instant. Then Sharelle hugged her purse to her chest and leaned forward, starting to rise. When she was on her feet, she felt suddenly distant, imagined she could see herself lean a little, totter unsteadily. She closed her eyes and tried to control the vision, but everything blurred.

Bert Bekin caught her and put her back in the chair.

Sharelle opened her eyes slowly, thinking she had had a delicious nap. She looked around and saw the two advisers, one on either side of her chair. She grinned weakly, remembering ."I'm O.K.," she said slowly.

"You sure?" asked Bert.

Sharelle nodded. "I have to be. Let's go."

31

━━━━━━━━━━

Y OU can't do that!" Amy Pritchard gasped wide-eyed.
"Sharelle, you just can't! It's horrible!"

"You promised," Sharelle warned.

Amy closed her mouth and stared a moment. "I know,
I know, but—"

"You promised," Sharelle said again firmly.

Amy nodded unhappily.

"I couldn't stand it if everyone knew," Sharelle said
then. "I couldn't stand it if everybody started to fight
me."

Amy bounced George on her lap, taking her eyes away
from Sharelle after a moment to stare into the playroom.
The other students and children had left a few minutes
earlier, and the two remaining girls had promised Ms.
Cummins they would lock up.

"I couldn't do it," Amy said almost under her breath.
"Oh, Sharelle, I couldn't. I don't see how you can. Please,
think about it some more."

"That's all I've been doing, Amy," Sharelle said, moving Renee from one shoulder to the other. The child
squirmed a bit and obviously wanted to be set down on
the carpet to roll around. Renee was beginning to be able
to scoot forwards, not quite yet on hands and knees, but
by edging inch by inch using her knees and elbows. "I
can't think anymore. I'm beat."

"Sharelle, there isn't one girl here, not one, no matter how awful things are, who would do this," Amy declared.

"You're probably right," Sharelle agreed. "Except for Paula, remember?"

"That was different!" Amy said quickly. "She had a lot of other problems."

"But she came up with the same answer," Sharelle said.

"She wasn't half the girl you are," Amy said decisively.

Sharelle smiled. "I know," she said without modesty.

"There has to be another way," Amy said. "I mean, no matter how bad things are, they can't go on forever. If only you'd wait."

Sharelle shook her head. "That's what I don't want to do," she said firmly. "If I'm going to do this, I have to do it now, before it's too late, before Renee gets older, before *I* get older. We've only been together a few months, Amy. It *has* to be easier to forget that than a few years."

"Well, sure it is, but I don't think you'll *ever* forget, Sharelle. I couldn't. No mother could."

"I know that, too," Sharelle admitted. "I just have to remember all the time why. If I can do that, it won't be so bad."

"Are you kidding?" Amy was incredulous. "Who cares why? The thing Renee's going to know all her life is that her mother didn't love her enough to keep her! That's a terrible, awful thing."

"She won't have to," Sharelle said calmly. "I'm going to write her a letter. I'm going to try to make her see why I did this, how it was best for her. Maybe she'll see that *because* I loved her, I gave her up."

Amy shook her head. "I would never feel that way," she said. "What I'd have is the fact, Sharelle, the fact that I was adopted, no matter what kind of excuses my real mother made."

"They're not excuses," Sharelle said. "They're reasons."

"Sharelle!" Amy said then, brightening. "Suppose I could help?"

"How?"

"Well, suppose I talked to my folks. I mean, the house is big enough. You and Renee could come and live with us till . . . till whenever, whenever you wanted to leave, whenever you *could*. I mean, just think. Renee'd have someone to play with. I'd have someone to pal around with and so would you. We're both at the same school, after all. What would be so terrible about living together, too?"

Sharelle smiled. "Nothing," she answered. "Nothing. Except it would be too much, Amy. It would be charity. I don't know. It's one thing to ask people you don't know for help. It's sort of strange taking charity from your friends. I don't think it would be such a hot idea."

"But, Sharelle!" Amy protested. "It's not charity! It's just an answer. It's a way out!"

"No." Sharelle shook her head. "No, it's just deeper in the same hole for different reasons. It would just show me every day what I couldn't do for Renee myself."

"Sharelle, you're not thinking straight," Amy told her. "Listen, friends do things for each other. It isn't charity. It isn't to show someone else how strong *you* are and how weak the other person. It's just something you do because you care."

"But that's exactly what I'm already doing," Sharelle said.

"You're being pigheaded," Amy said angrily. "Honestly, Sharelle, we're talking about your own daughter. You have to forget about yourself for a little while, it seems to me, if you really want to do something good. I'm just offering you the chance."

"No, you're hoping you *can* offer the chance," Sharelle corrected. "I'm *not* thinking about myself. No, I'm really not. I could probably grit my teeth and hang on, but who knows what effect it would have on Renee? I mean, I'm old enough to fight back a little. But she's just beginning to understand, to hear things. You think I want her to hear the kinds of things I'd have to put up with? You think that'd be so all-fired healthy?"

"She'd *be with you*," Amy said distinctly.

"She'd probably end up a basket case, too," Sharelle said without smiling. "Maybe *I* will."

The two girls sat in the darkening schoolroom.

"I've got to do this, Amy," Sharelle said in a monotone. "The way things are now, maybe I can get out from under someday. But alone. And maybe Renee'd get out from under, too, but also alone. There just isn't enough strength in the whole world to get both of us clear together. Everybody talks about help, but there really isn't any. The cards are stacked. Oh, I know you mean well, and I'd probably say and do the same things in your place if I was listening to someone like me say all this. But honestly, I can't do what I know *should* be done for a child. Other people can. Other people *want* to. It's sort of odd, you know? I mean, O.K., I *know* I can have children. Think of all the people who can't. Think what having a kid like Renee would mean to someone like that. I'm not ever going to forget her, you know. There probably won't be a day in my whole life when I won't wonder where she is and how and what she's doing. But there also won't be a day when I won't be glad knowing she's taken care of, knowing her new family adores her and can give her all the things, all the love and toys and education and the warmth of an honest-to-God happy home I couldn't."

Amy said nothing.

"It's strange," Sharelle continued. "Even with a baby, I'm alone. Maybe all this would be different if . . . if the father, you know, had been around, if I didn't have to fight so hard all the time alone. But I do. And that's that. I thought having Renee would maybe give me stuff I needed, stuff I didn't have. I was wrong."

"I don't believe that," Amy said quietly.

"I know you don't." Sharelle smiled. "And neither does

your family. Maybe that's the biggest difference of all between us."

"Sharelle, I am *offering* my family to you." Amy pronounced each word independently, slowly and clearly.

"I can't accept them," Sharelle said very softly. "I just can't."

32

SHARELLE had rejected the idea of putting Renee in someone else's care while she experienced life again alone.

It wasn't worth it, she thought, to have to go through the thing twice. Given the hand she was dealt, there was only one way to play the game, only one winner—Renee. If she put Renee with another family for a while, even for a few weeks, Sharelle felt she might melt, that she might change her mind, and so sure was she that what she was doing was for her baby's sake, to keep her then would be almost cruel. And if she played the hand out to the end the way she wanted, to have to go through two partings would be unbearable. What she was doing had to be done positively, certainly, and quickly. She would have a lifetime of regrets, perhaps, but at least these last few weeks of being together would give her memories to run on.

Every day became more and more precious to Sharelle. She prayed for good weather. She watched over Renee's health jealously. She tried to memorize everything the baby did: how she smiled, the sound of her laughter, the touch of her skin, the way she smelled. She took Renee to the beach to share the first moment's discovery of what an ocean was, of what water was, even though the January clouds hung over the city and fog made their clothing damp and uncomfortable. She handed Renee faded leaves and more colorful flower blossoms. She counted the baby's toes in a singsong and played number games with her.

She stayed as far from Melba as possible. Those weekends when Melba would go through her Saturday and Sunday routines, Sharelle arose early and bundled Renee up and left the house. There wasn't a doubt in her mind that when her mother discovered what was afoot, Melba would decide that Sharelle was unfit anyway, that she was irresponsible and selfish and cold, and that she could have seen all this coming a mile away. Sharelle doubted Melba would actually regret anything that happened.

Her grades began to fall. Her attention span was limited, and her mind elsewhere, recalling the list of requirements she had given Bert Bekin and Ms. Sampson, the qualities she wanted to find in Renee's new parents. She daydreamed through school, coming alive only during that one morning hour and the lunch period she spent in the parenting program. She seemed dazed otherwise, and she even began to lose weight.

"Sharelle, look at me," Kevin Simmons said rather severely one afternoon after he had driven her and Renee home. They were seated in the car in front of Sharelle's house, and the car's motor had just been silenced. "What is going on with you?"

"Nothing," Sharelle replied lamely.

"Oh, sure," Kevin said. "You look like death warmed over, you're skinnier than tinsel, and suddenly you hardly even know I'm around."

Sharelle did not speak.

"Come on!" Kevin insisted. "What the hell is wrong?"

Sharelle looked sideways at him, her hands still fussing with the baby she held. "If I tell you," she said quietly, "you have to promise me you won't say anything. I mean *anything!* I don't want to hear one word out of you!"

"Jesus!" Kevin whispered, shaking his head. "You're really bananas lately."

"Well?"

Kevin looked at her steadily and then he smiled. "O.K. Go ahead."

"Promise?"

He nodded.

Sharelle suddenly didn't know how to begin. Kevin knew all about Melba, knew about the times Sharelle had sought help from the social agencies of the county, knew about Dallas. But now she was afraid in a new way. She thought she knew exactly what he would say, and she didn't want him to say it. Mentally she crossed her fingers.

"It's . . . it's about Renee," she started.

Kevin waited but Sharelle said nothing more. The suspense was too much for him. "*What* about Renee?" he finally coaxed.

"I'm going to have her adopted," Sharelle told him bluntly, taking a quick peek to see Kevin's face as it first went blank with surprise and then as it clouded with what Sharelle imagined was a storm of objection. She looked quickly out the side window. "You promised not to speak," she reminded him.

"I haven't said anything," he told her. "Yet."

"Well, just don't," Sharelle scolded. "I know what I'm doing. I know why. I don't need a lecture."

They sat a moment in silence. Sharelle couldn't stand it. "I can't do it, Kevin. I can't. I can't give her what she needs. Someone else can. Someone else can and will and she'll be happier. God, I know she'll be happier!"

Kevin said nothing, true to his word.

"Well, aren't you going to say anything?" Sharelle demanded.

"What?" asked Kevin in return. "You want to hear what I think?"

"No!" Sharelle said instantly. Then, almost as quickly, "Yes. I do."

Kevin reached over to Sharelle's lap and lifted Renee into his own arms. Sharelle turned in her seat to see. After a moment Kevin's eyes returned to her own and she saw not anger, but sadness.

"Jesus, Sharelle, don't you know about *us?*"

"What us?" Sharelle countered.

Kevin shook his head. "Remember the us at Christmas time?" he asked. "Remember when we didn't just *dance* at ten o'clock in the morning?"

Sharelle had to smile. "I remember."

"Didn't that say anything to you?" Kevin asked plaintively. "I mean, I thought a lot more was happening than just sex. I thought we were *talking* to each other."

Sharelle nodded. "We were," she admitted.

"Then why do you have to live as though nothing happened, as though you're the only person in the whole world with problems? I mean, what the hell am I for, if not to share things with? You don't think that together we couldn't handle all this?"

"I don't think it would be fair to you," Sharelle said.

"Who's talking fair?" Kevin asked. "I'm talking *together!*"

Sharelle shook her head violently. "It wouldn't be fair to us, either of us, *any* of us, together or not," she said.

"How can you say that?" Kevin asked. "How can you decide for me what I can handle and what I can't?"

"I'm not deciding that!" Sharelle objected. "I'm just telling you how I *feel!* Listen, neither one of us knows what's happening half the time. We don't know what next week has for us, next year. What we even want to do with our lives. You think I'd let you be strapped like this, tied down for goodness knows how long, and make you forget about any kind of future?"

"What about Renee's future?" Kevin wondered.

"That's what I'm taking care of," Sharelle told him. "That's something I can do something about. But not yours, not your whole life. No college, no real career

You'd have to go to work. So would I. Who'd take care of Renee? Who'd take care of *another* Renee?"

"Wow!" Kevin smiled. "You really are looking down the line!"

"I have to," Sharelle said, reaching over to retrieve the baby. "I have hopes, too, you know. I don't want my life just to stop here."

"That's sort of selfish, Sharelle," Kevin judged.

Sharelle nodded. "I know. But I can't feel guilty, I just can't. I mean, Renee will have her life. I should be able to have mine. I want more, Kevin. I want to go to college, too, and maybe even graduate school or something. I want to go out there and really make a difference.

"You don't think taking care of Renee, making sure she grows up and learns and understands the world, is worthwhile?"

"Of course I do!" Sharelle defended. "But what about *my* learning what goes on? Shouldn't I be able to do that?"

"Sure," Kevin allowed. "But why can't you do that and keep Renee? I don't see what's so impossible."

"It's not impossible," Sharelle admitted. "Look, I know all this sounds mean and unloving and selfish. But I can't help it. There just isn't the same hope with Renee as there might be without her. I love her. I have loved her. Let someone else have that chance. She's a baby. She'll love almost anyone. And almost anyone, Kevin, can do more for her than I can."

Kevin shook his head and stayed quiet. "It makes me sad," he said finally. "In a way, Sharelle, even though you know how I feel about you, in a way I think, I *feel*, this is wrong. Just plain wrong."

"Well, it's not," Sharelle returned. "It's nothing like that at all. It's what's best for her."

"It sounds like it's for you," Kevin said.

"It's that, too, I guess," Sharelle sighed. "If I'm being honest."

"Then I don't approve," Kevin said firmly. "You haven't told me one thing that makes it work, makes sense, Sharelle."

Sharelle nodded. "It sounds sort of bad to me, too," she admitted.

"Then change your mind."

"I can't."

"Why not?"

"I just can't."

Kevin slapped the steering wheel with his open palm. "You make me want to shake you," he said quietly.

"It's not my fault," Sharelle said softly.

"Not much."

Sharelle turned quickly to him. "It's not!" she shouted. "You don't understand!"

"Then make me!" Kevin shouted back. "That's all I'm asking!"

"You've seen her!" Sharelle cried.

"Who?"

"My mother, for God's sweet sake!" Sharelle shouted. "What am I supposed to do about her?"

"What has she got to do with any of this?" Kevin asked.

"She has everything to do with it!" Sharelle replied. She turned her head quickly, because she felt tearful again and she was determined to keep her promise to herself. "She needs me," Sharelle whispered.

"What?"

"She needs me!" Sharelle repeated.

"You could fool me," Kevin said. "*She* doesn't think so."

"I know that, dummy!" Sharelle answered. She couldn't help it. There were tears in her eyes, at the back of her throat. "I can't help her and keep Renee at the same time," she said in a low tone, trying to keep control. "Renee drives her crazy. She wants to love her but she can't. It's too much. She makes life hell for me, for the baby, for herself. She's so screwed up, Kevin. She hasn't anybody besides me. No one's there to help except me. And I can't let Renee grow up around her. It's not healthy."

"Look, you have a roof and you eat," Kevin said reasonably. "Your mother's on her own. Hey, she tells you that all the time. I believe her. Why can't you?"

"Because I know her!" Sharelle defended shakily. "I know her, I see things you don't. Look, I know it's hard. I didn't want to tell you any of this. It's just that, well, I don't know—I felt I ought to, I thought I *wanted* to. There's a lot I don't understand. I can only tell you I'm doing what I think's best, and I feel right about it. I can't keep Renee and do for her, and stay here and do for Melba."

"But they're not the same thing, they're not even equal," Kevin objected.

"Yes, they are!" Sharelle said hotly. "That's what you don't understand. They are. One's just as important as the other, one's just as much in need. No one else can help my mother. Someone else can help Renee.

Kevin shook his head. "I'm lost," he admitted.

Sharelle reached over and patted his hand on the steering wheel. "I'm trying hard not to be," she said.

Kevin nodded. "I know," he said quietly. "Maybe you really need your mother more than you do Renee."

Sharelle withdrew her hand and sat motionless a moment. The baby squirmed on her lap. She needed changing.

"It seems to me," Kevin said slowly, "that you're fighting to earn something from your mother, not *for* her, Sharelle."

"Maybe."

"But what you want can't be earned, really," Kevin said then. "Maybe I'm wrong, but it seems to me a lot of things can be: trust and faith and admiration. But love? No, I don't think so. That's a gift, Sharelle. That's some-

thing people give because they want to. You can't go
about campaigning for it, no matter how strongly you
feel. If you give up Renee, and your mother doesn't come
through for you the way you want, where are you?" He
paused. "I'd say nowhere. I'd say that, Sharelle. I don't
see it any other way."

33

SHARELLE and Linda Sampson and Bert Bekin all sat in a row along one side of a conference table in an office down the hall from Ms. Sampson's. There were folders and clips and pencils and coffee cups and stray notepads and papers in front of them that Bert tried to organize as he spoke.

"Keeping in mind the kinds of feeling you had," he said to Sharelle, "the sorts of ideas, I've been able to come up with four families so far. Not all of them are exactly what you want, I know, but maybe if we work through the lists together we can begin to zero in."

Sharelle nodded expectantly. She knew what she wanted for Renee. She never for a moment doubted it could be found. She had made a list weeks before, deciding which requirements were real and sensible, which not. She had been left with six entries on her notepad, and all of them seemed equally important.

Bert reached out for a file that lay atop a pile in the center of the table. "All right," he said, opening it. "I'll just read you what's here, and you tell me how you feel about it."

Sharelle tensed in her chair and waited.

Bert read what he found, omitting the name of the couple as he had warned earlier he would have to do. They lived in San Diego County; the husband owned a dry-cleaning store. He was twenty-nine, his wife two years younger. He had been to college although he had not graduated; his wife had finished schooling upon high-school graduation. They were Presbyterians, had two cars, an annual income of about thirty thousand a year. They were eager and enthusiastic and outdoorsy

Sharelle listened carefully and, in her lap, held out fingers whenever one of her own criteria seemed to be missing. When Bert finished the file, he looked up at her Linda Sampson sat quietly, also watching Sharelle.

Sharelle felt suddenly nervous. People's fates were being altered here, and she was in charge. Not really, she reminded herself. The couple had come to the County on its own accord. But it was Sharelle who could make them happy. She would have liked to.

"Let's go on," she said finally. "Read me someone else."

"But, Sharelle," Bert said, "if you'd tell me whether we're warm or cold, I could save us time. I mean, I know most of these people. I could weed some out if we're no where near what you want."

"Please," Sharelle said.

Bert nodded. He picked up another file and opened it

This couple was in its forties. Both worked. They lived at the beach. They had had one child naturally who had died years before. They had an adequate income and a considerable amount of money in the bank saved. They were the only childless people in two large families.

Sharelle did not judge them, either.

Again Bert asked her for an opinion, a hunch, a gut response. But Sharelle declined. She would know when she heard.

So Bert Bekin ran through two more folders, two more families without offspring. Each time he waited and each time Sharelle asked him to go on.

"Sharelle," Linda Sampson said finally, having remained silent all this time, "we're trying to work with the things you said you wanted. Certainly some of these people qualify?"

"They do, but only partly," Sharelle told her case worker.

"Well, how?" Bert asked, barely keeping the exasperation from his voice. "Sharelle, we've got to have more help than we're getting. Otherwise we have to go through hundreds and hundreds of applications, and without getting any feedback from you, we're just wasting time."

"I've already told you what I need," Sharelle said quietly.

"Tell him again," Linda suggested. "Please."

"All right," Sharelle decided. She counted the fingers of her right hand as she explained.

"First," she said, "I want the husband and wife to be in their thirties. They've tried and tried and nothing's worked, and they're not too old, you know? I think that's important, not being too old to enjoy having a child around."

"O.K.," Bert said, making notes on a lined pad before him, even though he had already done so before. "Go on."

Sharelle nodded. "They both have to have graduated from college," she said firmly. "I want them to know about ambition and hard work. Oh, and they can't have other kids around," she added quickly. "I want Renee to have their full attention. I want her to get everything these people can give, not have to share it."

"But, honey," Ms. Sampson interrupted. "sometimes it's a great deal healthier for a child not to be the only child. How else can she learn to share, learn to give and take and find out about life's little tricks and setbacks?"

"She'll learn about *those* soon enough," Sharelle replied.

Linda Sampson smiled. "Got me there," she admitted.

"Fourth," Sharelle continued, "if both people have been working and saving, that's going to make me feel a whole lot better. That means they *can* actually do the kinds of things I couldn't ever."

"At least not now," Linda Sampson added.

"Now is what we're talking about," Sharelle reminded her almost angrily.

Ms. Sampson nodded and did not reply.

"Fifth, I want Renee to live in the country somewhere. I want her to be out in the sunshine and have clean air."

"All right," Bert said, looking up from his pad. "You want someone not too old, who has no other kid, with loot, who lives in the country, and who graduated from college." He leaned back in his chair. "You know, Sharelle, a lot of that we've just been hearing about."

"I know, but not all in one house," Sharelle told him.

"Are you being realistic?" asked Bert.

"Yes," Sharelle said sternly. "I am. That's the one thing I'm sure of."

No one spoke for a second. "I think she's right, Bert," Linda Sampson said firmly. "I think Sharelle *is* realistic, has been. We'll just have to keep plowing through."

"There's more," Sharelle said quickly.

"Oh God," Bert muttered.

Sharelle couldn't help but smile when she heard him, but she went on. "I don't want the people to drink," she said flatly.

"At all?" Bert asked.

"At all," Sharelle answered. "And I want them to be Catholic."

"Catholic!" Linda Sampson's eyebrows were raised. "When did you decide that?"

Sharelle shrugged. "I don't know. But it's important to me. I can't help it, it just is."

Bert sighed more loudly than was necessary. "At least that narrows the field," he guessed. "All right. I'll go back to square one and start all over again. Thank heavens for computers!"

He stood up and started for the door. "You stay right here," he told Sharelle. "I'll only be a few minutes."

Sharelle watched him leave.

"Sharelle?" Ms. Sampson said after a moment. "Tell me something. How did Catholic get in there? In your mind, I mean. Why should that matter so much?"

"It's hard to explain," Sharelle replied.

"Try," Linda Sampson urged. "We've got time."

Sharelle pulled her hands up to the table top and interlaced her fingers as she leaned forward. Her expression was earnest and her voice steady. "It's a friend of mine," she began. "It's someone I know. He's Catholic, you see. And . . . well, I don't think I've ever met anyone in my whole life who tried so hard to be good. Who *was* so good, at helping people, at making you feel worthwhile. It seems to me maybe some of that comes from God, or the Church, anyway. It's what I'd like Renee to try to be. Maybe this will help her. I think it might." She smiled. "It can't do any harm, can it?"

Ms. Sampson smiled and shook her head. "No," she agreed. "A firm belief of any kind only helps people, I think."

"That's what I thought," Sharelle said. "I mean, maybe if my mother . . . if Melba had any of those feelings, maybe—"

"Sharelle, I want to ask you something."

"What?"

"If I could get your mother in here, if I could get her to see a therapist of some kind, someone she could talk to, unburden with, would you reconsider all this?"

Sharelle was stunned. "I . . . I don't know."

"Think about it."

"You couldn't do it," Sharelle said.

"Are you so sure?"

"No," Sharelle admitted. "I just don't see that happening. Not with Melba."

"Would you let me try?"

"If you want," Sharelle said. "But I'm not sure what I'd do."

"Does your mother even know what you're planning?"

Sharelle shook her head. "It's not her affair."

"Oh, Sharelle," Ms. Sampson said sadly, "it is. Sure it is. You're giving away her flesh and blood, too, not just your own. How do you think she'd feel?"

Sharelle's voice sharpened. "Glad," she said quickly. "Relieved."

"I can't believe that," Ms. Sampson said.

"Believe it," Sharelle advised.

Ms. Sampson spent a long moment examining Sharelle's face. "You know," she said softly, "You're doing this for her in a way, Sharelle. Oh, sure, for Renee, too, I don't mean you're not thinking about the baby. But you're doing it mostly because of your mother. Don't you think she should be consulted?"

"No, I don't," Sharelle said quickly. "This is my life, my affair. Maybe I'll make mistakes, but they won't be *her* mistakes."

"Sharelle, you're letting your mother run your life," Linda Sampson said. "I don't see how you can fail to understand that. Even though it's Renee we're dealing with here today, it's your mother who's standing in the shadows, pushing and pulling."

"Well," Sharelle said quickly, "she's not going to do that to Renee, that's for sure. I'm big enough, but Renee isn't. It wouldn't be fair."

Ms. Sampson decided against discussing fairness just then. "All right," she said gently. "As long as you let me try to reach your mother, that's all I asked. Sharelle, there is one thing I want to know."

"What?" Sharelle asked doubtfully, almost rather sourly.

"I want you to know that I think you're being brave," Linda Sampson said plainly. "I admire you, even though I'm not altogether thrilled about what exactly you're doing or your reasoning. But I do think you're trying hard to solve something very difficult. And you get good marks from me for that. I just wanted you to know, that's all."

Sharelle looked down at her hands and prayed that Bert Bekin would walk into the room soon.

He did.

34

I know, Sharelle," Annette said simply, keeping an eye on both tiny girls as they rolled around each other in the center of Melba's living room. Their squeals and laughter were like background music to both sisters.

"What?" Sharelle said, watching Renee on the carpet.

"Sharelle, look at me," Annette commanded. "I *know*."

Sharelle looked up, squinting a little, trying to see if Annette were telling the truth.

"Believe me," her sister said. "I figured it out a long time ago."

"You did?"

Annette nodded. "I didn't want to believe it, you know," she said quietly. "I hated the very idea. I hated you for a while, too. Then I decided probably it wasn't your fault."

"It wasn't, not all of it," Sharelle said softly.

"That's what I mean," Annette said. "I hated Dallas for a few days, then, but Andrea got sick and somehow I forgot. Well, I didn't exactly forget. It just didn't seem to be so important suddenly, not when she was in and out of the hospital all the time, just hovering, trying so hard to keep breathing. I needed all my strength, I guess. And thinking about you and Dallas would just have drained me. I couldn't keep it up, not and pray for Andrea."

"When did you know?" Sharelle asked.

Annette smiled. "That isn't really important, either, is it?"

"I'm just curious," Sharelle said.

"Well, it wasn't so hard, you know. I mean, Dallas was never very keen to hang around, to have you and Melba over. And then when the baby took sick, and he tried to grab Renee, it just came to me. That just sort of cleared things up in my mind. He's not a terrible person, Sharelle. He's not."

Sharelle smiled a little bitterly.

"No, I know what you're thinking," Annette said. "It's easy for me to say. I love him, after all. I want to keep on loving him. I have to say that." She smiled. "I don't have to say that, Sharelle. It's just true, that's all. I'm not asking you to forgive him anything. Just maybe understand a little."

"I do already," Sharelle admitted.

Annette nodded and watched the children again for a moment. "About the other thing," she said.

"What other thing?" Sharelle asked, looking up worriedly.

Annette sighed. "About giving Renee up."

"How'd you know?" Sharelle demanded. "No, I don't need to know. There's nothing you can say."

"Yes, there is," Annette disagreed. "There's a couple of things I want to say."

"Don't."

"Sharelle, I'm not fighting you on this," Annette said. "I couldn't. If I were absolutely honest, I'd have to admit in a way it would be a relief. With Dallas, I mean. A reminder . . . a painful one . . . would be removed. But don't think that's so important as your knowing that you don't have to give her up because of Dallas, because of his threats. Whatever your reasons are, don't make him part of them."

"He isn't," Sharelle said somberly. "He isn't."

"Good," Annette said, leaning back on the couch. "He's done enough damage."

"You can say that again."

Annette smiled sadly. "I don't have to."

"How'd you find out?" Sharelle asked again insistently.

"I thought about keeping Renee, Sharelle," Annette said, ducking the question. "It's important that you know that. I thought about it. And I decided I would if you wanted me to. I mean, that way you'd see her grow up, you'd be around. You could even take her back some time if you wanted." Annette crossed her arms. "I also decided you had to ask. I would need to know *you* needed that, *you* wanted it."

Sharelle's voice was edged. "Why?" she asked. "So it'd look like I was sorry about everything, about what happened with Dallas?"

"Maybe," Annette admitted. "It sounds small, but maybe."

"How did you know?" Sharelle demanded once more.

"Melba told me."

"How did *she* know?"

"A woman came out to see her at work," Annette said. "Someone from Welfare, I think."

"Oh, terrific," Sharelle sighed.

"She said she had spoken with you, Sharelle."

"She did, but she didn't tell me she was going to tell Melba everything."

"Well, she did," Annette told her sister. "Melba was just furious. Not about giving Renee up, but about your thinking she should see a shrink."

"I never said that!"

"No, but apparently the woman from Welfare did. She wanted Melba to go to some sort of family counselor."

"Well, who says that's a bad idea?"

"No one except Melba," Annette replied. "You know Melba. *She's* all right, it's the rest of the world cock-eyed.

She said she just laughed at this woman, sent her packing."

"That doesn't surprise me," Sharelle said. She leaned down and helped Renee reach for a rubber ring. "What'd she say about Renee?"

"She was sort of confused," Annette said. "She said she knew you were that kind of person."

"She would."

"She was about to really let go but Dallas came home and she stopped. I think she thought you thought you were punishing *her*."

"I'm not," Sharelle said quickly. "Just the opposite."

"I know, but that's Melba. Anything we do is either for or against her, it's that simple. She calls you irresponsible and selfish and spoiled."

"She also tell you what really happened Christmas Eve?"

"No. What?"

"Never mind."

"She won't talk to you about this, you know."

"I figured that out already."

"She can't," Annette said.

"I know that."

"She loves you, Sharelle," Annette said then. "It's tough for her to say or show, but she does."

"You could fool me," Sharelle replied, hearing Kevin's voice in her own.

"There are just a lot of things she can't handle."

"No kidding."

"Don't be unforgiving, Sharelle," Annette said.

Sharelle turned in her chair, her mouth open, her eyes wide with disbelief and anger.

"Don't say it," Annette said quickly.

Sharelle shook her head. "God, it's hard trying to be grown-up," she muttered, standing up quickly then and starting to pace, throwing her arms out futilely to her sides as she turned.

Annette watched her for a moment. "Easy, easy," she said soothingly.

Sharelle spun on her, her arms flying, her voice cracking. "I'm doing the best I can!" she shouted. "You think this is easy? You think I want to never see her again?" And she gestured wildly towards the two children still at play nearby. "I'm fighting for three people, Annette!"

"You don't have to," her sister said.

"Says you!" Sharelle challenged. "You should live around here, you'd know!"

"I did."

"You got out! I couldn't! I can't!"

"But . . ."

"And if *I* can't, Renee can't!" Sharelle continued. "This is the only way, I know it is! There's just nothing else to do, Annette. Nothing!"

"Don't be so hardheaded," Annette said. "There must be . . ."

"Oh, sure, there are, sure there are ways," Sharelle shouted. "Ways that make other people pay as much as I do. You think that's fair, either? You think I want charity? You think I want to load my troubles on other people? You think that's fair? All I'm trying to do is make sense out of this mess! How do I do the most good and the least hurt? That's the question, Annette! That's what I fight all the time!"

"Don't fight so hard," Annette advised calmly, gently.

"Well then, what about just plain me?" Sharelle demanded. "When do I get my turn, when do I get my chance? Do I have to give that up just because people tell me to?"

"You could wait a little."

"Wait? And then what? Wait till I'm so far behind can't ever catch up? Wait till I start living a life like Melba's?"

35

SHARELLE told no one at the parenting program that Renee would not be back the following week.

The activity around her and Renee was rushed and noisy, with everyone looking forward to the weekend.

Sharelle slowed down, purposely. She tried to think which of Renee's toys to load in her backpack, which to leave. She decided only the small and personal things were worth packing. After all, Renee's new family would want to buy her things, toys and books and clothes. There was no sense in taking everything. Some other child could use what was left, some other mother.

Ms. Cummins was busy bustling around the outer classroom as the babies and their mothers departed two by two. Sharelle lingered, looking quickly at her wrist-watch to see that the bus that would take them back across town wasn't due for another twenty minutes. She leaned over Renee and removed the baby's diapers and changed them for the trip home.

She worked almost automatically now, her fingers skilled and her hands knowing. She could think about something entirely different even while she cared for her baby. She had kept the log of Renee's physical and mental growth, but she wondered idly if someone shouldn't draw up a chart for mothers, too. It would give them confidence.

"Sharelle?"

Sharelle looked around. Patrick. At her elbow, dressed

in a windbreaker and jeans, carrying a load of books from his medical study.

"Hi," she said, surprised.

"I came to say good-bye," Patrick told her almost shyly.

He couldn't know! Sharelle thought.

"The seminary," Patrick explained. "I start next week."

She sighed.

"So," Patrick said, "I wanted just to say good-bye. I mean," he looked away nervously, "I've . . . I like you. I wanted you to know that. I wanted you to know I cared."

"I know that," Sharelle said quietly. "I do."

They looked at each other. Sharelle turned and left a hand on Renee to keep the child steady atop the bassinet while she talked. "Patrick," she said, "tell me again, about . . . love." She was pleased she had found another word. Actually, instantly, she knew she had found the *right* word.

"What?" he asked, smiling.

It was Sharelle who looked away for a fraction of a second, disconcerted. "You know," she said. "About saving yourself."

Patrick grinned. "It's not that so much," he said. "If you believe, if you really believe, all you're doing is not taking sides. If you love God, and then through Him you love everyone else, it's easier maybe to help people. You can stand a little ways apart, sort of, and see other people's problems a little more clearly just because they're not really your very own. You have a little distance, I guess, is what I'm saying." He paused and then smiled at himself. "I like to think it's a generous thing, you know? You can give so much more because you've already given so much."

"Given up so much," Sharelle wondered.

"No," Patrick told her. "Not that. What you've done is chosen. You do have a choice. We all do."

Sharelle suddenly felt as though he had pierced her with the clearness of his thought. "I . . . we'll miss you," she said, almost choking both on her words and on her need, which she instinctively could not uncover. She thought perhaps Patrick would not judge, but she didn't want to take that chance, nor to force him. She wanted him to think of her as he did just now. The idea that she might disappoint or shock him was intolerable to her.

Patrick grinned. "Hey, I'm not *leaving*," he said quickly. "I want to be a priest, not a *monk*. I'll still be with you, I'll still be in the real world."

"I know, but . . ." Sharelle shrugged, feeling foolish.

"We'll always know each other," Patrick said.

"Will we?"

"I hope so, Sharelle."

Again they looked silently at each other, Sharelle letting herself feel aswirl in Patrick's blue eyes even though she knew she would hurt later for it. A thought came to her and she wondered if she dare utter it. She sounded it to herself, and decided she couldn't say it aloud. It sounded almost make-believe to ask someone to pray for you. It sounded as though you yourself weren't strong enough to handle life.

Patrick leaned quickly across the few inches that separated them to kiss Sharelle quickly on the cheek. He stepped back and smiled at her. "Bye," he said, starting to turn.

"See you," Sharelle called out, hearing the same words from Patrick every time they had parted.

He waved over his shoulder. Then, at the door to the playroom, he stopped and turned.

"Sharelle?"

"What?"

"I will," Patrick vowed. "I promise."

PART
SIX

36

SHARELLE fingered the small bundle she held in her lap. The sun over the ocean, weak at its peak, had died and the landscape around her seemed uniformly pale and washed-out.

She looked down at the brown paper sack for which she had returned home on a moment's inspiration. Earlier in the day she had taken Renee to the address Bert Bekin had given her. She had seen her child in the arms of someone else, carried away from her into another life. Not the woman who would officially be listed as Renee's new mother, but a Welfare worker who had been gentle and caring and who obviously knew what the transaction of one small body meant to its mother.

It had been a sudden thought: why not give *everything* to Renee's new parents? Give them the pictures Uncle Jack had taken of Renee in the hospital, for example, so that the new mother and father could almost feel as though they had been there the first day Renee had breathed and cried. Give them the baby's birth certificate, too, although Bert had explained the county already had copies of this. Give them the few toys and little clothing Melba had not burned up on Christmas Eve.

It was not a big package. It seemed almost sadly meager for such huge meaning.

Sharelle opened the bag and looked in for a moment or two. She did not take anything out to look at it. She had examined and remembered everything as she packed, grateful that there was no one at home to see her handle these things, see her hold them to her chest one last time. Sharelle had waited until Melba left the house for work before wrapping Renee warmly and taking her across town. If, as Annette had told her, Melba knew anything at all about what Sharelle was doing, she had never spoken of it. Well, that would have to come, Sharelle decided. Some time. It would come at a bad time, she knew. There was no good time. But she could face it. She couldn't guess Melba's attack but whatever it was, whatever direction it came from, Sharelle was determined to withstand it, to try to make her mother understand without feeling responsible, to try to make Melba grasp one single idea called love. It wouldn't be easy.

Sharelle sighed to herself and looked over the deserted sand. There wasn't anything easy about any of this, she thought. Not from the beginning, not from the very first moment when she had only half-understood or guessed what was happening, what it could all mean.

She asked herself: If I knew, would I?

The answer was unclear. Part yes, part no.

There were parts of life—frightening parts, secret parts —about which she now knew something, knew enough no longer to fear. That was good. The cost of such learning had been high, but still knowing as much as she did now *had* to be a benefit later.

If she asked the question on Renee's behalf, the answer was the same. Maybe what people had said, what she read, was true, that there was always, *always* something in a child's brain that remembered and was hurt by having been given away, given up. But if Renee was lucky— and she *had* to be, otherwise everything Sharelle had done was in vain—if Renee's new family was loving and thoughtful and gentle, she might not mind so much.

Sharelle had considered writing a letter to her daughter, one short letter that said she *was* loved, that she *was* wanted, and trying to explain how and why her mother had made her decision. But then Sharelle had decided in a way this would be unfair to the baby's new family—whenever they decided to give Renee the letter—and also unfair in a way to herself. It was asking too much of a child to understand the pressures and events that might have taken place many, many years before. Renee would judge her, and Sharelle felt she couldn't stand that, couldn't stand it surely if later Renee were to turn up on her very own doorstep and ask, Why?

What she had to do, just as Renee would do soon, was start over.

Sharelle smiled sadly at her own thought. The difference between herself and Renee was that Renee had a new family, brand-spanking clean and fresh and loving, and Sharelle was stuck with her own, old, set in its ways, unforgiving.

Choosing Renee's family had eventually turned out to be a compromise. Bert and Linda Sampson had explained to her that what she wanted, the entire package, just didn't seem to be available, and that if she wanted to go through with Renee's adoption at all, she would have to put some of her standards to one side.

Sharelle had fought hard, balancing one thing against another. At least most of what she wanted for Renee she had gotten. The couple were young, in their early thirties; both had gone to college and the wife was in graduate school still, studying psychology. They had plenty of money and a nice house in the country north of San Diego and a little east, nestled in the mountains beyond the reach of autumn fog and summer smog. They had no other children and everything on their application indicated they believed in education as much as in material comfort.

What they weren't was Catholic.

Sharelle had thought long and hard about this. It came to her finally that Patrick had been blessed with native goodness and trust, the way all children were, the way Renee was. What he and God had made together of this, what Renee and God could make of *her* talents was something over which Sharelle, or any mother, could never hope to have control. Renee would blossom naturally, and all Sharelle could do, ever, was hope. That was all *any* parent could do.

Bert Bekin and Linda were relieved, and pleased. Their job was at an end.

"Not exactly over," Linda Sampson had told Sharelle. "It's going to be awful for you, Sharelle, for a while, maybe for a long while. I hope you'll feel you can come back and talk if you have to, that you can unload some of what you'll feel, what you can't really avoid feeling. We *are* friends. I really believe that, I want that. I know that's a poor substitute for what you've given up, but it's real just the same, and genuine. Believe that."

Sharelle had nodded that she would try.

What she dreaded now was trying to sleep. She knew she would awaken in the middle of the night and miss the regular breathing of that tiny body in the room with her. She knew she would miss the rolling giggle when Renee was tickled, the odors of her babyhood, the surprise she felt as Renee began to learn and understand. She wondered how, if ever, she would fill those moments of stunning, sudden emptiness.

She felt positive about what she had chosen to do, about Melba's needs, about her own plans for a future. Still, to not know . . .

Well, there was a lot she did know. And wasn't that what she had asked herself a few moments ago?

Besides, she had a life to live, as much as she could, as well as she could.

She would stay at Lincoln. She had come to feel real there, and she knew that whatever hopes she did have for a future could be as well realized by staying on and working hard there as well as anywhere else. Besides, she felt she needed to stay near Kevin—for a while, certainly, perhaps longer.

The rest of her future was hazy, as hazy as the overcast that now hung above the ocean in front of her.

She clutched the bag in her hands. She knew she would have to hurry to get to the reception home in time to hand over what remained of her daughter's things. She had no idea when Renee would be called for, but she felt certain that Renee had to be delivered with as much of herself and her short past as possible. She would want to know as much about a child, she decided, if she were in the position of being a new mother as she could.

She stood up and wrapped her sweater tightly around herself. There was a wet chill in the air and she started quickly to walk away from the waterfront to escape it.

Somewhere, over a hill it seemed, there came in the damp air the echoing sounds of a church bell.

Sharelle stopped still a moment to listen.

Patrick Fitzroy.

She smiled to herself and started to walk again, a little more slowly, a little thoughtfully. Without trying, the tune of one of the songs she had heard him play on his guitar came back to her, and then, faintly, a word or two. Then more.

She walked up a short hill, her shoulders hunched inwards, her parcel held tightly against her body, humming. She remembered. "The door's still open, the fire's alight."

Oh, how she hoped that was true! It didn't matter so much *whose* door was open, or even who had lit the fire. As long as that could still be true, as long as she could hope, she could continue, keep on moving through life towards that one safe place.

A thought came to her. Perhaps it was *she* who had to keep open the door, she who had to keep the fire glowing. Perhaps it was only herself who could *make* one place safe.

There was so much she had to learn.

Were it possible for us to see further than our knowledge reaches, and yet a little way beyond the outworks of our divining, perhaps we would endure our sadnesses with greater confidence than our joys. For they are the moments when something new has entered into us, something unknown; our feelings grow mute in shy perplexity, everything in us withdraws, a stillness comes, and the new, which no one knows, stands in the midst of it and is silent.

—RAINER MARIA RILKE
Letters to a Young Poet

Acknowledgments and thanks to:

Dr. Edward S. and Jean Neufeld, for patience, shelter, and inspiration; Alan and Beatrice Grover, who gave me a Paradise in which to work; Richard Alvarez of the Los Angeles County Adoption office, for answering queries directly and quickly;

the students at San Diego's Abraham Lincoln High School, for being perceptive, funny, hospitable, and honest; Eleanor Jensen, Sue Jensen, and Kathy Regan, of the San Diego Public Schools, who humored me, were generous with their time and students, and helped point the way;

Richard H. Solomon, who has been of inestimable value to me;

the extraordinary young woman whose story first amazed me and then led me to admiration.